SO MUCH LOVE

SO MUCH

McCLELLAND & STEWART

LOVE

REBECCA ROSENBLUM

Library and Archives Canada Cataloguing in Publication

Rosenblum, Rebecca, 1978–, author
    So much love / Rebecca Rosenblum.

Issued in print and electronic formats.
ISBN 978-0-7710-7243-7 (paperback).–ISBN 978-0-7710-7244-4 (epub)
    I. Title.
PS8635.O65S66 2017   C813'.6   C2016-901417-7
                                             C2016-901418-5

ISBN: 978-0-7710-7243-7
ebook ISBN: 978-0-7710-7244-4

Typeset in Perpetua by M&S, Toronto
Printed and bound in the USA

McClelland & Stewart,
a division of Penguin Random House Canada Limited,
a Penguin Random House Company
www.penguinrandomhouse.ca

1 2 3 4 5   21 20 19 18 17

For Mark Sampson,
with so much love

PART ONE

Marriage

Just before the winter semester wrapped up at the end of March, one of my Canadian Poetry students disappeared—not just from my class but also maybe from the earth. Catherine Reindeer left the restaurant where she worked at the end of a day shift, but she didn't come home that night, or any night since. They found her purse in the parking lot the next morning. She was a good student, good enough that she didn't need me to review her essay topics or suggest background readings. But she was chatty and didn't seem to have friends in the class, so sometimes I was the recipient of her thoughts on Gwendolyn MacEwen, Michael Ondaatje, Julianna Ohlin. She spent a lot of time reading the biographical notes at the backs of books, always interested in discussing whose marriage had been happy, who worked a day job in addition to writing. She was—is?—a pretty girl, confident, a bit older than the rest. She had a husband, the newspapers said, unusual for an undergrad. I don't remember a ring. I liked talking to her, but I didn't know her well. Now that's she's gone, I think of her constantly.

Throughout the rest of the semester, her classmates held vigils for her, and her husband and mother appeared on the news—and then I had to give her an Incomplete in the class. I've moved on to teaching summer session, which is always full of kids who look for an easy pass: stoners, guys who leave their skateboards in the aisle. I don't have much else to do this summer. I finally finished my Ohlin monograph and sent it off for consideration, Gretta and I are in one of our silent spells, and everyone I tolerate socially seems to have gone to a cottage. All I have left to occupy my time is hosing bird shit off the patio chairs and attending Gretta's family events. So maybe the damn CanLit survey I'm teaching is getting more focus than it deserves. Extra intensity can only benefit the students, but it's odd being stressed out in July— unnatural. It's the fifth week of term and already I have a tight spot in my left shoulder blade and pre-class dread. As I approach the Humanities building, where the class meets, I feel my jaw clench.

The last lamppost I pass still has a tattered purple poster from one of the vigils they held for Catherine and the high-school boy who went missing around the same time. You could feel a raw terror all through town then—two gone and no one was safe. Kids clumped together after evening classes to walk to the bus, everyone glancing over their shoulders. They had the vigils because there's strength in numbers, I guess. I had thought about going to one, but in the end I couldn't see what standing on the east lawn surrounded by strangers and holding a candle in the dark would accomplish. There are still a lot of posters up on campus, but they're old and coming apart and there hasn't been a vigil since summer term started.

My teaching assistant, Alan—who hates the students and his job and probably me but loves literature—is slouching beside the west doors, smoking.

I stop in front of his dirty black dress shoes. "Morning."

He doesn't shift his gaze. "Morning, sir."

I could watch the cigarette burn right down and he wouldn't say anything more. "See you in class." He nods, a tiny dip of the chin. It's this lack of interaction that drives me to overthink my lectures—between Gretta and Alan, I'm getting a bit desperate for conversation, or at least some eye contact. I go past him inside. On my way downstairs, I pass a couple of my spring-term students. They smile but don't really look at me either; I am seen but not engaged. They were in Catherine's class. I wonder if they knew her. The girl on the left, big-eyed and big-hipped, is prettier than her skinny friend. Gretta has intuited over the years that when I see a girl, I don't just see "pretty"—I see skin tone, the cut of a skirt. This is not Gretta's favourite thing about me, even though I do it to her too. Or especially because I do—no compliment I've ever given on her pronounced yet elegant clavicles, her long, enveloping curtain of hair, the blue-veined skin at her wrists has ever been well received.

The Humanities building is old stone, which appears glamorous from the outside, but in the basement classroom I've been assigned, all that the stonework façade gets us is damp and small windows.

Alan slumps into the front row and pulls a paperback out of his pocket. It's actually the book under discussion today, *The Rainbow Poems* by Julianna Ohlin. I don't know why he bothered to bring it—I'm sure he has it memorized. It's probably just a guard against any student trying to speak to him.

The students are trickling in, but no one even glances at me. Hard to tell whether they feel intimidated or are trying to intimidate. They are likely just not paying attention. In the front row there's a guy in an oversized striped shirt squinting at a bright iPhone, drumming his fingers on the desktop. Even the nerds overwhelm me these days—they can be so dismissive of anything outside the gleam of a screen.

We're far enough into the semester that I should know most of their names, but I don't. Somewhere around my fifth year of teaching, they just stopped sticking. Even the gorgeous girls in the third row are anonymous. I will remember their shiny hair, the few windblown strands across their foreheads, the faded denim shorts cut off above the hollows of their silky thighs, but not their names. I will watch them all semester and never discover if their carelessness is genuine: their clothes will never get nicer, the hair never tidier, but they'll pass lipgloss back and forth during lectures and toss their hair like models in a shampoo ad. I can never stop watching them. I wish I could because I'm sure they notice.

The students are settling down now, shuffling into seats. Soon, I will have no choice but to begin—already those without friends to talk to are watching me impatiently. What are they expecting? Truth and beauty? Library reserves and deadlines?

The only way to swim is to dive in. "Julianna Ohlin was a brilliant poet who happened to be from right here in Iria, an unusual confluence of virtues. She even attended this university for a semester." Some voices fade away as soon as I raise mine; some determinedly finish their sentences, but after about twenty words I hear my own voice, dropped a half-octave from normal conversation, echoing alone in the high-ceilinged room. "I'll use this lecture to introduce her work and give some context about her life and heartbreaking early death." I have them now, though by no means for keeps.

I read aloud a poem, the one about the pointless magic of sunlight on crumpled aluminum: *Dull in fresh air / like smog after rain.* Not a great poem, just a famous one, one they can all recognize and feel good about. And if I'm being honest, I do like it: I can relate to the everyday-ness of the poem as if I could live inside it. "We'll be dealing with the only two books Ohlin published, and yes, you should own them. They are *Sometimes the Door Sticks* and *The Rainbow Poems,* which was assembled from her notebooks after her death."

I relish this too much—imparting, declaiming, making them know what I want them to know. But they are unquestionably with me: I can see the whites of their eyes.

Phrases flash by like fish in a river: "almost Byronic bravado," "sibilant longing." For a while I half tune out on my own speechifying. Then students start to shift and fidget—they aren't whispering yet, but the rustle of their skirts and cutoffs sounds like whispering.

"Other than a few short poems in some journals no one had heard of, Ohlin published nothing in her lifetime—her first book was a couple months away from being published when she died at the age of twenty-seven. All her fame and success—a lot, for a poet—came after her body was found in a flax field outside Calgary. She probably believed she was a failed poet. She died thinking that."

This would be a good time to taper off into the video clips, but I don't want to waste the day, waste Julianna. I can only devote one class to her. Much of the excitement people felt about her—and maybe part of what they still feel—was for the work she was *going* to do. To talk about her gifts is to talk about what was still to come, after she matured, explored her craft, had more experiences—poems she will never write.

The tragedy of her death hits me for the thousandth time when I see it reflected in the students' faces. Julianna really was a person once, a fleshy girl like these ones, with their long limbs, fruity perfumes. And Catherine, that girl grinning on the rain-sodden vigil posters who once got an A- on my midterm exam, she was a person once too. She had a husband, and now that man does not have a wife. Somewhere in the city, Catherine's husband is grieving and waiting for news. How does he pass the time? Even during the worst days of our marriage, and there have been plenty of those, I've always stayed awake until Gretta came home for the night, even if we didn't speak once she returned. Catherine has not been home in four months, but she could still escape from the terrifying narrative the news is positing, from that ripped poster, and return to her life.

I pause to catch my breath and give the students a moment to think. "Any questions so far?" One of the pretties in the third row leans forward. Her hand rises, a bony wrist with a leather bracelet, cinnamon-painted nails. "But *how* did she die?"

"Oh. Well, she was murdered . . . most bodies found in flax fields are."

"But just . . . like, by a stranger? Did they catch the guy?"

"How do you know it was a guy?"

An accusation of unconscious sexism is one of my go-to stall tactics, but she only shrugs. "It's usually a guy."

I shrug back. "You're right. It was her boyfriend, actually. There was never any mystery, really—or if there was, it was cleared up when he ran his car off a bridge a couple weeks later. Unless you're a drug dealer or in the mob, most people who get murdered get murdered by a loved one."

She glances at her friends before speaking again. "But not always. Like, last spring. Catherine Reindeer went missing and so did the boy from the high school just east of campus. They didn't know each other, so probably it was a stranger . . ."

The words fumble in my mouth but eventually drop out: "They're still missing."

This is a wrong turn, and the hour is wearing on. I am not talking about style or complexity or elegance. I am not even talking about the tragic loss of Julianna, or thinking about it, because I am thinking about Catherine's careful bibliographies, her typo-less essays. How, hanging around the lectern one time, waiting for me to shuffle through the stack of graded papers and find her essay on Layton's poetic diction, she mumbled, "I think maybe once I've studied enough poetry, I could maybe write some of my own." I asked her why she needed to wait, why not just give it a try now and see. She said, "Better to know what I'm getting into. Due diligence and all." Possibly the least poetic line ever spoken, but she did seem wise to me, at that moment.

I jolt to realize that I have not spoken for what must be over a minute, judging by the students' bemused stares. I stumble to the laptop and make my customary scene hooking it up to the projector. Finally, Julianna flickers across the screen. In the first video clip she's very young, maybe seventeen, dancing as part of a fellow student's performance art piece, all draped scarves and lugubrious arm movements. Thirty seconds later she's a little older and reading aloud an early draft of the same poem I just read them, solemnly enunciating her words into a microphone, her neck tangled with yet more scarves. The next clip is a news report accessorized with her high-school grad photo; the anchor wears a jaunty green tie but casts his eyes down appropriately. He's back in the final clip, this time with a darker tie, as the accompanying footage shows a sheet-covered gurney trundling onto an ambulance under a cloudless sky.

By the time I get the lights back on, everyone's blank-eyed and pale. I meant the class to be intriguing, intense, *poetic*. I meant to connect with these kids, cut through the thick air in the middle of the classroom and say something that mattered to them. Gretta would say I went in too heavy, too close to the bone. As I scan the room, everyone looks as if they've just seen a girl die.

And then I have to go home and get ready for the wedding of a couple I barely know. My summer suit is right at the back of my closet, where I left it in 2006, after the last formal wedding of one of Gretta's distant cousins. Somehow, since then, the jacket has gotten tight in the arm-pits. The only comfortable way to position my arms is as if I'm offering a tray of drinks.

The bride, Lisha, is a third cousin of Gretta's whom I've only met a handful of times, and the groom is a man whose name, as far as I can recall, I was never told. I doubt the bridal couple cares much how I dress, and with my mind still back in my silent classroom with my struggling students, I can think of no alternative outfit so I set off uncomfortably for the church.

Since my walk home from campus, the sky has eaten the sun and the buildings no longer cast a shadow. The interior of the car is pressingly hot, like being inside a lung. About three blocks out, I realize that I only hazily know the way to the wedding venue, and the Google Maps print-out is crumpled on my office floor. I haven't seen my awful BlackBerry in weeks. But Gretta will know where we have to go. She grew up in that beige suburb, where people on the radio are always commenting that schools are underfunded.

Traffic is as sticky and dense as the air. Even with the air condi-tioning on and the windows sealed, I still feel the humidity creeping in. I pass the restaurant where Catherine Reindeer was last seen, the one she worked at. It gives no sign of its dramatic role. It's supposed to be one of the nicer places in town—I always meant to take Gretta there but never have. Now I feel like I shouldn't. The parking lot, where Catherine's purse and cellphone were found, is crowded—so is the patio. The chalkboard out front advertises specials of mussels and 2-for-1 martinis. As I pass in the crawling traffic, a young waitress in very high heels stands at a patio table, pouring from a pitcher.

Even though it's only 3:01, Gretta is already waiting at the curb in front of her shop, looking south, leaning forward intently. She's changed her clothes since I saw her leave this morning, from jeans and a button-up shirt to a long purple silk dress fading in and out of wall-paper shades, from pale to brilliant, violet to lilac. It is shapeless and sleeveless and hangs away from her body as she tilts on the sidewalk. Her much younger assistant gave her the high-heeled sandals, tied with ribbons crisscrossing her shins, up and under her hemline. The whole outfit—the dull dangling earrings, her hair loose down her back—makes her appear younger than she really is, and different too, freer and more relaxed. I know she'll be uncomfortable in an hour—sooner, as soon as anyone looks at her. I also know that by the end of the evening she'll be sorry she wore any of it.

All this before the car even comes to a complete stop.

She enters with a heavy whiff of grape gum, slams the door, puts on her seatbelt. Her bag slides to the floor with a fabric-muffled *thunk* that could be either books or blocks of wood.

I put the car into gear and start moving. "Hi, Gretta."

"Len."

"I'm fine, thanks."

"Didn't we say two-thirty?"

I bite the inside of my cheek. "Three."

"Yes, and then we remembered cottage traffic and so . . ."

"Two-thirty?"

"Yes."

"At least this wasn't one of the times I decided on your behalf that you wouldn't mind waiting. I just forgot."

She flicks on the radio, twists the dial, flicks it off. "The 414 on-ramp is up ahead. It's a left merge." A beat. "You should get over."

"Yeah, I know."

She hunches toward the window.

It isn't until we are finally on the 414 and through the trauma of the merge that it occurs to me that I didn't actually apologize for my lateness. That ship has sailed. The only things I have to talk about now are my morning, the posters on campus, my grim presentation on the dead poet. But those all belong to the category of things Gretta doesn't know about, that belong only to me. So instead I go for that marital standard: "Did you have a good day?"

Gretta rolls down her window and spits her gum into the weeds and gravel beside the road as we whoosh by.

—— ᙍ ——

"I thought the beadwork was just lovely." That's Denise talking, some cousin of both Gretta and the bride, with very feathered hair and a fluty voice. Everyone at the reception is conversing along those lines, though. "And the dress was nice and flowy, the beads didn't weigh it down somehow." Maybe it's just a boring reception, or a reception of boring people with nothing else to talk about but lace and seed pearls and taffeta. If Gretta were speaking to me, I'm sure she would say something about the architecture—"It's funny how dour these modern churches are, isn't it?" at least—or comment on the Bible verses they read in the ceremony, some note of surprise about the unconventional James 18. I haven't contributed anything to the conversation with Denise beyond smiling, currently with closed lips over a too-hot bite of crabcake.

Other than that, I've been alternating drinking champagne with scotch and soda and waiting for some interesting ironies to emerge from attending a wedding with my wife while we are in the middle of a near-silent summer, one of those periods in our marriage when the whole thing goes dark. Tonight has been a letdown so far. Gretta didn't let me indulge in any sort of arm-linking, hand-holding, or other for-appearances-only shows of affection that might have given the evening a hopeful tone, as if we are about to start working our way back to real affection. She watched me with the same resigned tolerance she does at home, left six inches between us in the pew, and looked exhausted when people hugged her thin shoulders.

There is no argument, no issue we could work through, apologize for, forgive, resolve. There's just a dull, sad distance that's been present for months now. It's been so long since we could be together without this film of disappointment, I find myself feeling almost homesick for Gretta, though I know she is somewhere in this same crowded room, likely eating a crabcake of her own.

"It's nice to have a happy occasion to celebrate." Denise's hair is cut or pinned into wings in front of her ears. Behind her, through enormous panes of glass, the lawn of the golf course is gold and silver in the sunset, very tempting to slip out into it. "Especially when every news report seems sadder and sadder these days, doesn't it?"

"Oh . . . Like the disappearances? Catherine Reindeer and that high-school boy?" I set down my drink to slice a large wedge of Brie from the round on the buffet.

Denise regards me with chipper attention, as if I've just entered the room. "Yes, exactly like that. Those poor kids. It's gotten to be so long ago now, they aren't on the news much anymore. Even when they are, there doesn't seem to be much hope left. I mean, all the newscasters make it sound like the worst has already happened."

"They weren't kids, really. Well, the girl anyway—I mean, woman." I put a fistful of crackers into a napkin with the cheese, in preparation for fleeing out the patio doors.

"Oh, no?"

"Well, she was in her twenties, late twenties. I guess it's natural to think of someone who has been taken against her will as a child—it's such a loss of agency." I chew my lip. "She was a student of mine, actually."

Denise accords me the appropriate blink of interest. There's no reason to talk to her about Catherine, but she's listening, and god knows it's on my mind. "A good student, very cheerful and focused in class. A pretty girl too, not that it matters. It took me a while to figure out that she was older. Mine was the only class she was in last spring— she could only take one a semester. She had to work the rest of the time, keep the bills paid. She was twenty-seven." What I don't say, because Denise wouldn't know what I was talking about or care, is that Julianna Ohlin was twenty-seven too when she disappeared—and never got to be twenty-eight.

"Oh, that's so interesting . . ." As Denise sips her wine, her gaze darts around the room. "Where's Gretta?"

"Gretta?" One of the crackers slips from my napkin, bounces onto the floor, and hops under the hem of Denise's long skirt. She pretends not to notice.

"Your wife?" Denise grins and punches me—gently but not that gently—in the shoulder. More crackers go skittering.

"Oh—sorry, Denise, could you just—" She obediently takes the napkin full of crumbs. I scan the room, brushing off my hands. "Gretta, she's—" I see the bleached tablecloths, the polished wood floor, a couple who were at my own wedding, a young woman with dark glossy hair.

At last: "There." I point toward a window glinting pink with the setting sun, almost directly across the hall from us. Gretta stands against the high windowsill, ankles tight together in her dreamy shoes. She is talking to a tiny brunette bouncing a tinier brown-haired baby in her arms.

"Oh. What a striking dress! So many shades of purple."

I bristle slightly—I would have used the same wry tone to describe that dress but a husband has certain privileges. I change the subject. "Is that Mary? When did she have another baby?"

"Len! Where have you been?"

I flap a hand. "You know, the urban jungle."

Mary is now tipping her arms toward Gretta's to pass the flailing child over while Gretta bites her lip, shifts her sharp elbows.

"They're calling her Emily."

In the last blaze of sun, Gretta's bare arms are a similar colour to the pale pink bundle she now holds, which clashes with her already-rumpled dress. She only glances at the tennis-ball-fuzzed head before passing the baby back to Mary as gently and quickly as she can. Uncomfortable, uncuddly Gretta. Mary strolls off to find more willing admirers. Denise moves down the buffet, smiling at someone in the distance.

Gretta is staring into space, space that after a moment includes me. She frowns. I tip my head in Mary's direction and smile. She shrugs, then reaches out to take a glass of champagne from a waiter with a tray of them. He says something and Gretta nods, laughs, says something back. He grins and stands for a moment beside her, basking in her brief smile, then moves off into the crowd, offering his wares.

That could have been me.

I remember what it was like to be young—a child, even. I remember the best seat on the school bus is the one above the wheel well, for the footrest, for the rarity. I remember the tilt of my hand on a sweatered waist at a dance, the answering smile that meant *go, stay, I like you, dance with me, yes, yes.* I remember the crunch of feet on gravel and blotches of ink on exam papers and bright blue superheroes falling from the sky. I remember how it felt to live a life worth remembering.

I've seen photos of Gretta from her yearbook years, when she was younger even than Catherine was when she evaporated, as young as Julianna in her dancing years, though never so hazy. Photos of Gretta standing prom-dress proud in an overdecorated living room holding a white-rose corsage, or blowing out candles on a thickly frosted cake, or lying laughing in a pile of bronze leaves. And the other shots, where her eyes are canted down, or she's drawn a book or her hair over her face. She was sometimes shyly veiled and at other times so direct and sure in her gaze that no one knew what to make of her. Or so her family has told me. But Gretta has always been fine with defining herself.

I've also seen her in the present tense, our present: lumped in her bathrobe, head bent and hair twisted tightly at her nape, reading on the chesterfield—she still calls it that. A book is in her lap and she dangles her upper body over it, her bare narrow feet propped on the ottoman. Her worn terrycloth robe falls open at the hem, letting the lamplight gleam off her dry, shaved shins. I try to tell myself that the girl with the cakes and flowers and diplomas was always walking toward me, always on her way to becoming what she is now: mine. But my imagination won't reach that far. By the time we met, Gretta had hardened into herself, become sharply self-sufficient. She had started leaving her vulnerability behind long before I ever met her. I could have loved her back then, perfectly, unreservedly, and we never even knew it.

It's raining when we finally leave the reception. I'm sure we stayed longer than either of us wanted owing to a pathetic inability to find each other in the enormous hall. By the time we reunite, diffidently, too tired not to be comforted by a familiar face, the rain has transformed the gravel parking lot into soup. I'm a step ahead of Gretta going down the stairs and as I slosh toward the car, my mind is on the ruin of my only good teaching loafers. I'm halfway across the lot before I realize Gretta hasn't followed me outside; someone has stopped her at the doorway. Someone—a man I don't know, his suit crisp and his shoulders relaxed, clearly not pinched by the fabric at his armpits.

My clothes are already so wet that more rain doesn't matter, although on another day I would scramble to the car on principle. But at this particular moment—watching my reticent wife chatting with a stranger—the downpour suits my mood, so I walk the rest of the way to the car, sit down on the hood and wait. After a few minutes, I watch her finally walk down the cement stairs to the parking lot, the man escorting her with his hand on the inside of her elbow.

She glances around the lot, for me, presumably. He—whoever he is—draws his hand off her arm to shield her face from the rain. It seems to me that his fingers brush her hair and he smiles in a way that assumes that because she can't find me, I'm not there. And she smiles back, a private beam like I haven't seen in months. I make my fingers into a megaphone and shout, "Gretta!"

She looks in my direction for a few seconds before she sees me. The man turns to go back upstairs, saying something while already walking away. Gretta laughs, waves, and starts to dash across the parking lot through the slicing rain. Her dress clings like . . . well, there's nothing like wet silk. Of course it's too dark to make out any details of panties, nipples, thighs, but I know them well enough that I can imagine.

Likewise, I don't see her ankle twist in the rutted gravel, but it is easy to imagine when I see her tumble, how her ankle wrenches as she collapses onto her stomach and elbows, feet splayed.

Just for a moment I think about the ruin of her purple silk dress. In the night and the rain, it appears brown, and with the mud, soon it will be. But it was pretty—too clinging, too wild for a woman her age, but pretty. Most other women in their forties would've looked far worse in it. I startle to recall, as she lies there crumpled, that I am a man with a beautiful wife. Somehow that has always been difficult for me to keep in mind unless I am gazing directly at her. I slide off the hood and splash over.

"Gretta, are you okay?" I try to peer into her face as I reach down, anticipating her cold wiry fingers sliding into mine, a quirked smile of embarrassed gratitude on her lips. But instead she pushes up onto her hands and knees, then downward-dogs herself up to standing. I pull my hand back and straighten up beside her, disappointed not to have the chance to help.

"Yes." The water droplets on her face are too profuse and speckled with dirt to mistake for tears, but I allow myself the error. "I'm fine." But she limps forward, favouring the twisted ankle. Once I realize she's not going to take my proffered arm, I stride ahead and unlock the car. She opens the passenger door, slouches into the seat without comment. When I sit down beside her, her gaze is fixed on the sun visor.

I put the car into gear and flick on the lights, thinking only briefly about the mud on the upholstery. And tolerance. And marriage. And that man, whoever he was, in the parking lot. So much of what goes on in Gretta's life, I don't hear about. She would say the same thing of me, I guess. The silence greenhouses in the sealed damp car.

When we reach the lot exit, I can't seem to judge the space between the oncoming cars, so I wait for complete darkness in either direction—no headlights approaching—before pulling into the road. Out of the corner of my eye, I see Gretta run her fingers down her seatbelt and touch the buckle.

I dig my fingertips into the hard plastic steering wheel, watching the hyphenated centre line flutter past, and finally mutter, "Long night," before I switch on the radio to the crackle of news, not what I wanted in the humid car. But Gretta cocks her head away from the window toward the words *plea* and *police* and goes so far as to touch my hand when I try for the dial. Her fingers are winter-cold and her dripping hair slides down her shoulder. I let her listen.

After the reports on the latest murders and union negotiations and stock-market tumbles, there's a surprising mention of Catherine and that high-school boy who disappeared, Donny something. They remain the same degree of missing as last I heard. They are only on the news now because the boy's family is holding another vigil. Somehow my heart doesn't break for the kid I've never met—a failure of empathy. The night glistens with rain and it's soothing to watch things slipping by the windows, too blurred to think about.

"Still missing," Gretta says. She tips her forehead against the streaked side window. "It's been four months for the girl, longer for him."

"Hmm?"

"Those kids who disappeared last winter, they're talking about them. Donny Zimmerman and the girl . . . Catherine Reindeer."

Even though Catherine is often on the news, and there's no one in town who doesn't know about her disappearance or abduction or whatever we're calling it (not murder, though, not yet), it's strange to hear Gretta say her name—I feel like she's torn a page out of my sub-conscious and read it aloud. What else can she see, inside my brain? My neck warms as I think of Catherine in a burgundy tank top with the right strap slipped off her shoulder, onto her biceps. Catherine up in the back corner of the classroom, giggling at a joke I'd made, the pri-vate thrill it gave me to make her laugh. My memories suddenly feel prurient, divorced as they are from their soundtrack—all of Catherine's witty comments in class, her astute questions get erased, leaving me with nothing but her pretty arms, her warm soft hair. "I'd . . . I'd give her an extension."

"What's that?"

Stopped for an amber light, I see the destruction of Gretta's inconvenient dress in the streetlight glow: drenched and twisted, torn to reveal a slice of muddy knee.

"On her final paper. She never had a chance to hand it in. Catherine. She missed the exam too, but . . ."

"Oh, Len." She twists in her seat to face me. "She was your student? How did I not know this?"

It's strange how stricken she is, like she suddenly knows just how much I've been thinking about Catherine's absence all these months. Her cold fingertips tap my wrist again and again, very softly. As if she knows everything.

I can't return the favour and read Gretta's mind—I don't know what she is thinking and the slick concession road after midnight is not a good time to look into her eyes. Probably she assumes that the missing girl and I were close, that I am privately devastated by the loss. And since the devastation is true, it seems irrelevant that Catherine Reindeer came to my office only a handful of times, mainly talked to me about prosody, rebellion, Leonard Cohen. But I remember her, a girl in a burgundy tank top over tanned skin. Her skittering laugh that seemed to miss some notes on the in-breaths, the way she told me her thoughts on the poems without the typical undergraduate quivering at talking to a prof. And the tension of that class where none of the kids seemed to be doing well, and my desire to be more than an antiquated letch, to listen to her and not just gaze at the slope of her stomach.

The possibility that she might be dead has blasted all that hazy memory with a new light. Staring through the thick rain, I try to focus on the headlights. I think about a eulogy I could never give. And about her thick-fingered hand gesturing as she made a point about Gwendolyn MacEwen. No one made the mistake of thinking that I knew her because I didn't, not really. I only watched, and remembered.

It's raining so heavily that the windshield looks like it is sliding away. It's hard to see, hard to concentrate. Gretta's hand is on my shoulder, she's asking me something. I shake my head, trying to opt out of the

conversation. I prefer my own version of events to the news, to anything Gretta would know. As long as no one knows anything for sure,
then Catherine is alive.

"Len!"

And if no one knows, I am free to write my own story. A flash of
headlights.

"Len!"

I swerve from the blond headlights bearing down on us just in time.
A spray of gravel sluices up as I blur the car onto the shoulder. I'm not
thinking, thank God: just watching the dull face of the guardrail pull
closer, then braking, swerving, clutching the wheel, Gretta's steadying
hand still on my shoulder. It only takes five, maybe ten seconds before
I'm driving on the asphalt again. I carefully duck my shoulder out from
under her hand, so she won't feel me shaking. Just another ten minutes
home. All silent.

I park sloppily under a streetlamp, still shaking. Gretta leans limply
against the rain-dark window, but she turns toward me when I turn
toward her.

"Am I drunk? I didn't think I was drunk, but I just didn't—Am I?"

Gretta touches my cheek with fingers that, even after a half-hour in
the warm dry car, are still icy. "My darling, I don't know."

The Girl for Me

It seems disloyal after all these years, but I've got to start buying different mascara. The Lancôme one I've always used wears so nice and soft—heavy makeup makes a woman my age look like a harridan—but it isn't waterproof, and I've been crying all spring.

When Catherine first disappeared in March, everything was still frozen, but within a week the spring melt began. Rivers of slush ran down the edges of every street and the police came again and again, tracking dirty slush into my foyer. They doubted that an adult, a grown woman with a job and a husband, could be taken—as if such violence were kiddie stuff, or showed a lack of willpower. They kept asking questions about any unhappiness with Grey, an affair, secrets I can't imagine my daughter would keep from me. Or him. I can't imagine any of it. And so, helpless, clueless, I wept and wept.

After four weeks, the police don't feel the need to visit anymore. Like with a bad boyfriend, I call them if I think of anything new to tell them or just to check in, but they never call me. Things are changing, the world is stuttering forward, and these constant tears have to stop.

I can cry at night, alone in my big bed full of pillows—perhaps I always will. But I've got to be stronger during the day. It will be a relief, maybe even a blessing, as Seva would say, to be back at work, thinking and talking and making people's lives slightly easier by helping them with their banking. I want to spend the day with people who have never had the person they love most snatched away from a parking lot; I want to pretend to be one of them.

I've been such a reliable employee for so many years that Janie has been generous about my leave of absence, even coming by for tea with some of the other girls from the branch. Not that anyone knows what to say, but they've come over the past three Friday afternoons, bearing pumpkin loaves and coconut brownies, little bits of news from work, and encouraging smiles. If Catherine had died, if she'd had a straightforward car accident on an icy night or a fall while hiking in the mountains, there would have been some discussion of God, I'm sure—all of that "everything happens for a reason" nonsense, but it would have filled in the silences. I'm not religious, and Seva and Leanne know that, but it's what they rely on in bad times, and I rely on them. We've all been working at the same branch since the strip mall opened.

Even if it had been a more uncomfortable thing, a drug overdose or driving under the influence—and we have certainly had our share of such tragic idiocies around here—there are things you can say. About forgiveness, about moving on, about appreciating the time we had. About never doubting the value of memories.

But Catherine's disappearance is nothing but doubt. No one knows who would do her harm, but equally no one knows why she would run off. Both options are impossible, and there is no third. There is nothing to say, no question left to ask. I read the poetry Catherine likes—the book she forgot on the sofa, and another by the same poet that I got from the library. The poems are about plates of pasta, cats in the dark, vegetable gardens—nothing to do with me, but they are something that she loved. And they are something to think about other than the empty space where my daughter used to be. No one wants to talk about that, but my colleagues aren't that interested in poetry either. So on this, the fourth Friday since my daughter disappeared, I ask the ladies about mascara.

"Really, I'll be glad to be back at the branch. But I'm worried about the . . . weepy moments." What I'm thinking of are the tides of tears that come over me without warning, wordless and hot, but we middle-aged ladies are masters of understatement.

Janie taps down her teacup. "I'm sure you can be excused from your wicket a moment if you need it. Any of us would be happy to cover for you; I completely understand."

She doesn't understand, of course, and I can't explain how I feel without taking her son's phone and throwing it in the lake so that every time she has a question or suggestion for him, or just misses the sound of his voice, there's no way for her to get in touch. And even then, she could find another way—email, Facebook, his friends—to be certain he was fine and then not worry. There is no real way to explain at all.

"But no one can cover for me long enough for me to completely reapply my face. I need some new mascara that can withstand . . . everything. And still look professional. Any suggestions?"

Seva nods. "There's lots of nice mascara at Shoppers these days. These ones that make the curl for you, ones that spread the lashes apart, all kinds of colours . . ."

"I just want plain black. What I've always worn, but waterproof. Nothing trashy-looking. Buying makeup at the drugstore seems like something teenagers do because they don't know any better."

"No, no. There's a much better selection than they used to have. They're not even that expensive. You can experiment with a few and find what you like best."

"I don't want anything like the garish stuff Catherine bought when she was in high school."

Leanne pats my hand at the sound of Catherine's name, and they all open their pale round eyes, waiting for me to say more. I feel like I should resist, but it's magical to talk about her. It's all I want to do.

"Catherine was never a rebel, but she did like her little treats—blue eyeliner and glitter lipgloss and all that. This was when she was, oh, fifteen, I guess. She had just started waitressing. She'd come home at night with sore feet, almost limping. I could have told her those cheap Keds did nothing to support her arches, cushion her feet, but she wouldn't have heard it. Tiny tennis shoes were what girls wore that summer, and she loved them. That was back when she'd say, 'It's not like I even really care about shoes,' which meant, somehow, that those shoes were cool. What they did to her feet was irrelevant. The work was hard, but then she had her own money to spend, to waste. She loved that. She loved those silly lipglosses, those awful shoes."

The girls are nodding, smiling, but with backs and foreheads tensed. I've spoken longer than I should have in the give-and-take of normal conversation, but they love Catherine too. She is the sweet girl they met when she stopped by the bank, occasionally my "date" for the holiday party, always on hand if I hosted a dinner here. They love her, but not the boiling, endless way I do. Which is why I stop the stories there, put the teapot on the tray, and promise to meet Seva at the Shoppers on Sunday, letting our little get-together peter out.

I wait until they're gone and I'm at the sink washing dishes before I let myself follow my thoughts as far as they'll go. It's dangerous to think of Catherine too much, especially when I'm alone. If Grey were here, we'd pick one little topic and go over every detail—how she could never be bothered to blow-dry her thick, heavy hair, how even at the end of the day when she took down her ponytail there would still be a trace of damp. Or that woman poet she liked so much—or maybe she didn't like her, but she was reading her books over and over in the weeks before . . . before. She was like that, so much energy, you didn't always know what she loved and what she just felt strongly about. We can talk and talk about Catherine, Grey and I, and almost always manage to stop before one of us breaks down. We can do that because we both love her equally, if such a thing is possible.

Alone, I worry I'll go too far, think too much, and then not be able to get up off the floor. But remembering my beautiful girl is devastatingly tempting. Oh, my Catherine. So interesting. So lovely to think about. Her strange theories of how the world works. The rare moments when she wouldn't do the expected, "normal" thing. Her refusal to get a student loan, so horrified of debt that she took only the courses she could pay for in cash, which was why her degree was stretching out into its seventh year. Her contempt for her friends who competed in figure-skating competitions. Her childhood terror at the idea of French immersion.

She was only four when the neighbourhood school mailed me a flyer about French immersion classes—it seemed a wonderful opportunity to me. One night on the back porch as we played shadow puppets I told her that next year, when she went to school, she would get to learn French. In fact, I had the bunny shadow say it, hopping up and down the crumbling brick of our back wall. I even improvised a French accent, told her she would love French, *mais oui*.

But Catherine unclasped her hands from making the goose shape and squawked angrily, "No, I will not. I will not learn French."

I was baffled—still so inexperienced as a mother even after four years. Though Wayne had never contributed much in the way of parenting, he had left only six months earlier and I was feeling especially unmoored. I tried to explain the benefits of learning a new language, something different and exciting, something I myself would have loved to have done. And Catherine in her pink-and-white overalls just plopped right down on her bottom and wailed. I can still picture her hot wet face, sobbing that she would never "say that stuff," that she only wanted to say "true words." I never found out where she got the impression that French was a scary language or even where she learned that French *was* a language.

Years later, she laughed at the story and claimed not to remember her tantrum. When I pressed, she said, "Iria's a pretty small place, Mom, and I'd never been anywhere. I probably thought I'd have to move away to learn another language." She was giggling—I hope I laughed too, although I can't remember that part. The memory of Cat is clear, though—I recall her grinning pink-lipstick mouth as clearly as I recall her childish panic. My memories come into clearer focus every day—I suppose it's the longing that makes me conjure her so strongly.

They would have let me say all this and more, Seva, Leanne, Janie— they would have listened all afternoon and been glad to. But so much has been taken from me, I have to keep some memories for myself.

—◊—

LashBlast does not sound like the sort of cosmetic a woman in her fif- ties—a public face at a major bank branch—ought to be using. But it is only $9 and Seva squeezes my arm encouragingly, so I buy it.

Afterwards, I insist on walking home alone through the rain. I have had more physical contact with Seva in the past four weeks than during the whole seventeen years we've known each other—not just arm squeezes and hand pats but full-bodied hugs and tearfully wet kisses on the cheek too. Same with most of the girls from work, actually, not to mention cousins, neighbours . . . No one knows what to say, so they try to *do* instead. If they're not caressing and consoling me, they're keeping my freezer full of chocolate-chip muffins and tortellini soup just when I have fewer guests to feed than ever before. I always thaw someone else's muffins when I know a friend is coming over with yet more food. I feed them as they feed me, so at least they feel welcomed and appreciated, and I can make some room in the freezer for the new things. I've rarely been hungry since Cat's disappearance, but even when I was eating normally, what would a single woman do with an entire lasagna?

Tomorrow, I go back to the bank. I feel I should call Grey and tell him I won't be home, even though we don't usually get together until Wednesdays. I want him to know where to find me, just in case there's news. But I think he was scheduled to be back at work soon too—I can't remember if that was this week or next. Maybe I should finally get a cellphone. Maybe I should leave poor Grey alone. We live the same days, I imagine—days filled with tea and muffins, and brief quiet visits with friends who have nothing to say. Watching game shows and heartbreaking news reports where they don't mention her. Losing concentration on the second paragraph of a book. I know he hears from the police more than I do—either because they think of him as being closer to her than me, or they think of him as a suspect, he's not sure which. But if there was anything new to report, I know he would call me. Every moment he doesn't, I know there is nothing new to say. So I don't call either.

Today, I will clean the entire apartment and then go downstairs with the battery-powered handheld vacuum cleaner and do the car. It's terrifying to admit it, but I have done this most days since she's been gone. Clean has always meant *clear* to me, meant I could see clearly and get the more important things done.

Catherine, when she lived with me, was messier: jeans on the rug crushed down into the figure eight she stepped out of the night before.

Cereal bowls by the bed with a crust of milk hardening. I was never a judgmental parent, never pushy unless there was an urgent need. I tore up those French immersion forms and Cat did terrifically well in regular English school. I didn't question her decisions, and that made her feel she could talk to me, at least about some things. There was a lot I could never forgive my own mother for, even for the things I knew later were meant to help. She told me on my wedding day that if I married Wayne I would regret it. I did and I did, but who was she to tell me? So I shut up about Catherine's choices unless she was about to step into traffic, and for that I was rewarded with her walking through my door again and again with all her stories already on her lips.

Wayne hated how, even as a toddler, Cat would come to me and not to him with a picture she'd painted, feathers found in the grass, a cookie. "She's the girl for you, all right," I remember him growling.

Once she moved out to be with Grey, somewhere around her twenty-first birthday, and I moved into my new apartment, Catherine rarely called first, just appeared at my door, or already in my living room. She found a tree that grew out back, thick and heavy, which she liked to climb up to reach my second-storey windows. She said she didn't want to disturb me by buzzing the intercom—she came at odd hours and if I was asleep or out she would just leave again. I offered to give her a key, but she didn't seem interested and I never got around to it. Though she would never admit it, I knew she wanted to climb the tree for the sake of it. I don't know everything about my daughter, but I know that much.

Whenever she came with Grey, they entered through the front door. Grey isn't much of an athlete. I like that fellow, the way he edges as close to her as possible on the couch, on the street, on the bus, smiling into her hair. I've not lacked for gentlemen since Wayne, but no one has ever been captivated by me like that. Not romantically, anyway. For the first few years of her life, Catherine often wept if I walked out of the room. She must have stopped doing that around the time she went off to kindergarten, but I just can't remember when. As much as I remember, there's so much more I forget.

My first day back at work is busy because a computer update for the entire branch doesn't go well. Programs keep freezing or giving error messages or crashing. I have to reassure any number of harried clients that their funds are safe, that these are only interface problems. Leanne and Seva keep brushing past me, placing a hand on my forearm or on my shoulder, a platter of tea biscuits in the staff room at 2 p.m. They ask, "How are you?" over and over, but it seems like there is no right answer. I just shake my head and say, "Getting through, getting through."

My eyelashes feel heavy and sticky with my new mascara, but otherwise I am light as air. I thought I would feel naked here with the public teeming in, but I am the person in charge, behind the desk, the one who knows the most about what is happening and what to do next. A few regulars murmur, "Oh, Sue, I *heard*," but I only have to nod somberly once and point out the new mortgage promo before the conversation is over. When I go to the ladies, the mirror over the sink shows a smooth, serene face. Even my lashes look feathery and soft. This day of calm professionalism is such a change from sobbing weakly in my bathrobe and staring at her Facebook page. I never understood Facebook and still don't, but there are so many lovely pictures of her there. I should have taken more pictures.

And yet when my shift is over—the day shift, the most coveted one—and the after-work crowd is bustling in and the younger tellers who work the 12–8 are steeling themselves, I go into the back to get my coat and bag, and I start to shake.

I am alone. I have been so attended to all day, so carefully watched by the girls, but now that I am by myself, my shoulders and back and thighs and stomach tremble under the weight of all those minutes I did not think of my beautiful daughter.

Did I really spend the day answering questions about service fees, bounced cheques, online errors? Did I really smile warmly and say that I completely understood how difficult it was when a woman wearing a silk scarf with cherries on it could not access her loan statement for twenty minutes? Even though my Catherine was taken from a parking lot after a long day of work, taken so quickly and violently she let her beloved yellow Kate Spade purse fall into a puddle and stay there? *Taken*—I finally let myself think the word I didn't want to imagine. But really I've been circling it since the moment I knew she was gone. There is no other option, no solution to the mystery that makes sense other than a crime, a captor. Catherine was taken.

I lean over the table in the staff room, brace my hands on it. I can't get my breathing right. I have not seen my daughter in four weeks and three days and yet somehow I didn't think of her for hours because some people needed American dollar transfers, overdraft protection, postdated bill payments.

I have no idea how long I stay like that—not that long, maybe, since no one else comes in. I want to see Grey, even though it isn't the right night. He's probably always known what I have just admitted to myself, that she would never have left him—*us*—voluntarily. She was so honest that if she'd fallen out of love, she would have just said so. I don't need to tell Grey any of this. I'll just go sit beside him and talk about whatever he wants, knowing that we are grieving the same grief.

Back in the washroom, I unzip my makeup case as I walk toward the mirror, prepared to touch up at least my eyes, maybe redo my concealer. I need to look more or less chipper in order for the girls to let me leave on my own. Otherwise I will be in for another night of spaghetti with someone's husband and kids. But in the mirror, my cool face is still altogether intact—fluttering dark eyelashes and clear bright eyes. I could fool even myself.

The walk from the bus stop to Catherine and Grey's place isn't far, which was one of the things she liked about living here. At the corner, I see a poster for her—of course there's more of them in the areas where there are people who love her. The photograph is one Grey provided, the context unknown to me. She's grinning and reaching for a glass held by someone cropped out of the frame. The same poster has a plea for the boy too, the one who disappeared a month or so before her. He was much younger, only a high-school kid, and his photo shows the awkward grin and styled hair of a school-picture day. His collared shirt is incongruously formal next to casual Catherine. I wonder if I should call his mother. Maybe it would help, pain shared from one mother to another. Or maybe I wouldn't be able to bear adding a new loss to my nightmares.

When I find myself standing across the street from the house, I wish I'd driven, so I would have somewhere to sit and think for a moment. Standing still on the sidewalk is a strange thing to do—dog walkers and schoolchildren appraise me as they pass, but since I'm still bank-tidy in my pantsuit and hairspray, they keep moving.

I don't come over often. Even when Catherine was still here and everything was fine, I didn't, though it's only twenty minutes away and a charming little house with a flower border and some kind of pink stone tiles on the steps. In the living room are crowded bookshelves and a lovely blue couch. Catherine would always make me a cup of tea and put a plate of cookies in front of me when I visited. She made me feel like a guest, and I hated it. When I was—when I *am* with Catherine, I like to be the mother. I prefer to see her at my table, eating my cookies.

I hate approaching their red-painted front door when I know she's not behind it—that knowledge keeps me glued to the sidewalk, staring at the house like a spurned girlfriend. Grey and I tried alternating our Wednesday nights between their house and my apartment, but now he comes to my place every time. He seems not to mind—I told him it was easier for me and he didn't ask *easier how?* The answer to that unasked question is that it's easier to pretend I still have someone to mother if I'm cooking him spaghetti or putting the cookies in front of him. Then we watch an inane TV show about people buying houses. I can't believe he likes it, much less that Catherine does, but I humour him. I like to see him point out the stylist she likes best just for the sake of hearing her name.

Catherine did love house-hunting, and she loved this house. When they decided to buy a place together, she was still living with me, and she'd wander into the living room with her laptop a dozen times a night, murmuring, "What do you think of this place, Mom?" She liked to talk about square-footage, lathe-and-plaster walls, "good bones," finished basements. Once, I urged her to go see a listing I liked—pretty garden, wide driveway—and she gently chided me: "Mom, this is a strange layout. You see, the upstairs bathroom isn't accessible from the hall. You have to go through the master bedroom. Awkward." "But it's just the two of you—what does it matter?" "Well, for *now* it is." My heart thudded with impossible surprise—of course I'd thought of grandchildren, but I hadn't dared to hope. Catherine never said a word to me about having kids before or since. But this sweet little three-bedroom house with its sunny fenced yard is the fruit of all that gleeful labour, and I always imagine it bursting with skateboards and puppies and science projects and tutus. My hands shake in horror at how much I've lost.

It's cold, nowhere near the nice part of spring. The yard looks grim, the grass wet and dead, the flowerbeds only mud heaps. When I see a curtain twitch in the kitchen window, I finally cross the street and climb the stairs.

"Sue. Hey, it's good to see you." He's surprised that I've shown up unannounced, but we are long past the point of asking each other questions about how we're coping. Catherine would be pleased, I think miserably, that the awkwardness between me and Grey has finally dissolved. His hug is brief but satisfying—his meaty shoulders are so different from the slender, sweatered ones of my colleagues.

We've seen each other every week since she's been gone, but in my mind, Grey is always how he looked the first few days: wild-eyed, unshaven, dirty hair pushed up in spikes around his bald patch, a nervous hand covering his mouth. I have been remembering him that way even though he pulled himself together, physically at least, very quickly, much faster than I did. Today, like most days, he wears a hoodie and jeans, but his hair is combed, his beard neatly trimmed.

"C'mon in," he says, but I am already trailing him down the hall. The living room is tidy, or at least not visibly chaotic. He's either vacuumed recently or he has been avoiding this room. I've never known a man like Grey—devoted, beaming to see his wife walking toward him. Someone who vacuums.

"Can you stay?" He waves his hands idly by his sides. "I mean, did you come for a visit, or . . ."

I nod and smile, or try to smile, while unwinding my scarf. "Sure, that would be great, if you aren't busy?"

"Absolutely. Let me put the kettle on, and get us something to eat."

"Oh, no, don't trouble yourself . . ."

He shrugs and disappears into the kitchen, the words "No bother" drifting behind him. I sit down on the couch that Catherine so loved.

The first thing they bought new, together, once they had the house. It is stiff to sit on, but elegant, and such a bright, happy blue.

I hear the clank of the kettle and the whir of the microwave. He comes back with a plate of soggy-looking muffins. "I defrosted these. So many people brought stuff—at the beginning. I don't know what they thought I'd do with twenty-four muffins."

He sits down heavily in the complex Ikea chair I gave them, all curved wood bars and flat cushions. I took Catherine shopping when she was moving from my home to this one, and asked what she wanted as a housewarming gift—that chair is what she chose. Somehow, in her mind, it went with the new blue couch. I couldn't imagine why she liked it; she felt so far from me then, crouching in the store's fluorescent glare, cooing over that ugly chair. In that moment, we were probably as distant as we've ever been because I could not understand why she loved Grey either—the chair was probably just a metaphor. I liked him fine, but back then I couldn't see what there was to love about this awkwardly boyish but actually much older man. Catherine was inscrutable in her passion for him, and for the silly chair. I understand him now; perhaps one day I'll get the chair too.

For now Grey seems terribly uncomfortable perched in it. Of course, it might not be the chair.

"How are you, Grey?"

"Oh, well, you know—okay, I guess. I have a lot of muffins. Work's been easy on me since I went back. You're back this week too, right? At least it's something to do, right?"

I nod, surprised that he remembered. "Yes, it's good to be back. Bought a new mascara for the occasion. Everyone was kind."

He smiles tightly. "Your eyelashes do look nice."

"Do you . . . have you heard anything new?"

He shakes his head slowly. "You?"

"Oh, no. Well, I'm sure they'd call you first."

He shrugs. "I don't know what to do anymore. I feel I should be *doing* something. Like how can I just watch TV and eat salad or whatever. In the evenings and stuff. I should be—I should be . . ."

"What?" I lean toward him—I want to know what I should be doing too.

"Out, I guess. Going out, talking to people, looking . . . It's ridiculous, I know. But I feel like I should still be looking for her."

"I'm sure the police are doing everything, well, everything there is to do."

"Yeah, I know, I know." He pushes his palms down his thighs like he is sluicing off dirty water. "I trust them, I just don't have anything else to do. I feel bad watching the shows she liked. She hated when I watched stuff without her. I've been reading a lot, but . . ."

"Me too. Poetry mainly, things she likes. That Julianna Ohlin, the writer who lived around here."

"Oh, yeah. I just finished one of hers. *Sometimes the Door Sticks*—that one?"

I nod a little.

"She was really engrossed in that one right before . . . Then after she was gone, I searched all over and couldn't find it. Maybe she had it with her, I dunno. I had to get my assistant to order me a copy."

"Oh, she left it at my place, actually," I say. "It's not bad. I like the one—I like the poem where the speaker is standing at the bus stop and it's just coming on dawn—that one with the bird?"

"I think it's called 'Service Disruption.'" Grey picks up a muffin and carefully chews off one side. "I like that one. It's funny—*the gullwing arcing like the socket of a headlamp.* I don't completely get it, but I get why Catherine liked her. Ohlin."

"When she was first—first gone, I didn't sleep. Not really at all. I just read the books that were lying around, and she'd left that one on my couch. I read some of those poems over and over. Now they feel, I don't know, important. Connected with her. I just keep reading them."

"I know, right? Everything feels like a message. Like the last text she sent me, saying she'd see me soon? Or the clothes she had in the laundry when she disappeared. I didn't do laundry for almost two weeks, but then I ran out of underwear and when I dumped everything out there were little red panties at the bottom." He suddenly stands—I can't tell if he's just embarrassed that he said the word *panties* to his mother-in-law or if it's something else.

"Do you sleep, Grey? Are you getting enough sleep? Or any?"

I see his shoulders hunch up and down in his neat shirt, but he lowers himself back beside me. "Oh, some, I guess. It's weird. I lived alone for so long before Catherine and never really minded it. Now, I mean, of course I miss her—I love her. But also the bed feels so huge and awkward. There's no one there to keep the blankets from all lumping up on my side."

"I've lived alone as long as you've lived with Catherine, and I half expect I always will. But alone is just a lot of space for your thoughts. If your thoughts are good, being alone is no big deal. Since she's been gone, my thoughts are . . . I look forward to our Wednesdays so much, Grey."

"Me too. You have so many good stories about her." His jaw trembles slightly around the muffin he is gnawing on.

The tears flood my eyes, quiver a moment, and then spill, filtering through my stiff black eyelashes. A blush creeps up my neck, and I hurry to wipe my face with the back of my hand. When my eyes clear, though, I see Grey is weeping too, glassy tears streaking silently down his chin, but his only action is to gently pat me on the shoulder before pouring us more tea.

"You do too, Grey, you do. I love the stories you tell about her. That one where she got the Great Dane to jump in her lap when you guys were camping."

He chuckles, a bit hiccupy. "She's a funny girl, all right."

"Did I ever tell you about the time I tried to enrol her in French immersion?"

He sniffs and picks up his cup. "No, tell me." His eyes are still wet, and so are mine, but for once feel I can ignore the tears, and the fact that we both know I've told this story so many times before. This is the place to weep for Catherine, for as long as we want.

Before (Some Things)

The sushi place is in a strip mall behind another strip mall—Catherine couldn't even see it from the road, though it has a fluttering yellow Grand Opening banner, dimpled with snow and hung crookedly across the window.

"I don't know. I don't even like cooked fish all that much."

"Sure you do," Grey says. "You like shrimp and stuff."

Grey is already out of the car and pressing the lock remote just as she pulls the door handle to get out too. She cocks her head and looks at him through the windshield until he laughs and hits *unlock*. As she steps out of the car, the wind flips the banner over backwards—a sound like thunder in a grade-school play. The lot is full of slush puddles that will not be kind to her new brown suede boots, which are soft and slouchy with a low round heel. She is a waitress every day but Tuesdays and Wednesdays, in a restaurant much nicer than this, so she's vain today in her frivolous shoes—she really doesn't want them to get wet.

"Shrimp is shellfish. That's not like fish-fish, right?"

He takes her arm to steady her as she steps wide over a puddle. "This place has shrimp. You'll like it. You'll see."

It's warmer inside, if humid. There is a narrow lobby between the two sets of glass doors, a space heater blasting, the only ornament a bulletin board advertising local babysitters with feathered paper tabs at the bottom. Catherine immediately zeroes in on the missing person poster for Donny Zimmerman, the high-school senior who went missing in February. Each poster is different—she's seen at least a dozen around town, and there's always a few new details, another photo. She pictures his mom tirelessly making poster after poster, every time adding some new piece of information or better picture to bring him home. This one has a colour photo of him surrounded by green grass and soccer balls, and mentions that he's six-foot-one and one hundred and eighty pounds, allergic to soy. Some of the other posters she's seen mention a birthmark on his shin, chestnut brown hair, the kind of shoes he was wearing. Catherine already knows most of this; she knows a lot about Donny Zimmerman for someone she has never met. She can't help reading all the articles in the paper and being drawn to the posters: that big-toothed smile, that heart-breakingly young face. She wants him to be found, to go back to playing sports and driving his snazzy car, but he's been gone close to five weeks— the posters are getting ratty and some have been taken down.

Grey and Catherine are seated in a cushionless booth with a view of their car through the window. There's a narrow white vase on the table holding a single orange carnation. Catherine pokes at a petal—real. She nods, satisfied, but Grey isn't paying attention.

Catherine studies him as he studies the menu: the grit of stubble along his jaw, the bare patch on top of his head, wider every year. He is so serious, bending over the list of entrées, she smiles.

"What?"

"What do I know about sushi? You can order."

"I'm not an expert or anything. Just pick something that sounds good."

Catherine almost opens her folded menu, then doesn't. "I *want* you to order for me. Like the olden days. Like you were the head of the family."

"Ha! Is this a sexual thing?"

She grins. She's only ever unselfconscious about her crooked teeth with Grey.

"Okay, then—" He starts reading his menu again. "You seem like an eel girl to me, oh, and something with avocado in it, right?" He watches her face for several seconds, then nods. "Right."

Behind Grey's head and slightly to the left is a bobbing pink baby, lofted up and down by a woman in the next booth. The little girl might be more toddler than baby—she has soft feathers of hair bunched into pink elastics on either side of her head, and she's smiling and making eye contact, just like a real person. Her mother, or whoever the lady holding her is, joggles her up and down. It seems she has comforted the child out of some small tragedy; glassy buds of tears dot her round cheeks, but her mouth is still, her eyes clear. Finally, after a long moment of staring, she smiles wetly at Catherine, her pink tongue exposed between her tiny sugar-white teeth.

Grey is chatting with the waitress, happily gesturing with the menu—she knows his demeanour without looking away from the baby. As the waitress departs, Grey glances over his shoulder, following the path of Catherine's gaze. He turns back, smiling too, his tongue in the exact same position as the baby's.

After lunch, they go home and Catherine lies on her belly on the couch, reading. Her laptop is on the coffee table, so she can take notes if she twists her whole body off the couch. It's not comfortable, but it works. The book she's reading is called *Sometimes the Door Sticks,* today a poem about a heart beating beside the poet in the night that does nothing but echo her loneliness. Catherine has felt that way a few times, nights she couldn't sleep after a fight with Grey but still had to lie beside him, watching the rise and fall of his sleeping chest. It feels worse to be upset and not comforted by Grey when he's right there than to be upset alone. She wonders if she is missing the point of the poem, but Professor Altaris will be happy enough to know she found *a* meaning; he's not a dictator about interpretation.

Grey's feet thonk-thonk in the hallway above her and then she hears him rustling in the office and sometime after that in the basement. She is working toward a thesis for her essay about how the poetry that makes a reader uncomfortable or vaguely irritated might be challenging a reader's sense of self. Is that a good thing? She isn't sure yet. According to the jacket copy and the Wikipedia entry she read earlier, this poet, Julianna Ohlin, seems to have had a life a lot like Catherine's, at least up until now. They both waitress, they were both young when they hooked up with their partners, they both liked school and books. But Julianna's life was harder—she was truly poor instead of mainly okay like Catherine. And she had to move away from her family when she was practically still a kid. And her boyfriend was violent and probably murdered her in the end. And yet she still wrote these poems that Catherine can hold in her hands and mind years later. All Catherine writes are term papers and dinner orders and that's about it. And yet the girl in the poem about accidentally running over the tomato plant in a truck, drunk, late at night seems like she could be Catherine in another life.

She flips over onto her back to take a break from the book and rests her laptop on her belly so she can scroll through her news feed. One story is about Donny Zimmerman, only it isn't really news—just a reminder that he is still gone, people are still upset, the police are still trying. Catherine can't help but imagine what it must be like to be his father, his mother, his friends from school. A disappearance is different than a death—there's nowhere to put your grief, exactly. The parents keep appearing on the news, trying to seem composed though they are less and less convincing. She can't even fathom what the worst-case scenario must be for them, but clearly they have thought it out, in terrifying detail—you can see it in their tight faces, their professional wool coats hanging open despite the cold. She has watched Donny Zimmerman's elegant parents, bitmapped and jerky on the cbc.ca clip, pleading with anyone who might know anything about where Donny was to contact the police. The intensity with which they spoke to the camera, all the cords in their necks straining, made it clear they didn't believe he'd run away with a girl or wandered into the woods while wasted and died of hypothermia. There was someone for them to talk to through the screens and lens. They believed he had been taken. Catherine's mind can't go that far—the couch is too comfortable; Grey is too close and comforting, his shuffling steps audible in the house even when she can't see him.

It's tempting to go down the rabbit hole of reading the comments: the conspiracy theorists who say he was in a cult, the girls who knew him in school and clearly had crushes on him, but Catherine has to be at work in an hour. That means that she should leave now if she is taking the bus. She closes the laptop on Donny's tragic grin and tumbles off the couch half on purpose. She's in the bedroom, bending to fish her uniform blouse out of the basket of clean clothes, when Grey appears.

"You want to go so early?"

"Yeah, if I'm taking the bus I should go soon." She straightens, presses her blouse to her chest as if assessing the fit.

"But I can drive you."

"It's snowing."

"I don't mind. If I drive, you won't have to leave yet."

Catherine nods and, seeing that Grey is poised to speak, unzips her dress and pulls it over her head. From behind the fabric, she hears him say, "I think we should have a kid."

"Oh?" She leaves the dress up, over her face, and tries to guess his expression by his tone. She plays this game often—whenever Grey calls to her through the bathroom door or up the stairs, speaks to her in the dark. She is not always right, and sometimes she doesn't find out if she was right or not because Grey leaves or the mood changes before she glimpses the shape of his mouth, the squint of his eyes. "I thought we already decided we're going to have kids."

"I mean soon. I could get you pregnant right now, if you want."

She brushes her lips against the rough linen of the dress—it feels fantastic. "Well, I do want to, but eventually. It's just I'm still in school. I don't want to be a waitress forever. I can get a better job once I've graduated. And there's still so much on the mortgage and—I think it's important to wait for the right time."

"It's the right time when we decide it is."

She feels him tugging up at the hem of the dress, above her head, and she clenches her fingers into the fabric even as she leans her body in, searching for his.

A baby. She has been watching strollers at the mall so long, she's stopped even pretending she doesn't stare. When Daria comes into the restaurant with her little Stevie to pick up a paycheque, Catherine's arms are the first extended. As soon as she hears him squawking out front, she is aware of the hard flat surface of her sternum between her breasts, where the baby should be held. When Daria hands his squirmy body over, the fit is so perfect she can almost hear the click.

Her dress suddenly whooshes up over her head and Grey's face appears, slightly flushed. Her skin goose-pimples and warmth floods her face as she stands in front of him in her bra and panties, even though she has been half-naked all along. It's just seeing him see her that makes her nipples perk up and her scalp tingle.

"Do *you* want a baby?" She bends to the basket again, snatches out her skirt.

Grey's hands circle her waist and pull her back upright. "Lately, I've been thinking about it. It's the house, I guess. I never thought a guy like me could have a nice house and decent furniture and a decent job. And a wife . . . a wife like you. Sometimes I walk around this place and I'm like, *Wow, really?*"

Catherine laughs into his shoulder. "Yeah, me too."

"And that's you, Catherine—you figured it out for us. If it were left up to me, I'd still be in that little apartment with that ugly brown carpet . . ."

"Now that we have nice carpets, the next step is a child?"

"No . . . just that it seems possible." He backs away from her slightly and brushes his thumb across his mouth, but his other hand still firmly rests on her hip. "We pay the mortgage on time and take out the recycling. We show up to work every day. We're happily married people who eat a well-balanced diet and are kind to our parents—it's people like us who have babies. I really think I could care for a little baby, be responsible for all its needs." He starts to step around the bed still holding her: they are dancing, sort of.

"But would *I*?"

"You would. You would if you wanted to, Cat. You have a way."

Catherine shakes out her blouse, then tosses it on the bureau. "You always have too much faith in me. I don't—"

"It's so weird how these things don't wrinkle. The fabric looks just like cotton."

"But it doesn't feel like cotton. Are you really going to drive me? It's snowing a lot." She points at the window.

"I am a man of my word. When have I not done what I said I'd do?"

"I don't know." She is thinking about taking off her panties, about being late for work—they still have maybe half an hour, a little less, until they should leave. Plenty of time. "It's probably happened."

He steps back slightly, eyes wide and curious. His shirt has come partly untucked from the right side of his jeans, so she slides her hand across his hip, over his belt, and into the space between fabric and flesh. The skin there is cool, even though it's warm in the house. He comes closer again, sliding one thigh between hers.

"But most of the time, I'm a pretty good husband, right?"

She tries to look serious. "Yeah, you're all right."

Her shift is a not-unpleasant blur—she long ago learned how to be polite to people without listening. She stays locked in her daydream about a powder-scented little baby in one of those pretty patterned-fabric slings she sees people wearing in the park, just the pink bald baby heads peeking out. The idea that she doesn't have a degree or a career or really any kind of life plan dances around the edges of the daydream. Sometimes Catherine feels like she is barely a person. She is still trying to do enough things, read enough books, have enough life to build into a character. She doesn't even have her driver's licence yet; she keeps saying she's going to take the test but never gets around to it. Who could she be to a baby?

She pockets her tips without looking, a surprise for later, and takes her first break outside, sitting with Daria on some old office chairs someone left by the dumpsters, spinning around until they are dizzy, watching Claude smoke. She doesn't feel up to reading in the corridor tonight, even though she has her Julianna Ohlin book in her bag. When Catherine stops spinning, Claude is complaining about a movie he saw, something with a dragon in it. No, not complaining about the movie, Catherine realizes, just about the audience.

"The worst—running up and down the aisle, spilling popcorn, crying when the dude got killed."

Daria kicks off Catherine's ankle to spin in the other direction. "Serves you right for going to a kids' movie matinee. What did you expect?"

Claude shrugs. "My girlfriend wanted to go—I wasn't listening when she said the title or I would have argued."

"You don't like kids?" Catherine pivots the chair to the left, digs in her toes, pivots to the right, clomps on the ground. She didn't change back into boots to come out here and her feet are going to be slush-wet for the rest of the night.

"I don't like *parents*." Claude drags on his cigarette so the cherry flares. "Don't have them if you're not going to raise them to act like humans."

Raise them, Catherine thinks. *Like cattle.*

"Hey, thanks for the awesome advice, Claude! I'll totally take that under advisement." Daria's boy is only a few months old. You can still see the soft mound under her blouse where her pregnant belly used to stick out.

Claude smiles at Daria but doesn't answer. He's had a crush on her for a couple years now, but the baby confused things—now he doesn't seem to know how to talk to her at all. He turns to Catherine instead. "How's school?" Claude is nineteen and goes to the same university as her but full-time. He just does a few hours a week at the restaurant during the school year; his parents pay for the rest.

Catherine takes one class a term and works full-time. "I'm starting my final paper."

"In what? *Literature?*"

"No, on why money is awesome. Isn't that what you always write about?" Catherine stands up, and the chair clanks and tips backwards in the dirty snowbank. "It's about a poet, someone from around here."

Daria stands, then rights Catherine's chair carefully before starting up the stairs. "Poets in Iria—imagine that," she says.

"She's pretty good, actually."

Daria shrugs, and even Catherine isn't positive she believes herself.

"Well, I mean, the poems sound good—everything fits together. Sometimes I'm not sure what things mean, like is a screw falling down the kitchen drain a metaphor or just an actual screw?"

"What difference does it make, if you like the way it sounds?" Daria says, holding the screen door open. Claude shuffles through, then glances back before disappearing into the restaurant. "It's not like I know what half the singers on the radio are saying," she adds.

"Well, I have to write an essay on her poetry, for one thing."

Daria laughs, and Catherine wanders to the washroom before going back to the dining room. She is caught between two daydreams for the rest of the evening—the one from earlier in the evening of her and Grey's spare bedroom painted a soft green all over, with cushions, a white crib, and the squeaky cry of a kitten—she can't quite fix the sound of a baby in her head. But now the pretty blond poet from the back of her book is mixed in somehow. Catherine pictures her looking the way she did in Professor Altaris's video in class, tense and serious but wearing a beautiful violet dress, reading poem after poem to the kitten baby who is lying unseen in the crib.

After her shift, Catherine walks toward the bus stop. If she goes home after work she has to take the slow, dank, late-night bus, but if she goes to her mother's she can walk. Also her mom will probably be asleep when she gets there, but Grey will be up playing video games with the sound off, waiting for her. He'll want to have beers and continue the conversation from earlier. She keeps going past the stop, past the lighted streets of downtown where the tourists come to drink within sight of the water. It's just coming on spring, still slushy but not too cold and the wind is gentler. Soon the semester will end and she hasn't decided about her summer class. Maybe a course on poetics, or something on Greek comedies cross-listed in the Classics department. Or nothing at all— there's always the temptation to take the summer off and just go to the beach with Grey every weekend, spend the evenings she's not working out in the yard reading, barbecuing, fixing up the garden.

She walks to a twisty little neighbourhood of tall, narrow houses, most of them subdivided into apartments, most of them falling apart. If she had a baby, would she get her degree? Her mother never did; maybe that's why Sue hasn't pushed her to finish hers faster. Would she get up the guts to take a creative writing class around daycare and storytime? Something in her says *too soon*, but another part thinks of snuggling a baby against her body and says *now now now.*

The building her mother lives in is nicer than most on this street, but that isn't saying very much. Catherine changed into jeans after her shift, and the tree out back is easier to climb in winter, without the obstacle of leaves. Still, she briefly loses her grip halfway up and when she braces herself against the trunk her left cheekbone grazes a branch. It stings, but not badly. She's usually happy enough to do things the easy way; the tree is an exception. It's her favourite way of getting into her mother's apartment and Sue leaves the window ajar all year. The tree is not that tough to climb, but when Catherine leans off the branch and swings onto the windowsill, she always feels like she has scaled Mount Everest.

Her mother is wearing her red velour bathrobe and isn't very surprised when Catherine hops awkwardly into the room.

"You want tea, honey?" Sue half stands, her magazine slapping to the floor.

Catherine snatches up the magazine, automatically flipping it over to see the cover. *The New Yorker*—her mother is addicted to it. "No, thanks." She is unbuttoning her coat, sitting down, shrugging it off. There is no other place so warm as here.

Sue settles back in her chair but gazes intently at Catherine. "You have a fight with Grey?"

"No. I don't usually come here for that, do I? I just didn't wanna take the bus."

"Oh, Cat, no one wants to take the bus."

She toes her boots off under the table, trying to remember if they're slushy or dry enough to leave there. "It's okay if I stay, though, right? You don't mind?"

"What am I doing? Nothing. But don't you have a lot of homework?"

"Just a paper."

Her mother leans her elbows on the table. "What's it about?" Sue is a bank teller, with many rhinestone broaches and a comforting manner. The other ladies she works with talk about people they see on the street, and sales at the grocery store, and the new television lineup each season. Sue has *The New Yorker* and Catherine for poetry.

"Someone from here. Julianna Ohlin. She—"

"Oh, her." Her mother does not have bangs, but if she did she would have blown them off her face. "I remember her."

"You don't like her work?"

Another red velour shrug. "I just read a couple of poems, but not until long after she was dead. But my friend Lainey used to babysit her, so I knew her a little bit. Lainey would bring her to our place on the way to the library, and I'd give them popsicles. She was just a little girl then."

"Really? You knew her?"

"Well, it's not like this is Margaret Atwood. Just a woman with a nasty boyfriend. That's what the papers said, anyway."

Catherine tips her head to the side. Her own father had been a fairly nasty guy, from what she can recall—yelling, the shattering of Sue's only bottle of perfume, a firm smack to her own small hand as she reached for the remote control. Though Julianna Ohlin got murdered and Sue, as far as Catherine knows, bears no physical scars.

"No, but she was still a good poet. She can surprise you with weird lines, double meanings. She's funny when you're not expecting it. She died before she got famous, but a lot of people really liked her book." Catherine feels more confident, this time, saying the poems were good. She can't stop hearing the rhythm of the one about mopping floors in her head.

Sue shrugs again, the vee of her robe widening slightly. "All right, I guess I should try to read some more of her poems. You got anything I can borrow?"

"Sure. But you never heard anything about her, as an adult?"

"I heard that sonofabitch boyfriend of hers broke her neck after they moved away."

"Yeah, but nothing about her book? It came out the year after that. 1996, I think."

Sue reaches for her tea. "I probably heard something, but I never read it. You know that modernist stuff was never my thing."

"Yeah, yeah, Tennyson or bust."

"Oh, I'm not that narrow." Sue taps her empty cup down. "You really think she's good, the Ohlin girl?"

"Well, yeah. But I feel like I don't like her poetry as much as I should."

Sue keeps watching Catherine but doesn't say anything.

"She was a waitress too. She wrote poems about serving potato soup, getting orders wrong. About all the stuff I do—laundry, walking outside when it's hot, feeding the cat."

"You don't have a cat. You don't even like cats."

"I like them okay, I just think I'm allergic. But what I'm saying is—I feel like I've already lived her words, so they're too familiar. Is that weird?"

Sue stands up and puts her cup in the sink. "But you haven't, not really. Because even when she was washing her dishes just like you wash your dishes, even if she used the same soap, her life was not the same because her boyfriend was a rep-ro-bate and Grey would kiss your feet."

Catherine shakes her head, looks away, not because Sue is wrong but because she knows she's right—he would. "It doesn't all come down to the love of a good man, you know. People's lives are more complicated than just one thing that happened to them."

"Yes, but sometimes that one thing can colour everything else. You don't know because you got lucky the first time, finding him when you were only twenty years old. I haven't always liked everything about Grey, but he loves you 100 per cent and that's enough for me. You've never had to know anything else."

"I had other boyfriends. Remember Kev? Two whole years."

"Sure, but you were a kid—it was a high-school romance. You went out with him and did god knows what, but you still came home every night. Nothing really changed. But Grey changed your life. Even when he's not around, even if you're doing something that has nothing to do with him, it's better for you because of him. You could learn a few things from those poems, try to see things from the perspective of a woman who lived the other way."

"I'll try, Momma."

"So if you're sleeping here, you send that man a text. Don't make him worry." Her mother nodded sharply. "There's sheets in the ottoman. I'll make you some eggs in the morning."

"I've got class in the morning."

"I'll be up, don't worry. Good night, sweetheart." Her mother squeezes her shoulder like a football coach, sturdy and pushing.

Catherine flops onto the bare couch—her back and hips are tense from fatigue, her feet tender when she rubs them on the arm of the couch. It was a long evening, full of anniversary dinners and girls' nights out. But what she's thinking about are high chairs. If she and Grey had a baby, they'd need one. Lots of other stuff too, of course, but she's thinking about high chairs because of the spindly blond wood ones they have at the restaurant. They all get sticky with mashed pears and chicken gravy—she can smell it on her hands after she's had to carry one. But the babies like them, even though they're belted in—there was a red-headed baby in the corner tonight, patting a pile of spaghetti into pulp.

She always showers after work before getting into bed even though Grey says he doesn't care. Would she be so precious if she was only sleeping in two-hour shifts between breastfeedings? It's impossible to imagine. She texts, "Sleeping at moms" to Grey. She hopes he won't be annoyed—he was probably waiting up. "I love you," she adds and shuts off her phone before he can reply.

Lying on her mother's ancient red-corduroy-upholstered sofa, she's reminded of how much she loves her bed, hers and Grey's, a queen with a stormy blue duvet and a clutch of pillows at the head. It makes her homesick to think of the dark wood headboard, the low night-stands—nothing in the room is expensive but it's all theirs, picked out, purchased, and placed exactly as they decided. But a baby, a baby would challenge that precision: shrieks and wails, fingerprints and stair gates. Crayon on the walls, spit-up on the carpet. A baby would be perma-nent. Grey is ready for that, has been ready for a while, probably—he loves their domesticity, calls her his family. Usually their ten-year age difference doesn't matter, but here it might. When he talked about that possible child he seemed so confident, so grown-up, and she can't imagine feeling that way herself.

It's after midnight when she dips into her bag and pulls out the poetry book by the writer whose boyfriend was cruel, who died young and left behind no babies, only poems. She flicks the book open at random to find a poem about a bus, then one about a cat: *Archie, fur fanned over the edge of a cushion, eyes drooped low.* Would writing a poem be like having a baby? Would having a cat be like having a baby? Her imagination won't take her that far. She's too tired to read, so she flips on the TV, but the news has yet another story about poor Donny—an interview with his mother this time, with her rumpled blouse and heartfelt pleas. Maybe a poem is not like a baby because once you write one, it can never really be taken away. Eventually Catherine falls asleep clutching the book to her chest, thinking of that boy still missing, of the parents who dream of him.

—⁓—

There is something wrong with the car and now Catherine is going to be late for her dinner shift. Grey has been "working from home" today, which is usually just code for making caramel corn and playing video games. He does this a few times a year—no one seems to mind. Except today he hasn't been doing those things. Instead, he has been trailing her around the house all day, pausing in the doorway while she showers, sitting in the living room without a book while she reads. She keeps wandering over to give him a kiss or touch his hair as she walks in or out of a room, but he just cocks his head as if listening to her, though she hasn't spoken. Then he offered to drive her to work, even though the weekday buses aren't bad.

Catherine is still putting on her boots when Grey comes back in and announces that the car won't start.

"Oh." It's too late for her to take the bus—they've cut it too close. "Well, I guess I'll call a cab."

They wind up standing on the front lawn in chilled silence until an angular purple car slows down in front of the neighbour's house, briefly stops, then pulls up toward them.

Grey says, "Cabs never look like I think they're going to."

"You watch too many movies set in New York." She leans into his parka and kisses his cheek, then walks toward the taxi. When she opens the door, her elbow brushes his arm. "What?"

"I thought I'd come. For the ride."

She glances at him, then gets in, bumping her bum across to the far side. She gives the address to the bored driver as Grey bustles in, his parka rasping against the seat.

The cab backs too fast down the drive, wobbling in the rutted snow.

"You're being weird."

"What?"

"You're gonna have to get a bus back, then call CAA and deal with the car. It'll take all night, if you want to drive to work in the morning." She is staring at the taxi driver's identification on the back of the headrest. His name is John Lloyd, which surprises her, but then again, this is Iria. She has watched too many movies set in New York too.

"It'll be done before you get home anyway. Not your problem."

"True. But . . ."

"Look, if you're freaking out about the baby, I just wanted to tell you to forget it. Or put it on hold. Whatever. I'm not pressuring you."

When she faces him, his gaze locks onto hers instantly. The cab swings around a curve and she leans into the fluff of his parka. *The baby.* With the definite article, as if it already exists somewhere, only waiting for her permission to come out of hiding.

"I'm a lot younger than you."

"I know, Cat. I haven't noticed it makes a difference." He taps her knee, just a brief press of fingertips.

"But marriage is *more,* more than what I had before. I added you to my life, but I kept on going to school and working and seeing people. You became a part of all that, and didn't take anything away. But a baby—"

"You'd still have me, you'd still have your life. I wouldn't expect you to quit school or anything. The baby wouldn't be only your thing."

"Of course, but would I be able to work and study even if I had time? I don't know if I could focus on anything else if there was a baby. It might take too much of my brain or—I don't know."

She's thinking of all the times she babysat the Saunders' kid in high school. She could never believe a baby—only a few months old when she started sitting for him, not even twenty pounds of formless flesh— could keep breathing, maintain a heartbeat, even just exist with any reliability. So while he slept she'd creep into his bedroom and put her hand on his sleepered back and wait for the upbreath, the tiny expand. She did that every time she babysat him, a couple times a month for years, until he was a running, laughing child. She believed it kept him safe. The nights she'd try to stay downstairs with her homework and the cast of *Friends,* all she could see was tragedy—Mrs. Saunders sprinting down the stairs tear-streaked, shouting, "How could you let him just lie there?" The 911 call, the ambulance, the slow dark silence once everyone had gone away. How could a parent ever trust that disaster wasn't coming in the next beat?

How could Donny Zimmerman's parents have known—or Julianna's? That they would have these lovely children, perfect human beings—and then they'd be gone. But also, how could they not? Having a child was too much risk, too much wagered on a single, frail vulnerable body. How could they survive the loss?

Grey has turned away to tug on his hood, but he's talking, little dribbles of thought escaping from his mouth. "Wouldn't it be interesting, though, an amalgam of you and me? I wonder what it would look like.

But it doesn't have to happen, there's lots of ways to live a good life. We could travel, see a place other than Iria. Would you like to see Europe?"

"We're here." She leans into his face, not a kiss, just a press of cheek on jaw. "I love you." She cuddles into the grit of his stubble; she wants to stay in the cab.

He tries to pull back, murmuring, "I love you too. You're the whole point."

She keeps her arms locked until the cab driver shifts and says, "That will be $12.85." He has no accent and his name is John Lloyd, but somehow Catherine still feels he is from a faraway place.

—⁂—

Two nights later, and two days before the worst thing to ever happen to Catherine happens, she and Grey go to a dinner party at her mother's place. Sue has also invited her next-door neighbour Dayvid, her friend Seva from work, and Catherine's cousin Polly.

Since she has Grey with her and they have brought a cake, Catherine comes into her mother's building through the door. Once in the apartment, she takes her boots off by stepping on the heels and marches directly to the kitchen to set down her cake. It is frosted and elegant, and as she walked across the lumpy, unshovelled sidewalk from the bus stop, she was worried about ruining all her efforts. They took the bus so they can get drunk. "Well, not too drunk," Grey had told her, digging in the change box for bus fare. "It is your mother's house." Catherine nodded. "Maybe just pleasantly buzzed."

Catherine lifts the edge of the box and peers inside. The scrolls of chocolate frosting don't seem to be blurred. She lets the lid fall shut. "Hey, Mom, I made you this cake," she calls over her shoulder. Now it's no longer her responsibility.

"I'm right here, don't yell."

Catherine hugs her mom.

"You're still in your coat?"

She shrugs and starts unzipping. "I was worried about the cake."

"You worry too much. It's just a cake."

"I know." Catherine lets her arms go slack so that her coat slides off, then catches it and drapes it over a kitchen chair. "But it's a really nice cake. Took me forever to do all the roses."

Sue nods, watching Grey approach from the hall. "Hello, son-in-law."

They embrace, then Grey glances behind her at the cake box. "Was it okay?"

Something bubbles menacingly on the stove and Sue steps toward it, shaking her head. "You two."

The evening is long and comfortable. There's something about having the two people who love her best in the same room that makes Catherine feel invincible. Indeed, there aren't any jokes she makes that night that the group doesn't laugh uproariously at.

"This is the best cake I have ever eaten," says Seva with her fork in her mouth and a smear of chocolate on the back of her right hand.

"It is very good," Sue says, even though her own piece is less than a third eaten. "Worth all that trouble after all."

Dayvid grins. He is an older single guy, stooped and beaming. "A toast to the baker!" He raises his coffee cup.

"But she's not just a baker, she's a scholar too," says Sue, gesturing with her wineglass. "She is writing an essay on a famous poet and how she was murdered."

"Well, it's not really about the murder, just the poetry, mainly . . ."

Dayvid is gazing at her with his cup still in the air.

"Thanks, you guys." Catherine air toasts, drinks, feels Grey's hand squeeze her thigh.

Swallowing zestfully, Dayvid sets his cup down and regards the table at large. "What's this about a murder? In Iria?"

Seva nods jerkily. "Oh, you must remember—that young poet. She wrote a poem that got in the newspaper, years ago. It was about Iria in summertime, something about when the sailboats flutter onto the lake."

"Oh yeah, I forgot about that one." Sue reaches carefully for the teapot, glancing into everyone's cups to see who needs more. "They put it on some monument, didn't they? At the harbour?"

"And she was murdered?" Dayvid seems oddly delighted by the story.

Catherine shrugs. "That was later, and it happened out west, after she moved away. But I'm just writing about her poems, how she chose what to write about, how she elevated these humdrum subjects with such beautiful language."

Dayvid leans toward her. "And so do you write poetry too, or just write about it?"

"Oh, no, just about."

"Well, you used to write poems. In high school." Her mother is finally finishing up her piece of cake. Everyone else is on seconds.

"You did?" Grey dips his head into the space below Catherine's face. "How could I not know this? I thought I knew everything about you. A poet, really?"

Catherine can feel warmth creeping up her neck and into her face. She's trying to recall the actual poems. Some of them were about silent lovers and 9/11 and other things she knew nothing about. But there was one about a hug a friend gave her before moving to New Brunswick, a sestina about the way the lake changed colour through the course of a day. She really doesn't remember much—for the past ten years, what she wanted to do was read, not write.

"Everybody's something in high school. You're not a diplomat because you were in model UN one semester, are you?"

Grey jerks back from her and grins with too many teeth. "Of course, I know what you mean." He reaches across the table for the nearly demolished cake.

Conversation shifts to books and what everyone means to read soon and good movies and the pleasures of bad movies, the still-troubling story of that still-missing boy. Polly is scooching awkwardly around the tiny dining room to get back to her seat after going to the bathroom, but she catches Catherine's mention of Donny Zimmerman.

"Oh, that poor young man." She finally drops into her chair. "His parents go to my church. We pray for them constantly, but I don't know what to think. I fear they are losing hope."

Dayvid shakes his head slowly. "How awful. Do you know them well?"

"No, not well, but we're a close church community so it impacts us all. We raised close to $90 at the bake sale to help them with the posters, and our sister church put some up in Toronto, even though he wasn't the sort of boy to run away."

Sue pats Polly's hand gently and gestures at the teapot until she nods. Standing to pour, Sue says, "I can't imagine. Let me know when the next sale is, Pol—I'll help, or at least come buy a few things."

Dayvid looks toward Catherine again. "You should donate one of your marvellous cakes. You're a great baker."

Catherine shrugs. "Not really. Anyone could have made a great cake with that much chocolate and butter and sugar."

It's a fun party, by any standard, but Grey and Catherine don't stay too late or get too drunk. Even though it's freezing, the walk to the bus feels so easy because Catherine no longer has to carry the cake. She puts her hand into Grey's instead.

When they are almost at the bus stop she slips on a slick of ice hidden under snow. Her heart clenches—she's tipsy enough to slip but not tipsy enough not to mind falling—and she lets out something close to a shriek. She only falls to a forty-five-degree angle before Grey catches her. She lies limp in his arms a moment, then scrambles up, and curls into his chest until her breath calms.

"I'm sorry I screamed. Do you think anyone heard?"

Grey laughs. "You mean your mom? Probably not, we're half a block away. I'm probably the only one that heard you."

"Well, you were the target audience." She pulls back and they walk on, holding hands again.

"You could write a poem. If you wanted to."

"I could write a poem. I could have a baby. I could do a lot of things." She shrugs, pulling up their linked hands.

"Do you believe that?" He is trying to look into her face again.

She keeps her eyes fixed on the street ahead, watching for the bus. "No. But I could probably do that too. Self-confidence is a learned strength." She can see a purple light through the trees at the edge of the parking lot. The bus is coming.

"Sure. You got time. We do. There's lots of time for everything."

"We should have a baby." It's terrifying to say it aloud. "I'm scared, though."

Grey grins, stares off at the purple light, then gazes back to her. "I don't think they let people who aren't scared have babies—too cocky. All sane people are scared of something that big."

The night is bright and clear; they are young and alive. Young enough. The bus is almost at the stop. She tugs his hand. "Let's run."

Castle

Obviously the lawn has to be mowed. That's the sort of thing that would be an important, neighbourhood-building, property-values deal in town, especially in the south end down toward the lake. But even out here, with the big gaps between the houses and the road ending in an electrical field, you can't be too careful. Certain things you can get away with at the outer edge of the suburbs: clotheslines full of flapping Jockey shorts, a rusty dented gate hanging askew, maybe even parking on the lawn, but you should still be thinking it all through, every decision you make. You have to watch yourself; everyone else sure is watching you.

It's hot and there's not much shade, and you only have a push mower over all those acres. At least it's gas-powered; an electrical cord wouldn't reach a third of the yard and imagine trying to do all this without even a little momentum. It's still a good bit of work. There's kids on the road with flyers they stick in the mailbox, asking if you want your lawn done. They'd do it too—nothing is too hard to stand between a kid and $20. But nothing says they'd do a good job—you can imagine the jagged lines, a smoke break in the back, maybe a little rummage in the shed. A man's house is his castle, and you don't want anyone to start feeling they can wander around the property with impunity.

The surprising thing is that people out here think of themselves as living in a town. Of course, everyone lives somewhere, according to the post office, but when the real estate lady first drove you out late last fall, those long loops of telephone wires over the empty green fields seemed to say *Alone*. Even the mailman wouldn't be coming to your house—all you've got is a pick-up mailbox on the gravel shoulder of a road with half a dozen houses sprawled out among the fields and stands of trees.

But a place like this, even if you can't see your neighbours, they can see you. A couple weeks after moving in, just before the holidays, before you'd come close to feeling safe and comfortable, some hayseed came up to you in the IGA and said over the "Frosty the Snowman" Muzak: "I see you bought the old Svenson place." Before you could ask how the hell he knew that, he added, "Seen you shovelling the drive. Don't envy that work, no, but it's a nice spot you got. Svensons kept it up good."

You just have to shrug, and maybe even say something funny about Frosty, but you sure do take note. A man's home is his castle and if it's under surveillance, that is certainly an act of enemy aggression. You have to get your angry face under control because when he sticks out his hand and says, "Steve Ossington, but people call me Steve-O," you're going to clasp his palm and say, "Dex." Even that's a gift, even that will cost you something, but it's like an investment. It's strange, how you've got to build relationships just to be left alone.

A castle must be guarded, so once you know you are being watched, take precautions. You put up the old thick white plastic venetian blinds you didn't think you'd need living across from a cornfield, but there's neighbours on either side, and they peer close as they slow-drive past. Absolutely you'll need heavy blackout curtains in all the bedrooms at the front. The basement window is tiny and around back anyway, so you feel like you can let the rabbits have some sunlight. But before it's even spring, you start to question that when a meter-reader winds up on your back lawn inspecting the brickwork, leaning low enough to see your private business, maybe even the rabbits, through that little window. So you plant hedges all along the side of the house, and that stops that.

You can fortify your house—can and must make it impenetrable to all the prying eyes in the world. But that doesn't extend beyond the property line.

It's around the first real heat of June that you meet Steve-O again, this time at the Shoppers Drug Mart, and he introduces you to Mrs. O, all yoga pants and overfull cart. She grins, thick soft lips.

Just stand with your Arctic Air deodorant and pack of Gillette disposables like you're looking at the insides of your own eyelids. That's the trick, to act like your eyes are shut even when they're open.

"Hey there, Dex—nice to meet you. I'm Janet, I'm sure Steve-O has told you all the good stuff." She slips into the line behind you while Steve-O ogles the gum display. She wants to talk, of course—about church, about sales at the drugstore, about your big flat lawn and the work of keeping it nice. The lawn has made you much more exposed in summer—you have to be out there at least once a week for a couple hours, put on a show for everyone to watch.

"I got a ride-on I could lend you, Dex," Steve-O says without glancing away from the gum. And yet, he's clearly been listening to this silly woman prattle on. The things marriage makes men do.

"Oh, don't worry about me, I don't mind," is what you have to say. What else could you say?

"No worries, I can get it in the back of the flatbed. Just a small favour among neighbours, really." He turns and grins, exposing the over-red gums of a smoker, and gives his wife a little side-arm hug around the waist for no reason you can see.

Honestly, favours are going to be trouble more often than not. At the end of an interaction, a man likes to think that the interaction is *done,* but with a favour something is always left hanging. Pay a man and you can walk away; a favour keeps you caught.

But Steve-O is all right, and it's already sweaty-warm out and so you can bend just a little. The first couple times, it's all fine—you slip Steve $10 for the gas and the guilt of it, but he's happy to haul the mower down the road to you—even though you could probably wedge the mower in the back of your van and spare him the trouble. Unfortunately, he says he *likes* stopping by your place and worse, his wife's always "along for the ride" (scarcely a hundred and twenty seconds down the road is hardly a *ride*—it's as if the man hates to be alone, which does not bear thinking about). She's the one with the comments: "Oh, such a lovely forsythia hedge!" "You might want to check that crack in the asphalt by the garage before it gets deep." Busybody. Steve-O just beams at her. The questions are worse than the comments because it's ruder not to respond: "Now, Dex, are you coming to the church bazaar on Saturday? Or did you want me to save you some butter tarts and bring them by afterwards?"

Of course that's exactly the sort of prying nobody needs, which is why when the heat's not too bad, you do the whole place with the push mower and that's just that. It's a small price to pay to keep her from demanding a tour of the house or god knows what else. It's been just you and the rabbits all this time, you figure you can go a little longer without Janet Ossington's company.

'Cept it's a long slop, out there in the hot sun—and so it's understandable that you might break down and ask to borrow that ride-on on the hottest days of the summer. The Ossingtons are fine, in their way, and generous too, so you try not to mind their prying chatter. But it's tough—Janet always seems to be after some piece of information or another.

One time when they were dropping off the ride-on, she told you some damn story about an overcooked lasagna. "I never know when Steve-O or the kids are gonna be showing up, asking for dinner. You, you got it easy, since you cook for just yourself and you would always know when you are gonna be there to eat or not."

This makes so little sense you wonder if she is hinting about the rabbits—judging you for being a single man with just a couple of pets, no woman to cook his dinner. Modern society doesn't much value independence, wants to see everyone paired up and locked down. But who knows what she's thinking, and you don't want to guess. So just politely tell her you've got to be going and wait for Steve-O to shepherd her to the truck. There's a lot of lawn to be mowed before sundown.

You've got to have a job—everybody does, or anybody worth anything does. What the job is doesn't matter too much, as long as it keeps the mortgage and MasterCard people happy. And the warehouse is cool enough in summer, sometimes there's pizza on a Friday. An order-picker—that's what you do, but it's not who you *are*. It doesn't pay to dwell on it too much. Go in, do your eight, go home. It's what a man's got to do.

Go on home, careful on the sharp bends on the way out from town. Heat shimmers in the air—it's hard to see proper when it's this hot. But you are almost there, and closest to home is where vigilance is most needed. Don't be blinded; see what there is to see.

Go up the driveway, black asphalt that you've patched and is now smooth and gleaming, like black ice in summer. Unlock the door and step into the cool of the air-conditioner—not central, just on this floor but still, something nice that makes your home feel that much different from the outside world. A literal temperate zone, away from the blazing craziness of everything.

Shut that heavy wooden door and feel it seal behind you, sealing you in with the cold and your things and your own self, away from the neighbours and colleagues and all those outsiders.

Look around—is it all as you left it? The stonework by the fireplace, dusted, ashless? You might, as winter rolls in, consider stacking some cordwood against the back wall—it is good to be self-sufficient. The slim, even black handles of the knives in their block—are they aligned? The sharp-cornered new bar of soap to the side of the bathroom sink—still powder dry, at right angles to the edge of the basin?

Downstairs in the basement, feed the rabbits. Spend time with them, don't just walk in, dump the food, and walk out. They have feelings too, aren't just dumb animals. They need your leadership, your presence. Play some games with them, show them that you can be kind and caring, but that you are always the boss. That is what they respond to, what they long for. A little bit of fun, a little bit of petting, and everyone sleeps better.

Once you're cool and comfortable, it's back out in the yard again—a man's work is never done. Today's only mid-twenties, so you're using the push mower. You do a nice even strip up, then a nice even strip down, then back out toward the road again, then back toward the house. You don't vary, you don't waver, you keep your lines straight against the one before. Your father advocated for the boxes within boxes, but few lawns are without encumbrances all the way round, plus doing that is a good way to get dizzy. Plus your father is dead, so who do you listen to now?

Up, down, alternating facing the glistening dark of your blocked windows or the blue expanse of the sky above the corn stubble. It's the end of summer but still hot, and the grass is still growing, though limper now, floppy. Not much more to go before the cold comes.

A fat maroon minivan pulls in the drive, and you don't know what it's doing there. Maybe they're just turning around and way out here, where there's no stoplights and no one looking, where everyone drives fast and listens to the radio and texts and throws trash out the window, they don't feel too comfortable turning in the road. You can get that—you're a man who understands the need for safety. You're a man who can offer the butt-end of his driveway for the occasional and brief use of a stranger, no doubt about it. You want the roads to stay safe and clear of accidents and the attendant scrutiny such things might bring.

But the van pulls farther into the driveway, and then there's the whirr-click of the engine shutting off. It's her. That woman, Janet Ossington, in snug jeans that stop at the wide part of the calf, and a pink tank top with wide straps. No Steve-O, though.

She walks round the van easy in her high-heeled sandals and comes right onto the lawn, her spike heels puncturing your sod. Doesn't waver. She marches right on over to where you are draped on the push bar of the mower, sweat running down your eyebrows and between your shoulder blades.

"Dex, Dex!" she calls as she approaches. The motor is loud—it's hard to hear. "*Dex!*"

She staggers in a hollow, probably dug by some damn rabbit or woodchuck. No, not a rabbit. But she keeps on toward you until she's forced to stop or walk right over the mower. She stares at you, and because she's not invited and basically is a trespasser it takes a moment to realize that she won't shout anymore, that she's waiting for you to shut off the mower and let her talk to you in a normal voice.

So you do.

She raises her eyebrows, squinches up her lips, and glances toward the van. "Dex, can Laura use your bathroom?"

Now it's your turn to squinch because not only *who the fuck is Laura?* but also what kind of strange demand is this to make of a *neighbour* while standing nearly in sight of her own house?

Is this a subterfuge? Is this an attempt at . . . what? What could she possibly want in your home? All she'd do, she and this Laura, is mess up the rugs with grass clippings and scare the rabbits and *look* at things. If there even is a Laura.

But there is a Laura—or at least someone is sliding the van door back and a fuchsia shoe touches the asphalt. The shoe is tiny and it's a small small girl who steps out of the van.

"Laura." The word is out of your mouth, whispered, before you even realize it. She's a lovely little child, soft flesh above her shoe, chubby pink calf and the tuck of knee, the dark navy ruffle of her shorts—

Janet shrugs, flipping her hair on and off her shoulders. "There's contractors working on the bathroom today, and they've got the water off. The toilet isn't even over the hole right now."

The second foot follows the first, the girl now standing blinking on the blacktop. A teal barrette holds her long caramel bangs out of her sleepy eyes and her mouth hangs dully open.

"They said they'd have it right by the end of the day, but Laura's only four and little ones can't wait. I was driving her to the truck stop at Stevens Corners, but when I saw you out mowing, I thought, *Old Dex won't mind a drop-in to use the facilities.* We'll be quick-quick."

And then, while you're still gazing at the pink cherub with her yellow T-shirt and elastic bracelets, the woman in front of you seems to see something she interprets as an affirmative—a nod, a smile, some small indication that you don't actually give. Janet pivots away and begins marching back to the blacktop.

Clear your throat, speak up, *speak up*, as she takes the little one's hand, because it's clear where this is heading. It's heading into the house. Your house. Your sanctum, your castle, your home. Imagine your glossy hardwood in the entry hall stained by the wet flecks of cut glass. You know Janet won't take off her shoes, despite the mat by the door. Hell, she probably won't even wipe them—she'll have gotten what she wanted, the inner view, and she'll be too busy looking, taking in your home and choices and rights and privacy and judging judging judging. Who knows what kind of trouble she could bring if she judges you lacking, inappropriate, wrong in some way. You imagine the rabbits in the basement, the startle and twitch as they realize that someone else is in the house, someone new. Their eyes widen even more and they open their tiny mouths—

"Get the fuck away from my house."

Janet is halfway up the drive with her daughter's soft hand tucked in her painted one. She takes a few more steps, slowing, twisting over her shoulder to meet your gaze.

"I said, get away. Who are you, coming here? No one asked you here." You're hot, sweating, shaking with exhaustion and rage—probably saying too much. But you need to be clear, need to make sure there's no doubt. "You take care of your own, I say—you take care of your household's needs, I'll take care of mine. Now get the *fuck* away from my house."

"Dex, I'm sorry, I didn't—"

You don't even have to raise a hand. She must see in your eyes how wrong this all is. Or who knows what she sees there, but she backs up toward the van as you come closer, finally running the last few steps. You can just follow slowly, not even speaking, yet the message is clear. She doesn't even open the side door, just scoops the child into the driver's side and shoves her across into the passenger seat. You see her eyes, rabbit bright, in the windscreen as she twists the ignition. As soon as she's got it in gear, you go back to your lawn.

Obviously, you shouldn't do things like that, can't swear at the neighbours, especially those who've lent you an expensive piece of machinery in the past. It's not classy, or neighbourly, or any of the things we're supposedly striving to be out here. But what could you have done, really? There are some things a man just has to do.

To Burn in a Bright Moon

Even though it's dark, Catherine closes her eyes. There's nothing she wants to see here, even if she could. She tries to think of something else, anything other than here.

A long time ago, before the worst thing happened, there was Donny Zimmerman's picture in the newspaper. She would see it and think, *Sad*. She read all the articles, but now she doesn't know which parts of the stories she remembers from what she read and what she heard later. She remembers his chocolate-frosting swoop of hair in his graduation photo, his high marks and loving parents who were both lawyers. He was on Secord High's basketball team: a late-night practice, a walk to the car in an empty parking lot—that was how Dex got him. She knew even then, reading the news on her laptop, sitting on her pretty blue couch back in her real life, that he was the sort of boy she would've had a crush on in high school. He would've known about her crush but been polite and even friendly if they were assigned to the same group project, though he wouldn't have ever asked her out. She knows Donny now, knows his fierce memory and love of cats and his jokes that are really just quotations from Monty Python sketches and not funny if you haven't seen those sketches. She knows the quiet thump of his beating heart against her face when she's resting against his chest so he can have the pillow, she knows his wide eyes straining to see out the tiny dirty window she cannot reach. She knows how he reacts to a pinch, a punch, a tender stroke along bruised ribs, the taste of apples. Catherine knows Donny Zimmerman in some ways better than she has ever known anyone.

And now he's going to die in her arms.

She never thought of Donny Zimmerman as an obsession. Back in the past, among the jagged scraps of memory, Catherine used to watch the news reports about Donny's disappearance—his parents' faces tight and miserable, his teammates lighting candles for him in the parking lot before every game. She'd watch half brokenhearted, half distracted while she finished typing her tidy little literature reports, her neat school assignments. Watching the news, maybe too much news, innocent and warm in her pyjamas, with all the lights on while her husband played *Mario World* on mute in the living room, Catherine may have wondered what Donny was really like, not as a crush or a headline, but as a person. Maybe he liked coffee, hated the Ramones, wanted to go to Scotland someday. That sounded about right to her, from what she saw in the photos.

There were so many photos—each poster and news report seemed to have a new one. He was a young man with a yellow button-up shirt, huge teeth, and a slightly crooked nose beaming against the standard cloudy-blue-sky backdrop in a school picture-day photo. A second school portrait showed him with a slightly younger face, blue shirt, more muted smile. In another photo, Donny is crouched on a green carpet of grass, surrounded by soccer balls he is pulling out of a net bag—he looks up at the camera like he has been caught unawares.

And there were many more—Donny in suits for dances, clipped out of basketball team photos, with thumbs up and tongue out by the pool. You could imagine an entire life in those photos—a tidy, perfect Facebook life, but still.

No, she had never thought of Donny Zimmerman as an obsession until she met him and realized how much she already knew about him. He was startled too—both that he had been in the news so much and that she had remembered it all. Donny was always real to Catherine.

She can't keep the tenses straight—she was at home watching the news and she didn't know him. And then she did. And now they are so close that even with her head full of another time, even though it is so dark in this room that she can barely see the outlines of his nose and ears when she opens her eyes, she knows how his face looks. She knows the firm pink curve of his lower lip and thinner double peak of his upper lip. She knows the crisp stubble that got fuzzier over time but never quite became a beard, though there are a few long patches on his chin and neck. He is so young, too young for a beard. She knows his bright eyes, the way they glitter in even the weakest light; though they are closed now, she can see them shine behind her own eyelids. She knows his breathing, the deep, shaky pattern of in and out these past few days. There are hiccups and pauses in the pattern now—more, she thinks, than before, though she has a hard time keeping track. She holds her breath until he starts again.

Catherine shifts back on the rug, trying to get the soft part of her forearm under his head. The way he's lying now, the whole weight of his skull is on the knob of her wrist. He has lost so much weight since he was in those basketball-practice videos they showed on *Live at Five,* but the head is heavy no matter what. There is no such thing as skull fat. Dex should have come down with dinner by now, she thinks, because the light has disappeared. But that could be a storm dimming the window, or cloud cover. Maybe Dex has just put something on the other side of the bushes to block out the sun. He would deprive them of even that, if he thought of it.

When Catherine first staggered down the stairs into the basement, she could barely see Donny in the flickering fluorescent light. He was just a silhouette of thick, wavy hair standing in clumps and spikes—he was no one to her, neither friend nor enemy. Donny was skinny even then.

Ever since Dex grabbed her, Catherine had known what was happening to her. She had tried not to know, but Donny's presence confirmed her terrifying theory. Taken. Kidnapped, and not for any ransom or reason. Just taken, to be kept.

When Dex beckoned her across the parking lot, dusk was falling and he just looked like a contractor in dusty steel-toed boots on his way home in an old van. He was sitting on the floor of the van, feet sticking out through the open back door. There was a map in his lap, a tube of Pringles beside him. He was a big guy, muscular and overalled, but he came off as placid and confused in the parking lot, just asking for directions to a building supply store in Turgrove. Why would he be so far off the highway, if he was heading for Turgrove, a distant suburb? She hadn't questioned it, had been tired from her shift, eager to help and to catch the bus, and get to Grey, dinner with Evan and Angie, her evening, her life.

It wasn't even late, or fully night, there were other cars moving around the parking lot. How did it happen? How did she allow it to happen? He waited for her to get close, then spent a few minutes asking dumb questions, getting east and west mixed up, making her lean over to see the map, before he hooked an arm behind her knees, and pressed his palm over her lips. There was something terrible in his hand, a rag that had been soaked in a gummy liquid, she couldn't place the sweet rancid smell. But even before she passed out, she never screamed. Not even one little whimper until hours later. She doesn't know why she didn't scream.

She woke up in a shadowy garage, her legs bent awkwardly under-neath her. Dex had opened the door to the van and was yanking her out by the armpits. She was slick with sweat and she could smell it from inside her open coat, thick and swampy, mixed in with the smell of dirt and motor oil. When Dex picked her up she tried to fight, but her limbs were just starting to respond. They fluttered limp and aimless. When he put her down, her legs were still weak and her face was wet with tears and drool and she wasn't sure; anything could have happened in the van. He hadn't struck her yet that she knew of, but what did she know; she didn't even know how long she'd been unconscious.

There is a gap here—she remained conscious, she hasn't forgotten, she just dances away from the memory, like fingers brushed against burnt skin. And then she's pushed, staggering down the stairs into the basement. Dex had been holding her wrists in his giant hand and when he shoved her down the stairs she was startled to realize she was free, or at least unbound. She had been struggling so violently and was still so doped, she had somehow imagined in her panic that there were ropes or chains on her, not just Dex's grip. She heard a sharp gasp, someone breathing at the other end of the room, a cough that sounded male. The first hit didn't fell her, but the second made her reel and then the floor just seemed safer anyway, so firm and cold. She crouched; she cowered. She didn't know Donny was weeping for her, pressed against the painted cement wall. She didn't know he was waiting to comfort her, as soon as Dex turned the lock in the basement door.

Now they sit together in the dark and she knows him well enough to stroke his face while she holds his head in her lap. His skin is cool and tacky with the sort of thick sweat you get with a fever. Donny's been dying for a couple days—there's a wheeze in his chest that could be pneumonia or a punctured lung. Neither of them have any idea what the problem is. She leans down close to where his face looms pale—it must be evening, the light through the high, tiny barred basement window is fading. "Are you hot?"

He twists his head and she feels his hair grating on her thigh. He says something, but she doesn't catch words.

"Not hot?"

There's a long pause, then a whisper: "Cold."

"Here, I'll—" She'll what, exactly? There aren't a lot of options. If the overhead light were working, she could find the blanket, but so little of the twilight penetrates the basement that it's a hopeless plan at this hour. It couldn't have gone far, but if one of them was wrapped in it when they went to the toilet bucket in the far corner and then threw it off—it could take hours to find. Sometimes Donny can find it by feel, but Catherine always loses track of what sections of the floor she's touched and has to start over. And Donny would be left alone while she searched. Instead, Catherine lowers her torso and squirms down to lie alongside Donny without letting go of him. She wants to be face to face: that way she can keep him warm, rest, and still feel him breathing, being alive.

Despite her careful manoeuvres, she accidentally drops his head sideways onto the floor. He lolls awkwardly and doesn't whimper as his nose grinds into the cement. He is too silent. If he has died without her realizing, if she doesn't get to say any kind of goodbye—that can't happen. When she finally positions the length of her body beside him, she leans her face toward his to see if his eyes have opened.

Ever since the last fluorescent tube in the ceiling fixture blew out a day or two ago, they've only had the dirt-encrusted window for light. Some sun does come through, but just a glimmer, striped by the security bars and the branches of the hedge.

But now night is falling and it's goddamn dark and Donny's face is all jut and shadow, and she has trouble making out if his eyes are open even with her cheek pressed to his. Then he says, "Cat," and she slumps with relief.

"Yeah, Don, I'm here. I'm here. What do you need?"

It could be a sigh, or just his usual raspy breathing. "I don't know. No. I don't feel good."

Some of the shadows are bruises, she knows. Dex took Donny upstairs early in the week and she could hear the blows falling. When Dex comes downstairs empty-handed, that's what happens—if he isn't bringing them supplies, he's wanting something, someone.

She can hear Donny's voice again, softer now, just breath shaped into words. There are no other sounds in the house, not even the TV. It has been like this for a while, she can't tell how long but longer than usual. Is Dex gone? Did he leave them? Could something have happened to him? When she strikes out against his chest or arms, he feels as solid and unbreakable as granite, but anyone could slip in the shower, bang his head, lapse into unconsciousness, drown in three inches of water, not be found for weeks in his sealed-up house. She knows there is no way out for her without Dex somehow allowing it. Even with Donny whispering against her face, she is still thinking about the ways out for her.

He is saying something rhythmic, not conversation but a chant. "'Why, look you now . . . how unworthy a thing you make of . . . me! You would play upon me . . . you would seem to know my stops . . . you would pluck out the heart of my . . . mystery . . .'" He keeps pausing to wheeze and gasp, but Catherine knows he is reciting *Hamlet* again. He was not studying that when Dex took him—his grade twelve class had finished it the previous semester, but he'd memorized big chunks for the exam and it stuck with him. In return, Catherine offered him all the Julianna Ohlin poems she could remember from working on her essay for Professor Altaris's poetry class. At first she tried to describe them— the bit about a stray dog finding half a doughnut in the grass, the sad moment when the truck tire crushes a tomato—there were lots of great little images that made Donny smile and nod, or at least gave them something to talk about for a while. She found she knew a lot of the poems off by heart—stanza after stanza of Ohlin's work unspooling rhythmically from her mouth, sometimes catching her by surprise. She wasn't sure she was getting the poems right. She had always found her memory to be more faulty than it seemed, convinced she'd gotten all the groceries when she was missing half. Had she invented some of the lines? They *sounded* right, so it didn't really matter if they were hers or Julianna's. Anything Donny and Catherine remember, think or imagine, they've said to each other so many times now that the stories and poems and lines and anecdotes belong to them both equally. Everything is shared.

She knows so much about him—the love of English class, the way his voice seems deeper when he sobs, every movie he can remember watching, how far he went with his first girlfriend. Only girlfriend, now, she realizes. "'. . . you would sound me from . . . my lowest note to the top of my compass . . .'" The wheezing is getting worse, and his voice is fainter. She leans in and tries to shush him, tells him to rest, but he just keeps going: "'. . . and there is much music, excellent voice in this little organ . . .'" He is losing the tone, the appropriate cheerful rage that he usually brings to these lines. He has taught Catherine the whole play; he doesn't seem to have any trouble explaining why characters acted the way they did. She imagines him sitting beside her in Professor Altaris's class, nodding at the lectures, sharing notes on meter, discussing close readings, borrowing books. He was supposed to graduate this spring— he could be in classes with her at the university in the fall. Except they are locked in a basement and Donny is delirious.

"Donny." He doesn't pause. "*Donny!*" She shakes him gently and his face tightens in pain; even in the dim light she can see the harsh creases at the corners of his mouth.

"Hey, Cat. Hey."

"How do you feel? How's your . . . breathing?" She doesn't even know what to ask.

"It hurts. I dunno. Did you call Kyla?"

She has to stop and think. She knows all the major characters in Donny's life, former life, but she can't imagine interacting with any of them. They are only characters to her, in the story Donny keeps telling. Kyla is his girlfriend. Yes. Catherine is so tired that it takes a long time for her to realize that Donny's question makes no sense. If she could have called anyone, she would have called everyone, months ago. They would no longer be here if she could have called anyone, ever, even once.

"This one time, at school, I was supposed to meet Ky after . . . and walk home with her."

"Yeah?" Suddenly he is speaking so easily, the words tumbling. This should be a good thing, but Catherine isn't sure it is.

"'Cept I had this English quiz, right? And . . . for some reason I bombed it, just couldn't answer one damn question. And it was on . . . *Hamlet,* and I love *Hamlet* . . . It was crazy, not knowing those answers— like having a stroke. And then, I handed in this—" his breath catches in his throat, a high-pitched hiccup.

Catherine loves Donny in the fierce way of love that has no other outlet. And because he has been so kind to her, ever since her first day in this place, giving her sections of his orange when she ate hers too fast. And because he is a sweet kid with an A average who never cheated on his girlfriend, and he doesn't deserve to die in a basement with a stranger he has never seen in good light.

But most deeply, Catherine loves Donny because he keeps her from being alone.

—⚏—

Catherine has never been alone, not really. She met Grey when she was twenty. That year she was taking her third university class, English literature since the beginning of time, and working the dinner shift in a strip-mall restaurant on the edge of the city. She had a few good friends, plus her mom was always there, and then she had Grey too. They met in the emergency room after a slosh from the deep fryer scalded her left arm. Sitting in the basement, she struggles to focus on that incandescent moment when her eyes first met the man she would marry. At first, the whole memory is pain—a hot blur of it. But when she thinks for a while, and there's nothing else for her to do but think, she begins to pull out the individual filaments, isolate the luminous moments within the pain.

That scalding felt exactly like the bone-deep fire she would've suspected, and even after all the Tylenol she had in her purse, her mind was just a blaring red veil. For a long time—she doesn't know how long—she sat in the slick vinyl chair of St. Anne's Hospital ER, clutching her arm wrapped in a dishcloth she was increasingly certain was not even clean. That's the centrepiece of the memory: how her body felt perched in that uncomfortable chair with her healthy right arm reaching across her body to brace the pulsing pain of the left one. She has saved this description of the agony all these years because there was no space for it on the intake form.

The restaurant manager, not very interested in her injury but vaguely afraid of lawsuits, had sent another waitress with her to the hospital. Aimee bought Ringolos from the vending machine, and then ate them one by one off her pinky finger, sitting hip to hip with Catherine, staring straight ahead. Catherine was sweating under her hair, woozy from the pain, convinced microbes were invading her body from the thick beige cotton dishtowel, but she still would've liked a Ringolo. To have at least been offered a Ringolo. A burn victim should have privileges and, in the fuss, she'd left her bag at the restaurant. Finally she just asked.

"Hey, can I have a couple of those?"

Aimee stared at her as if she were something dripped on her dress. It wasn't that nice a dress—the staff at Betty's had leeway with what they wore, but Aimee always wore black shapeless things. Catherine shrugged. "I don't have any change."

Aimee tipped the bag toward Catherine, who gingerly unlocked her fingers from around the grimy towel and inserted one possibly also grimy finger slowly into the red foil bag, trying to slot her fingertip into a ring without being able to see them. Aimee rolled her eyes.

Walking past, a man said cheerfully, "Ringolos are the *best!*"

That was Grey, and she would find out within the hour not only his name but also that he had fallen from a low rock wall he'd been climbing for no real reason. His friend Evan had brought him in to have his arm set and, waiting in the chilly waiting room, Grey clutched his arm in the same cross-body hold as Catherine did. As he sat carefully across from her, he nodded at her arms. "Hey, we're mirror twins." But they weren't really, because Grey's shoulders hung loose, and he chatted with his translucently blond friend about the CP24 weather screen in the corner in a manner that did not suggest he felt the same pain pulses she did. He was older than her, she knew by the flash of skin on the back of his head, but he was bouncy with nervous energy, and he spoke just a bit too loudly, like a boy.

Aimee sucked barbecue-flavoured dust off her finger, then glanced at her watch. "Okay, I'm gonna go."

Catherine crunched down on a thick potato-paste O. It was funny how the pain didn't fade, or become more tolerable as the night went on. Her arm was still a hot throb, a mini-sun stuck under the filthy dishcloth. She chewed and swallowed. "Go?"

"Yeah, well, my shift was five to eleven, so Dave's expecting me? And I gotta get my bus, right? Else I'll be here all night?"

The pulse, the scald. What could she really ask of Aimee, who wouldn't even share her snack foods without prompting? Make her miss the bus? In Iria, that really would waste the whole night. "See you, then."

Aimee's blond head loomed closer. "What did you say? You're all slurry."

"Just—just, good night."

—∞—

Catherine whispers whatever kind, sweet words come into her mind: *quiet, calm, soft, relax, okay, love, space, good night, perfect, gentle, eventual, night.* Then she recites one of the Ohlin poems she remembers, *In the motherly darkness, in the tight warm quiet of night.* . . . Professor Altaris said that poem was about secret anger, about hiding, and something that could not be said, but Catherine doesn't see that at all. Even now, when she's so angry for all that she's lost, for Donny, for all the cuts and bruises on her back and thighs, the poem doesn't seem angry to her—just comforting. She says it to Donny again, the part about the cat's cool ears and the swampy smell of home, and then continues through every poem she can remember, giving him the sound of her voice, her words.

He twists to face her, muttering, "What happened to Julianna? Did she write another book?"

She often tells Donny facts about the poet too, things she remembered from Professor Altaris's lecture or the biographical note in the back of her books. Catherine had done a lot of research for her paper, so she knew that Julianna had lived in the west end of Iria when she was a kid, that she'd gone to the same university as Catherine and maybe where Donny would go someday. Catherine struggles with how to talk about the husband, though—usually she just stops at that point, but tonight she is tired. Donny wants the stories to go somewhere good, for Julianna to be happy or at least successful, but she can't give him that, even though she really wants to. Still he's asking and she hasn't eaten or had any water or even peed all day, and she can't think of anything to do but answer.

"She had another book, but other people put that together from what they found in her notebooks after she died."

"No. How old was she when she died?"

Shit. Donny is hurting too much. She wanted to tell him beautiful fairy tales, but she can't lie—she never could. "She died when she was twenty-seven; everyone was pretty certain that her boyfriend murdered her, but it was never proven. He . . . drove his car off a bridge and killed himself, so it never came to court."

Donny's slender body goes limp against her. "Oh. That's awful. She seemed—I thought she must have been a good person because the poems are so . . . kind. How could she have died so young?"

He's thinking about whether they will survive down here, or for how much longer; certainly that's what Catherine is thinking. She suspects he wants Julianna's story to have a happy ending so that they will have one too. So she keeps trying to patch up the story, make it okay. Okay enough.

"She was a strong person, so she probably stayed a strong presence after she died. I mean, you know, sometimes you can feel the spirit of someone who has passed on, giving you strength or . . ."

"You mean like a ghost?" Donny's voice isn't mocking, and Catherine finds that strange—despite his sweetness, he has a teenager's sarcasm, usually. But he wants to believe.

"Maybe. I don't know. Sometimes a part of them stays with the people they cared about, don't you think?" She hopes it's true.

Catherine keeps murmuring, a long, slippery story about Julianna's spirit drifting above the city where she died. Poems float into her head and she grabs whatever scraps she can and says them aloud, then goes back to her story.

For a while, she thinks the words are helping: first Donny stops his anxious periodic whispers, and then the tension in his back and shoulders seems to gradually slacken. Then his breathing slows. The hiccups and pauses resume. A cough. Another jagged pause. Three more breaths, then no more after that. His ribcage isn't moving anymore.

She does not feel alone in the room, which is how she was expecting to know—so she doesn't accept it yet. But she has been sobbing for a long time, so hard she's gasping for air, crying in a way she hasn't yet no matter how much Dex hurt her. Part of her thinks Donny might wake up in a moment, and another part is hollowed out, numb from the knowledge that he is gone. His body is not cold, though, not while she holds him close.

Leaves, mother, air. The one I love looking down into the moon on my face . . .

She is not fully awake, and the room is so dark that Donny is just moonlight and dust in her eyes. But he feels heavy against her chest and belly. She will tell herself later that she did all she could, that she held him when he died, and even though she did not feel the exact moment his life slipped away, it had to have been while she was holding him because when else would it have been?

When next she's fully conscious, it's darker, the moon is gone, and his weight on her is dull and cool. She knows for sure then, stops hoping, but it feels wrong to push him off, to struggle out from under. Wrong because it would hurt his feelings, feelings that he no longer has, make him feel stupid and rejected—he is sensitive that way. Was. But isn't anymore.

She screams then, from how her brain bends under the complexity of what is not anymore, and having not eaten all day or seen the sun or her husband or been touched with mindless affection for so long. She screams and wails and beats against Donny's silent chest. And then she sleeps again, or something like sleep. There are no more thoughts for a while.

—m—

Grey told his story quickly, a touch contritely, to the nurse at the desk, and Catherine tried to appear as if she wasn't listening by watching the doors through which Aimee had disappeared. Catherine wasn't particularly interested in what was wrong with Grey; she listened because the only other distraction was an infomercial for some kind of washcloth on the television above her head. Along with her purse, she'd left her book on Britomart and the Red Cross Knight back at the restaurant; otherwise she would have been reading. Grey was not fascinating to her until she loved him.

He eventually came back and sat across from her again, beside his friend, who had bought his own bag of Ringolos in the meantime. This was Evan, who stood up at their wedding in his brother's suit, the cuffs slumping over his palms; who once pulled her to safety at the side of a pool after she bumped her head on the waterslide; who always invited her and Grey to Thanksgiving—she didn't know anything about him then either. Evan offered some Ringolos to Grey, who shifted the weight of his limp arm carefully onto his thigh, which finally freed his other hand to grab a fistful. With half of them in his mouth, he inclined his head toward her and mumbled through crumbs, "You okay? I mean, obviously not, but okay enough? Even the nurses look worried about you. You don't expect that from them."

Catherine started to shrug, then felt a crinkling flutter of pain and stopped. "I'm okay, I think I'll be okay."

Evan nodded but remained focused on eating.

"I'm Grey. Fell off that cement wall in the park by the water. What happened to you?" Grey would never again be so forward.

Catherine was sick-dizzy. Heat seemed to press in on her throat, cutting off her air, bringing hot bile into her esophagus. She could feel sweat gloss her face. It had only been ten minutes since Aimee left, maybe fifteen—actually, she had no idea—but she was clearly in far worse shape now than she had been then.

"Burn," she whispered.

Grey's eyebrows shot up and beside him, his pale friend grimaced. "Burn?"

"I slipped. Oil . . . is slippery. It slipped, the chute, the round thing, it's like a slide for the oil, it slipped, and the oil splashed on my—" She remembered seeing the shiny yellow oil touch her skin. There probably hadn't been an actual sizzle, but in her mind it sounded like eggs in a pan.

"You have an oil burn, that's what you're saying?" Grey's forehead furrowed. She didn't know he was Grey yet, even though he'd told her his name. It hadn't become synonymous with *him* yet. Back then he was just some guy, but the years of breakfasts and naps and birthdays since have overwritten those first memories—he was always Grey. He leaned toward her, his intact arm cradling the broken one so he couldn't reach out to touch her. "You don't sound very good."

"I don't even work in the kitchen!" Catherine said. "Aislinn was on fryers, she was supposed to do it, but the funnel slipped so I leaned down to try to grab it, to keep her from getting burned . . ."

"Aislinn is the girl who was with you?" This was Evan, peering at her from under deep eyebrows. "Where did she go?"

"No, that was Aimee!" Catherine was disturbed to find herself almost wailing. She took a deep breath. "She had to get . . . the bus." She trained her eyes firmly on the first guy, then the second, even as they seemed to be receding from her in the over-bright room. It was the one whose cradled forearm mirrored hers who returned the gaze. She remembers that even as she remembers little else from the rest of that evening, retreating into pain haze and fluorescent fuzz.

—⁊⁊—

It has been dark down here for so long that Catherine can distinguish the tiniest threads of dawn penetrating the thinning branches of the hedge and the bars and her dirty window, the light slanting across the shit-brown rug allowing her to see—faintly, in silhouette—where she left the crumpled blanket when she got up at some point. She has no clock, and hasn't kept track of days very well, but it seems like the light is taking longer to come each morning—the days are getting shorter. She was brought down here when spring was just on the horizon, and the cycle is turning again.

She watches the light grow stronger and more vertical until it is a diffused glow, beamless but striped with the shadows of security bars, lighting the room to reasonable brightness, so that she can see the numbers on the ancient TV dial, read again about Taylor Swift's problems in her one issue of *People*. "I think my eyesight is getting stronger," she tells Donny. "I swear I can see more these days with less light." She nods, still gazing at the window.

Donny's been gone for some time now. Dex hauled him away, flung over his shoulder like a drunk kid on prom night. Donny never went to prom. She keeps talking to him because she doesn't want the basement to be silent, and because she can't imagine another person there—her and Donny are the only ones who make sense in this room. She is still telling him stories about her childhood, the places she's worked, the books she's read. She is still reciting Julianna's poetry to him, whatever lines come back to her. More and more do, appearing in her mind in the mornings as the light winks in. The more time she has to go over each poem, the less she feels she understands—the stanzas keep changing meanings, or their meanings to her. She imagines being back in Professor Altaris's class, sitting quiet in a shiny plastic chair, listening and thinking and reading. Writing down titles she might get from the library, studying the bright blue PowerPoint slides on the screen. When she didn't understand something, she would just raise her hand and ask a question. So breathtakingly easy.

Even at midmorning, when the basement gets the most light through the hedge, what she can't see, not really, is herself. Catherine is convinced she's getting paler, but without Donny, who can tell her what she looks like? Even if he didn't say, she could tell by his face what he saw in hers: if he said, "Don't worry," she knew her eyes looked tense and darting; if he told her funny stories about pranks the guys on his basketball team played, her fear must have shown in her bitten lips. If he was silent but stroked her back, Donny was frightened of her rage. She's sure Dex cannot see her face, has some way of not seeing her eyes and nose and soft cheeks—how else could he grind them into the gritty orange runner in the hallway upstairs, strike them with the side of a bathroom scale? When the bruises and scrapes on her face were fresh and gory, Donny would kiss them, soft dry lips, a gentle press, like her mother would when she was a little girl. She did the same for him. What else did they have?

At the Clinique counter, the white-coated makeup ladies assessed Catherine as "olive-complexioned," which seemed to translate into dark-skinned, permanently tanned. But now that she has been indoors and away from the sun for so long she feels bleached to bone. She gets up and stands on tiptoe in the spot where Donny stopped being alive, the place she prefers to stay, but she can't see out the window at all from across the room. The only place she can peer up and out through the security bars and thick glass and the tangled branches and dead leaves into the smudged and muddy sky is directly below the window. Walking across the room is a long journey, but she eventually gets there.

Dex's basement is deep; he probably chose it with Donny and Catherine—or people like them—in mind. But still it is a basement, the ceiling looming not far above them. The windows were just shallow bands of glass striped with bars, but Donny could see out pretty well. He was taller than Catherine by a good six inches—a born basketball player. She would ask him for the weather report in the mornings when they woke up and he would stand at the tiny window, the sill level with his eyes, and tell her what he could see of the sky. It got more difficult as the summer wore on: Dex planted hedges and they leafed out fast. She suspected Donny made up a lot of it—the swooping crows, the glints of dandelions, a wandering raccoon—but she appreciated the stories, the sound of his voice, the reminder that the outside existed, that it could be seen.

Now the windowpane is cold to the touch and the leaves on the hedges have started to die. Has she ever really been out there? How could she ever manage it again? On certain hungry mornings, when Grey seems like a fairy tale her mother must have told her, she is convinced that her skin has gone too white and fragile for her to ever step outside again; so dark is the room that she would probably burn, even if only by the light of a bright moon. She thinks the time to go, if there was one, has come and gone.

When she woke up in the hospital, her was arm thick and stiff with gauze. The light spiked under her dry eyelids, and then Grey was there, on a bed across from hers. He was just sitting on the edge in his jeans and polo shirt, with his parallel arm in a cast, reading a copy of *People* with Jennifer Aniston on the cover, while Catherine was in a gown and tucked fully into her bed.

"Did you stay . . . did I faint or . . . Did you stay for me?" Her face was warm.

"Well." He shrugged awkwardly, with only one shoulder. "It was too bad you were by yourself after your friend left, and you seemed so scared. Besides, it took them a while to fix me up, so I wasn't waiting that long."

She shook her head, hair grinding against the pillow—pathetic.

"You said you didn't want to be on your own. No need to . . . I have time."

She squirmed. "I said that? I don't remember."

He nodded, the half-shrug again. "It's fine."

Catherine felt clean and light and her arm didn't hurt; they must have given her drugs. Grey was watching her closely. She said, "I'm sorry to keep you here so late."

He smiled, but soft and worried, no teeth. "It isn't late." He glanced around. "You can't tell because there's no windows, but it's not late— it's early."

She smiled, something in her veins making her slow and sweet.

"It's *morning,* Catherine." She jolted and saw Grey flinch in response. "The nurse told me your name. I'm Grey, by the way."

"Grey. It's morning. Today is morning. It's now."

—⁂—

Dex is in the basement, which is unusual. Lately, he just calls them up from the open door at the top of the stairs. Calls *her*. No *we* or *us* anymore. No plurals at all now. Dex bumps her against the wall, tries to draw her into one of his chase games, but he quickly gets frustrated—she's tough to catch in the darkness, and she knows the room so very very well. She knows how to skirt the edge of the morning haze from the window and stay invisible, how to use the TV stand and the toilet bucket and the door frame to the old cold cellar to her advantage. She barely falters. He still gets his hands on her and slams her into a wall once or twice, mumbling about her being a bad bunny and running too fast on her long legs. She rarely listens to Dex anymore; he doesn't make much sense and it drives her crazy trying to figure him out. She just scurries, both because he likes it and because she wants to. She's tried going limp many times, but if Dex gets angry because she won't play the game he wants, things get worse for her.

She hears Dex's heavy boots stumble and a loud *Oof* as he hits the TV stand. He must have tripped over the blanket. He mutters the words *Dumb cunt* and slowly goes back up the stairs. Catherine and Donny could never agree if it was better or worse when Dex dropped the weird game of them being rabbits and they were all just humans again. There are bangs from above. When Dex comes back down, he brings something long and white, something metal that clanks, and a flashlight. The wide gold beam of brightness snaps the room into focus, paints it strange and electric—she doesn't recognize what she is seeing. Is this where she has lived all this time, with these rusty pipes, this dirty rug, this sickly shade of peach paint? Is that where Donny told her about his first kiss, there on the brownish cement under the window? She used to know what the basement looked like, but the light blew out ages ago, or at least that's how it feels. It didn't seem so grim, so cement, so real. It was better in the dark.

Dex sets the metal thing down on the floor and steps up on it—a step-stool. Then he clenches the flashlight between shoulder and jowl and reaches above his head to unscrew one of the glass tubes from the ceiling. She forgot, during her weeks in the dark, that there was a way to make it light again. Now, she's not sure she wants it to be. In the darkness, the room could be infinite. It's only the light that reminds her she's imprisoned. No, of course not. Of course she's known all along.

"Here," Dex says softly, without turning, but still she startles. He rarely speaks to her. Donny spoke to her. He was her friend and they spoke all the time, the way friends do. But Dex is speaking now. "Here, give me a hand—hold this." What he thrusts at her is a frosted glass tube, gritty with dust in her palms and rattling. The glass is cool in her hands, the dirt dissolving in the sweat of her fingertips. He is going to make the room light, all the time, illuminating the space where she is imprisoned, the place where Donny stopped being. She doesn't know if she can bear it.

Something *pings* onto the floor and he wobbles down toward the sound, the flashlight's beam wobbling too. He gives up quickly and reaches back toward the ceiling, trying again to unscrew the second tube. The flashlight faces forward once more. She can see only the back of Dex's head in silhouette. It doesn't often occur to her that she hates him, because it is irrelevant but also because Dex is only pain, not a person. He is only the absence of everything else.

He hands her the second tube. These are weapons in her hands. Glass swords, not heavy but surely sharp if she broke them. Who does Dex imagine she is? Has he had her so long that he's forgotten she isn't his? Is she so weak and useless now that he assumes she can do nothing to him?

A hot white rains down on them: fluorescent light in the room where she lives and Donny doesn't anymore. Dex has gotten one new tube in and is stooping to get the other out of its cardboard case. This is where she lives and Grey is somewhere else, in a clean, well-lit room aboveground, maybe longing for her. She longs for Grey and for the rooms he is probably in, their sunny living room with the picture window looking out onto the yard, the bright blue couch, narrow but comfortable, where she used to flop with her laptop, writing essays and reading the news and wondering where Donny was. Donny was here and now he is not here. And Grey is not here. And she has no one to protect but herself, burning in a false moonlight. When Donny couldn't run, neither could Catherine. She had to stay still, had to be hugs and jokes and humanness for Donny because she was the only one he had. Now Donny is gone and Dex has inserted the second tube and the room is so bright and Dex is about to turn around and see Catherine's face, her pale and only face, and then he'll hurt her again because that's all he does.

Before he turns, before he turns, *before he turns*, she is screaming inside her brain. She raises the glass swords behind her own head and then, with all her wavering strength, brings them down against his skull. But he spins around too fast, she sees his surprised eyes as she strikes, a baffled look of hurt feelings as well as shock. She doesn't hit skull, she hits *face* and not as hard as she wanted. It's all going wrong but the tubes explode with a tinkling boom, like balloons made of glass. Something dry and sour fills the air and Dex's face is bloody, sprinkled with glass, his eyes scrunch shut. Did she get glass in his eyes? Horrified, she flinches, closes her own eyes before she realizes that to hurt him as much as possible is what she wants—and she strikes at him again, and again. Dex staggers, lurching down from the stool in a stride that is half fall, grasping for her, but finally pitches forward in a snowstorm of shining shattered glass, draping over the top of the TV. The light tubes have broken into stubs in her hands—she throws the shortest one away and grips the end of the other, which still has some length of glass to it. And Dex is moving and she wants him to stop but the tube is short now, she has to get so close. Closer and closer, closer than is safe to his grabbing hands and mouth to reach his soft, stubbled throat, but she punches and stabs at whatever vulnerable cords and arteries are there, unleashing rivers of bright red blood. There's so much, so wet and slick. With every thrust she loses more glass off the end of her delicate weapon. Finally she can't tell what is cut and what is simply pooled blood on his neck. She risks a push, the first and only time she's touched Dex willingly, and he follows the weight of her hands, slumps whimpering to the floor. Her hands are sticky—the broken end of the fluorescent tube has cut her too and now his blood and her blood are blending everywhere, this terrible intimacy.

He stops making sounds. She can't be sure if he's breathing, but she won't go closer to check. Maybe she wouldn't be able to tell. She's shaking so violently and the cuts on her hands are throbbing and the bright bright light in her eyes. The light tube is barely more than the metal cap at the end now, and she lets it fall from her hand. Catherine starts climbing the stairs toward the door, which maybe he left locked and maybe he didn't. Dex never mattered, and he matters even less now.

Her hand is slick with sweat and blood, and it hurts when she grasps the doorknob, but she does not look down. It is hard to look anywhere, the room is so bright. The sun will be a far greater challenge.

The House That Modern Art Built

All the houses in the subdivision were enormous and sitting on little tiny lots, so they looked like fat people pressed up against each other in bus seats. But I was doing the kitchen, which was decent, and once you're inside you don't see the outside. I guess that's what the morons buying these three-car-garage monsters thought too.

We had a list of custom specs from the particular moron who had bought this place, including crown moulding, which I thought was basically assfuckery in a mid-1990s nothing-scape like this one, but Edwin could say, *Sean, the customer is always right* a thousand times and still not get tired of the words. I liked working for Edwin because he gave me a ride out from town in his van, and because of the gorgeous miter saw he had. I'd been using it for the windows and now for the mouldings. I didn't love my job, but to aim the laser line and then slide the blade arm through the pine like air—it was satisfying.

The actual house was never going to be beautiful, but that wasn't the point—I was hired to do a job and I was going to make sure my work was amazing even if it was going to get swallowed up by the larger shittiness.

Like you can see this ugly-ass woman and be revolted when you first look at her, but maybe she's got really good teeth or gorgeous tits or something, so you can get through talking to her by just focusing on that.

That's what I was thinking as I got out of Edwin's van at 7:57. We were only going to get a few hours of work in before the sun was so hot the hammer would skid out of your hand. That's the way August is here: disgusting. But the subdivision was half-built with people already living in it, and they had some rule that we couldn't be loud before 8 a.m., so we mainly lost working in the cool in the morning. Just carrying the toolbox and some wood into the kitchen, I was sweating. I couldn't be drinking much water when I was working indoors because we were getting to that stage in the build where if you left something messed up or wet or whatever, you might get called out by Edwin, or even by the owners if they showed up for a surprise look-see. Sometimes it was worse than being at home with Julianna because if she bitched too much about stuff on the floor, I could usually make her shut up, but at a job, I couldn't talk back—not if I wanted to stay. I hated owners, hated worrying about spilling a bit of water like a little kid, sometimes hated goddamn Edwin, but I loved those saws.

The thing was, assfuckery or not, the work of damn crown mouldings was nice, even in a stupid room. The house had forty-seven neighbours just like it, slick white suburban boxes with no need for crown anything—but I liked cutting the simple angled lines, fitting the joins, smoothing the edges. Julianna was a poet, all staring out windows and imagining shit, but I liked real things, like the wood that framed the window. Things you could touch and feel proud of, instead of scribbles on a page. She told me someone in the city wanted to publish a bunch of her stuff as a book, which kind of blew my mind. Usually it seemed like me and her were in agreement that writing was just her way of wasting time, the way watching TV was for me. She did work at it, reading a bunch of poetry books from the library and writing the same things over and over, even though there wasn't any point. When she heard about getting to publish her own book, Juli got so excited I didn't say nothing to bring her down, but in my mind, I was wondering who was going to buy a bunch of pages about our stupid cat, Archie, and the time I was plastered and drove my brother's truck over her garden. I read her poems of course, but afterwards I didn't know anything more than I did before, didn't feel any better or smarter, which I think is supposed to be the point of poetry. When I finished my day, all the windows in the house would be framed in—you'd think she would have seen the difference.

When Edwin came in from helping the other guys pouring concrete in the garage, he was not as happy with my work as I was expecting.

"Speed it along, please," he said. Edwin didn't smoke, but he always talked like he had a cigar jammed in the corner of his mouth. "This guy, he wants crown moulding so he can say he got crown moulding. It don't need to be fit for a king. Quit with the perfectionism."

Now that pissed me right off. "You want me to stop and let Caleb or Joey do it?"

"Those losers? Fuck no. Just make up time in the dining room, and wherever else. This ain't fucking modern art, all right?"

I kept my mouth shut and hustled it through the dining room without barely looking at what I was doing—I couldn't stand to look. The day got hotter.

"This house job is going straight to shit. The owner is coming by every day, sometimes twice. He thinks we're too slow, lollygagging on all these fancy extras *he* wanted. He walks around with his hands in his pockets inspecting stuff he doesn't understand. I'm not even sure he knew what crown moulding was when he asked for it, maybe he just thought anything with the word *crown* in it had to be good. He sure did stare at it for a long time, sort of squinting, like he was trying to make it out."

"Oh, yeah? That's crappy." Julianna was getting dressed to go to work when I came in, which was sort of the problem with her job. She was a waitress at a fake-Italian restaurant because she never got paid anything much for her poems—not so far, anyway. Waitressing meant she was always out in the evening without me. She kept saying that she wasn't "out" if she was at work. But the fact remained, she was at the restaurant with all these douchey pasta-eating guys, who would pat her ass if they got the chance, of course, because she had a sweet little curve back there, and she wore these fucking shorts that I could not believe were part of a uniform at a family restaurant—a saintly white blouse and these tiny black shorts like a Hooters whore. One time she'd been leaving for work when Edwin dropped me off, and he was practically hanging out the driver's window watching her walk down the side-walk. I'm sure it was the same with whatever guys were passing her all the way to the restaurant.

"Today, hottest day of the summer, the owner just stood at the other end of the living room, fiddling with a tape measure like a little kid— pulling it out to watch it snap back. So fucking annoying. I was sanding up the ends before I started the window frames. I didn't like to work when he was there, but you gotta get something done sometime, espe-cially when he's pushing for faster work. Of course he came over and looked at what I was doing and asked what I was sanding the end bits for. 'It need that?' He asked me that!"

"Oh, jeez, I'm sorry, Sean." She was doing up her shorts; she had to tug a bit to get the button done. I always told her to just scrape off the sauce and eat that, not the noodles, because carbs were bad for her ass.

I don't know if she listened to me—I bet she didn't—but she still looked damn good, and had the tips to prove it. It was a blessing and a curse, that ass. "What did you say?"

"Well, I'd've loved to not answer. But it was pretty clear I heard. So I just explained to him how yeah, you need to sand if you want a tight join. And he just fucked off—left, and took the tape measure too. What a loser!"

I chucked my shirt into the corner—Edwin don't allow the guys to be shirtless on site because he says it's unprofessional, but in the van we all strip off fast—and was heading to the can when Julianna said, "Hey?" She was twisting her blouse over her stomach. "Sean?" Then she just stood there blocking the bathroom door while I was just sweating and dying to take a leak, like she didn't know she had said anything.

"What, Julianna? What?"

"I think Archie's feeling sick today. Could you keep an eye on him?"

"Archie?" She was watching me with her big dumb eyes, making me feel like I was the dumb one. "The cat? Oh, he's fine. Cats are rodents; they take care of themselves."

"He's not a rodent." I only got a step forward before she grabbed my arm. Her hands were like ice, and I remembered why I liked her again. "I've just been so busy, with the extra shifts at work and trying to get the book ready and all. And then today I realized he might be sick—"

I shook her hand off and took another step away. "Well, that is your own damn fault, Julianna. You have responsibilities here, you have a job that you need to keep, but instead you're wasting time, writing shit no one wants to read—"

"They're going to publish it, Sean, I told you! A real publishing house sent me a contract."

"Yeah, yeah, for how much again?"

"I told you, $500. That's not nothing—and I put a lot of myself into that book. It's important to me to get things right."

"And for $500 you're going to kill the cat you supposedly love and lose the only job you can get."

"I won't—I just wanted—"

"Go to work, Juli, or it'll be you and that cat both feeling sick."

"They want to eat gravy but pay dry," said Edwin—some fucking metaphor. After he kept talking a minute more, I realized Edwin was actually going on about the owner refusing to pay proper labour costs. It would've been nice to understand that earlier in the conversation.

This was the next night: he ranted all the way to my place and then he wanted to come in. I knew he was hoping Julianna would be there. But what can you say when your boss drives you home and goes, "Got any beer?"

At least she wasn't there, though actually that pissed me off too—she should've scheduled her shifts so we were both home at the same time occasionally. And the cat *was* there, running ape-shit circles around our ankles. Edwin was eyeing the bottle of 50 I handed him as if I'd fished it out of the sea. He was reading the label for a full minute, even though there were about four words on there. I oughta've shown him one of Julianna's endless poems—it would've taken him out of commission for a week.

Finally he took a swig, swallowed, and looked down at the orange mess swirling around his feet. "Your cat?"

"It's Julianna's."

"Seriously?" He bent down and gave it a testing pat, as if you could tell by the fur who it belonged to.

"Seriously. You know a guy with a cat?"

Edwin sat his fat ass in a chair. "I've known just about every thing in my time."

"I bet." We drank in silence.

Edwin leaned over the cat again and tugged at the silver tag on his collar. "'Remember us with no familiar name'? What the fuck is that?"

I rolled my eyes. "It's a poem. Julianna had some fucking idea about . . . I don't know. The cat's name is Archie, and the guy who wrote that poem is Archibald something, so it's like—she loves that poet guy. I tried to read his book, but I guess I'm not a fucking poetry genius because it was all just trees and sadness to me."

Edwin nodded and shrugged and took another sip of beer. Really, he wasn't a bad boss. He got the job done, and he didn't put up with shit unless it was his own. I could've almost liked the guy if he didn't have a hard-on for my girlfriend.

"What's she up to these days, Julianna?"

"She's workin'. Italian place by the arena."

He leaned back and narrowed his eyes like he was going to say something filthy and I clenched up. "Oh man, I love them garlic sticks. You eat free there?"

"Naw, I gotta pay unless she brings leftovers home."

"How long till the end of her shift?"

"Long. Hours." I did not check the clock on the VCR.

"Yeah. I bet if you go in there, though, she'll set you up, right? Extra sauce, the good wine instead of the shitty house stuff?"

God, he was so hot for her, even the food she served was sexy to him. "Dunno. I never tried that."

"You never know till you try." He set the bottle on the table and stood, hitching his belt. "You tell Juli I might be stopping in some suppertime."

I thought about clocking him one but I needed the job. I was so hot and tired, and I'd drunk that beer so fast, I didn't know if I'd heard what I thought I'd heard. So I just walked up the stairs with him, even though I didn't want to climb those steep basement steps behind his swaggering ass, but I knew the door stuck and if you weren't used to it you couldn't get it open. It felt good to watch him fumble for a moment, though. When I closed the door behind him, the goddamn spooky-eyed cat was staring at me. I can't take that shit. I knocked him with my foot just a bit and he flipped down a couple stairs—just to remind him to show a little respect. Cats land on their feet, my ass.

When I got home Friday night, I was pissed off because Edwin kept us waiting in the hot van for ten minutes while he shot the shit with the guy who installed the window glass. Then he kept a tenner off my pay because he said I'd busted a blade off the jigsaw and what he thought I would've been doing with a jigsaw out there I just don't fucking know.

There was nothing to eat. The only thing in the kitchen was a bunch of old notebooks on the counter, for some reason. I opened one at random and read a poem about ice on an ice-cream cone. It wasn't bad, and I would've told Julianna so if she'd been there to hear it. I went out and picked up shrimp pad thai, came back, ate it while watching a movie where a dog plays basketball. Then I went back and read the poem again. I wondered if the ice cream she was writing about was from the shop down by the lake we used to go to back home—she thought it was romantic to walk and eat ice cream and look out at the water. Or maybe it was about the time we tried to make our own and it was a mess.

The cat went up on the table while I was in the can and he stole a shrimp. I locked him in the pantry, tossed the cat-contaminated food, opened a beer, watched the rest of the movie, then Letterman. Nearly midnight and Julianna still wasn't home. I shotgunned another beer in the kitchen. In bed I felt like I'd stay awake, but then it was morning and Julianna was curled beside me in a white linen ball, so I must've fallen asleep.

—⚏—

Work continued to be bullshit all the next week—still hot, still dull, still the fucking owner begging us to make it fancy but then cut corners and Edwin agreeing. After all the time I spent on them cupboards, they put on ugly plastic door pulls. Like zits on a perfect round ass.

"You can't be telling the client what he needs. It's the client who tells *us*." Edwin was unloading boards from the truck—I didn't even know what they were for. There was something else now?

I tried to stay on topic. "Correct me if I'm wrong, but generally, doesn't the client tell us at the beginning what he wants, and then leave things be? Correct me if I'm wrong, but the client is not usually in the house while we're doing the work."

"It is what it fucking is, Sean. I pay you the same per hour whether the work makes sense or it don't. This ain't modern art, I told you. So earn your money and quit bugging me, okay?" He shoved the ends of some of the twelve-foot two-by-fours at me.

I grabbed the wood and breathed deep. I needed all the oxygen I could get. "Fine."

We plonked the boards on the lawn. As I started to go, he said, "I was right—your Juli *does* help a guy out with a few extra breadsticks and the good wine."

I stopped with my back to him; I needed to work out what he was saying, if it was another of his fucking *metaphors*: Did he just go eat in Julianna's restaurant, or did he actually lay her?

"What'd you eat?" I said it like it was a code, which is all metaphor is. "If you'd told me you were going, I would've said get the chicken parm. That's the best." I finally faced him; he was just smiling like an idiot, squinting into the sun.

"Them lasagna rolls, man—those are the bomb."

"What time did you go? To the restaurant?"

"Late . . . lateish. I figured if it was the dinner rush they wouldn't like her chatting with a friend—" Edwin was not Julianna's friend "—so I went just before close, like."

"Like."

"You're a lucky man, Sean, and don't forget it. She let me stay while they was closing up and we had a little chat. Sweetheart, that one. A real sweetheart."

"Chat?"

"Well, I just asked her what was new. Imagine my surprise when she told me she has her own book of poetry coming out in a few months. How come you never told me that?"

I just stared at him. The answer was, Why would I tell him anything? But I figured I couldn't say that without starting a fight. "I didn't know you were interested in poetry."

"Oh sure, oh sure, huge fan. So this is exciting, getting her very own book published. We ought to celebrate."

"Well, I'm glad you and Julianna had such a good talk." He didn't seem to be getting my tone, but that was an act. To get that tone out of me was the whole point of the conversation.

Edwin kicked at the pile of boards. He still hadn't told me what they were fucking for. "You two ever step out on the town? I know a place, a couple young sweethearts of my acquaintance introduced me. Dancing, good beers on tap, good-looking people, great place to raise a glass to Juli's success."

I opened my mouth and he just about thrust a hand in. "Not a pickup joint—classy. You could take your lady for a night of celebration."

"Well—"

"You oughta think about it. These girls that I'm taking out tonight, they're all right, but they'll go with whoever pays for drinks, y'know. Would be nice to have you and Juli there too, for real conversation."

I shook my head, nudged the narrow boards with my foot.

"You just think about it. We won't be waitin' on you, like." That wink again, my god, I ought to have punched his face in when he did that. "I'll give you the address."

At home, the place was just piles of dishes and books and crap, and Julianna on the floor like a child, with a bunch of papers out in front of her and that fucking cat in her lap.

"What're you doing?"

"Oh, hey. Just working on the order for my book." She didn't even get straight up when she saw me come in—had to carefully set the cat down and stack up her pages so they wouldn't get kicked. Shows her priorities. Finally, she scrambled up to big-girl level. "How was your day?"

"Bar none disaster. The owner is totally dicking us."

She patted my arm but didn't really meet my eye. "That's too bad, Sean. I'm sure Edwin will sort it out. I got some veal for dinner, if you want."

Of course she would bring up that bastard right away. I stared at her to see if she looked dirty, like a liar. When I met her, way back in Iria when we were both practically kids, she was a virgin, or that's what she said. Actually she wrote a poem about it, how I was the only one, ever. I wasn't sure. She was hot, Julianna—I knew that even though when you've fucked someone a lot of times, it's hard to see their hotness. But with her I could always see it. I guess it got pointed out to me a lot by how other guys stared at her. They wouldn't let me forget for a second.

"It was on sale. Frozen stuff." I guess she thought me going all grim was because she bought expensive fucking veal. Her giant blue cow eyes didn't tell me anything—after all these years, I still didn't even know if I trusted her not to lie. How fucking crazy is that?

"What's modern art?" I said it because I suddenly knew she'd know. She'd gone to university, though she dropped out when I got the job out here.

The cat had gone into the kitchen and was yowling for its dinner. Julianna was walking after him as she answered. "What do you mean?"

"You know, modern art. The expression, the thing people say."

"Like Clement Greenberg? Or like Ezra Pound?"

"No, not like history. I mean Edwin's always going, 'It's not modern art,' when I want something I'm working on to be better and he doesn't. Like he doesn't want me to do too good a job."

"Oh, that's an expression. Like, it's not that important."

It was like a punch in the gut. It was good to know that's what she thought of my work. Good to know she was so knowledgeable about Edwin's expressions. Just fucking great. She went into the kitchen to feed that cat she loved so much, not even looking back to see how I felt. As soon as the door shut I slammed my fist into the wall beside the window. Plaster dust waterfalled onto the floor.

Of course Julianna came running when she heard the crunch. I couldn't even tell if she was pretending to care when she touched my busted-up, bleeding knuckles. Or was she cooing over me even though she was wet for fucking Edwin? I shoved her and she skittered back, tripped on goddamn Archie, and fell onto the couch. The cat sank his teeth into her calf like it was a mouse. She squawked, her ponytail disintegrating around her face.

There was no choice. I had to see for myself. "C'mon, brush your hair; we're going out."

I watched her very, very carefully. When we first saw Edwin by the pool tables, she nodded and grinned and let him kiss her cheek. He insisted on buying the first round and when I tried to say *no thanks* went on about Julianna's brilliant poetic book—that's what he called it—and how he was going to say he knew her before she got famous. I was dying to ask what his favourite poem of hers was because I was betting he hadn't read any nor even knew what they were about. But what if he had? What if he said one of my own favourites, the one about the ice cream, or the one about a tomato plant growing in a gravel yard? So I didn't ask.

We sat at the bar with these two awful females of the sort you'd expect in a place playing Shania Twain followed by Aerosmith. Super-young, not pretty but with thick dark eyeliner and boobs that seemed to be resting on shelves inside their bras. It was an awful night, because everybody had some sort of plan or agenda, in addition to the usual one of just getting pissed drunk. Julianna was trying to get me to not be mad but in that idiot way she had of pretending not to know why I was mad in the first place, so she wouldn't have to stop what she was doing or apologize at all. She just rubbed up against me the whole night, all bug-eyed. Those sad girls Edwin brought just wanted to get their drinks bought and their bums patted every once in a while, so they could bicker with each other about who Edwin really liked. Edwin was happy to buy their rum and diet Cokes and pat whatever was available, but he was obviously after Julianna. He wasn't subtle about reaching around her to flag the waitress, clapping his hand down on her thigh every time he laughed. She didn't blink, and she even blushed when he talked about how she was creating true literature, as if those other sluts cared. He was so familiar with her, calling her Juli as if he'd known her forever, grabbing a sip of her drink when she looked away and then, when she caught him, just giving a little wink and licking his lips—it was obvious they'd slept together.

The thing was, I felt like Edwin was mainly doing it to get at me; sure, she was hot, but the two chicks sitting on the other side of him weren't that bad, didn't have boyfriends they fucking lived with, and weren't playing hard to get like she was. Not that hard, though— Julianna laughed when she saw him licking her beer foam off his lip, a wet chirp that sounded way too into it for me to believe all the surprised looks she gave to his wandering hands. I was a rock, though, just staring at the baseball game on the screen over the bar, minding my business, peeling labels off my empties, waiting out the night.

Finally, finally, it was last fucking call and we could let the evening die. Edwin knew we'd taken the bus to the bar, so when he got outside he offered us a drive home in his lousy car, but then Julianna went, "No way, you're plastered," like she was his wife or something. And he just hands her the keys, super-sweet, like they were the couple and I was just some asshole getting a free ride home.

She lit out across the parking lot—just like that, her long blond hair glowing a kind of silver in the streetlamps' glare as it swung just a few inches above her round little rump. Edwin jogged up to her with the two girls trailing behind. They didn't even glance back to see if I was following—I could've gone back in to call a cab or collapsed in the parking lot, for all they fucking cared. Eventually I went after them, just to see the nightmare through.

Really, I knew it wasn't Edwin's fault, although he was a fucker. It was natural for a man to want a beautiful woman, and anyway, Edwin never promised me he wouldn't. It was Julianna who had made me promises, written me little bathroom-mirror poems on sticky notes about staying *true forever,* all that shit— and it was her I held responsible.

When I got to the car, Julianna was already behind the wheel and the two girls—I never got their names—were fussing around getting into the back. Edwin goes, "Well, Sean, your woman has secured the front seat for you. Guess I'll make myself at home on the hump." He and the girls laughed like idiots. I guess they were drunker than I'd thought. He climbed in between them and slammed the door. When I went over and opened the passenger door, Julianna smiled up at me and without thinking I smiled back—a pure instinct smile. I felt stupid, but what could I say? I was just a loser who couldn't even buy a car or keep his girlfriend off other guys' dicks. Juli waited for me to buckle up before she pulled out.

I was ignoring Julianna, and in the back seat Edwin had somehow sweet-talked both of the girls onto his lap. Juli was being all prissy, asking, "Is that really safe?" The girls just laughed like hyenas and started yammering on about who liked Edwin more. "No, me!" "No, *me!*" Barely even words, but they sure could go on. Then one of them shifted sideways over his knee so that I, glancing back from the front seat, could see right till Sunday in the headlight from oncoming cars as we pulled onto the highway back to town. I kinda got hypnotized.

That's why it took a moment for me to realize the car was heading onto the soft shoulder and jerkily slowing down. I looked over at Julianna and her face was wet. "Christ, what now?"

She just kept on crying and braking and didn't take her eyes off the road.

"No, what's this? I say something to you? I didn't say no goddamn thing to you."

"A cat. There was—a cat!"

We'd come to a stop by that point. Them in the back were wasted, but they still could recognize we weren't moving. "What the fuck?" squawked one of the idiot twins.

"Just calm down, Juli, honey." Edwin actually leaned forward between his two blitzed beauties and put his hand on Juli's shaking shoulder. She didn't even notice, as if he'd done it a thousand times before.

"No, no. I gotta get the cat."

If I'd been sober I would've worked out that she'd meant *in the road there was a cat,* but I wasn't and now we were at the side of the highway in the goddamn dark and Julianna was both sobbing like a maniac and trying to get out of the fucking door with cars whipping by at a hundred miles per hour. So I grabbed her by her skinny arm and yanked her back in the car. "The cat is at home, you dumb bitch."

"The cat, I hit it. There's a cat on the road that's hit and I've got to help it."

Finally I got what she was saying through the beer fog. I brought my voice down so the others wouldn't hear—not that they gave a fuck. Edwin had lost interest and was necking with the blonder one; the one more like Julianna. "Yeah, well, don't add yourself to the graveyard."

"I can see it." She pulled herself toward the door again, but I got my fingers dug into her arm. "Sean, I've got to help that cat." She twisted and managed to get free of my hand, I don't know how. That girl was an eel. She opened the door and was out before I realized I'd lost her.

She was plastered to the driver's side door when I got to her—a semi had just gone by and the car was wobbling. "Get in the car, Julianna. I fucking mean it."

"I couldn't stop." She was talking like her teeth were chattering. "Jessie and Jennifer don't have seatbelts on and they would've gone through the windshield."

"Well, good you didn't kill no one over a fucking rodent."

"Cats aren't rodents!" she screamed, her mouth wide and spit flying. She started to lunge at some white streak a hundred metres back in the right-hand lane. Even I could see there were headlights coming.

She must have had something more to drink when I hadn't been paying attention.

I grabbed her arm again and the other one too, flipped her round and slammed her against the car. "You can't fucking run down the highway, Julianna. You need to take responsibility for murdering that cat and just get the fuck on with it."

She was crying so much she looked ugly. "I-I-I-I—"

I smacked her a good one across the mouth and came away with a hand coated in snot and tears and spit. "Get it together. Now you gonna drive or am I? Maybe me driving wasted is better than you sober, what do you think?"

"What the fuck?" Edwin had rolled down the back window, which Julianna was half leaning across. "What's going on? Leave the girl alone."

"Fuck off, Edwin. Get back to your sluts. This is none of your business."

She was trying to drop down out of my hands now and curl up on the ground. Thank god she didn't weigh very much.

"Jesus, Sean, this is fucked up." Edwin was trying to get the door open but Julianna was pressed against it and I put my hand on the top of the frame too. Fucking Edwin. He always had to get involved in every goddamn thing. The girls in the car were squawking but I couldn't see their faces.

The next passing semi flattened me against her. When it was gone I shoved my hand behind her back, opened the door, and crammed her in with the other two bitches.

"Edwin, take shotgun. I'm driving now."

I got us home just fine, though I did see the back door of Edwin's car was a bit dented where Juli had slammed against it. Served him right, specially since right after that he told me he didn't think there'd be all that much carpentry work for me the rest of summer. Fucking liar. But I made him settle things like a man, and that was satisfying.

When I got home from dealing with Edwin, Julianna showed me the bruises on her arms, her swollen lip. I told her what the fuck else was I supposed to do? She could've gotten herself killed. She didn't have an answer to that. And she was mad about me losing the job—even a crazy whore needs someone to keep her in veal and notebooks. We had a fight, and she wound up having to stay home from work for a long time after that. But it was good—me and her, just the two of us hanging out all the time, no outside interference. I think we both felt lucky, being together like that.

The Happy Ending

Gretta and I were happily married for a long time, I think. Maybe one is only ever qualified to assess 50 per cent of a relationship, if we accept the idea that other people are never truly knowable. And I do accept that. Or at least, I accept it with Gretta. She has always been tense, reserved, self-possessed, but I think the insight you get about someone when you're dating is a down payment. You only pay off that mortgage of intimacy twenty or thirty years later. It seemed fair—I didn't expect her to offer me full access to her secret heart after only a couple of years. And I wanted to rescue her from the iciness of being an orphan in her twenties, of living far away from home, of not being able to talk in large groups of people, of being alone. The glimpses I'd had were enough for right then. When she accepted my proposal she looked radiant, her dark hair a copse shutting out the sunlight behind her as she leaned down toward me, on my knees as the cliché dictates. "Yes, Len. I'll marry you. Yes."

For the first few years—seven, eight, nine years—I continued to feel that radiance regularly. Sometimes I still do, a glimmer, beaming over the squash casserole she learned to make from my mother's recipe, in her sigh when I touch her breast, in the way she responds instantly when I reach for her hand. But there are limits: I can't present the Gretta I know to others. My early attempts to bring her "out of her shell" failed awkwardly at party after party; in a bustling room of strangers and canapés, she would always be only herself, shell and all. But she loves me. Even if she were holding a crumpled tissue in the hand I wanted to hold, she would transfer it to the other hand, wipe her palm on her thigh, and offer me her fingers as quickly as she could, as if the offer might expire. Or if I needed it, she'd just give me the tissue.

The summer my mother was dying, I thought I would bankrupt her tissue supply; her allergies were no match for my grief. I'd come back from the hospital bathed in tears and sweat—it was a humid summer—but there was never a project, a phone call, a murder mystery with a bloody bathtub on the cover that Gretta wouldn't put aside for me. Over and over, we found ourselves out on the balcony, drinking whatever was in the liquor cabinet, going over the ways I'd failed as a son, and the ways I'd succeeded, and the ways we'd remember my mom when she was gone.

That summer, Gretta saved me from myself and my tendency toward poetic despair. And other times—the tenure struggle, the book I couldn't write—it was always her hand on my shoulder, talking me through it, listening through everything. I felt like I could never return the favour. Even during the years we were trying for the baby—the doctors never figured out what the problem was and then all the clichés came out of everyone's mouths (*not in the cards, not in the stars*)—it was still mostly my tears, my weakness that showed. I remember her standing by the window in the fertility clinic's waiting room, her straight back draped in a brown sweater, murmuring that it would be okay, we would always be okay, somehow. Her hand stroking the nape of my neck late at night, promising that I would always be enough for her. How could I have ever thought that could possibly be true?

I could never save her from anything, cushion her from any blow. And yet and yet . . .

Her father died a few years before I met her and fifteen years later I still know only the barest outlines of what remains the darkest time in her life. It took me a long time to realize she doesn't owe it to anyone— not even her husband—to fan out all that past pain like a hand of cards. It is hers to do with as she wishes.

The most she's ever said is, "When my dad was going, he was completely lucid. He wanted to see the phone bill, talk about things in Iraq, reminisce about my mother, but he could barely speak, throat all torn up from the intubation in the surgery. And it was so exhausting for him to write everything out. He felt so trapped in himself."

That sounds like my life, more every year. Something happens after you turn forty—things stop changing. The pathway through life, which seemed like it would lead over the horizon and unto death, fades away. Not because of a collision or a roadblock or anything so dramatic—we are simply where we are and perhaps we shall go no further. No fantastic career adventure or shocking physical improvement is in the stars for either of us now, though we are decently employed, decently attractive. And no child to watch climb the ladder of years and through her progress give us the illusion that we are moving forward ourselves. We simply are, together, and have so many decades left to evaluate this.

The vulnerability of being in love is all that you stand to lose. When I think of that man, Catherine's husband—I forget his name—I imagine his life as a perfect horror, hours and days of wondering. What can you do at dusk on a Saturday if all you've ever done is drink wine on your balcony with your wife? Because it does feel like that's all I've ever done:

I would no longer recognize the me I was before Gretta. Catherine's husband must feel the same, only now he's gone back to being that stranger. But perhaps they weren't the same kind of couple as us—more talking, more laughter, less silence. Who can imagine another way to be married once you've been doing it a decade your own way? It's like imagining another way to breathe. Catherine was so open, so chatty, though—it must have been a more conversational marriage.

Still, whatever I imagined of other couples during the worst depths of our arguments or the chilly quiet periods, I know if Gretta were to die or leave me, it would ruin my life. A person can grow to resent that level of need for someone. Perhaps she feels the same about me. Or not. I have felt the weight and the threat of that vulnerability, these past few months, whenever we spoke of Catherine's disappearance, each of us wondering how we would survive the absence and the ambiguity of such a loss. And even though we never discuss that fear, feeling it together creates a little intimacy—like laughing together in the dark of a movie theatre, staring straight ahead.

Most weekends, we're drained of conversation by Sunday afternoon, unable to find another reason to open our mouths without the stimuli of other people, other places. And yet, there's still the desire to be in the same room—I'm not sure what it is we want, the physical closeness, or just the comforting face. And still the silence. So we sit at the dinner table this Sunday night over chicken penne and white wine, and my hand creeps toward the pile of mail. I shudder at the click of her fork against her teeth, then glance up, guiltily, to see she has produced a library copy of *The Macabre Matter* from nowhere and opened it near the beginning. She manipulates her fork in the pasta one-handed. Penne is good for that. There is a delicacy, and a kindness, to the way she raises her eyebrows over the edge of her book. She is waiting for me to approve, knowing I will.

She passes me the parmesan cheese, noticing I've forgotten it without looking up. And despite a fat issue of *The New Yorker* that I can see peeking from the mail pile, I spend another minute thinking of the news and weather I'll be able to report the next evening, at the next dinner (baked fish, I already know—Monday). After a day away, I can feel more like a provider. And what can I provide besides the hilarious things my students do, articles I've read, what I'm writing or might write. Hell, what I had for lunch if she wasn't there to eat it with me. More and more, I want to tell her things.

And yet, and yet. Though we never attained the closeness I thought we would—shimmering insights into what the other is thinking or feeling, perfect immersion in each other's lives and relatives and hobbies, deep unwillingness to be apart for more than a day—none of the cozy cuddles depicted in commercials for insurance or hot chocolate—we exist in a kind of quiet harmony. The easy meals, the amenable relatives, the wide white bed. I do like to look across an expanse of sheets or pasta and see her, the way the lamplight hits her straight and narrow nose, the pursed pink of her lips. I couldn't rescue her from a pinprick, from a rude gesture in traffic, and yet here we are, in the middle of our lives, together. Despite the lack of fantasy patina, I'm grateful for her, for us.

Heading home at the end of the day, I get that familiar homesickness just before I arrive. After a tough day—and now that I'm in my forties, I'm starting to feel like they're mainly tough days—I still want to just spill it all out to Gretta and see if she can tell it back to me like a bedtime story. This desire has been growing all summer and fall, maybe since the beginning of spring when Catherine Reindeer first vanished, or since we each realized the other was devastated by the loss of this stranger. Or near-stranger. Maybe that was just one agony too many; we are kinder to each other now than we've been in years. We still don't talk much, but her face when she's genuinely listening to me is a comfort I could fall into. I don't need advice, or any kind of commentary—after fifteen years, I know what she would say almost as well as what I would. This far into paying off the marital mortgage of intimacy, niceties like "How are you?" have become irrelevant—I know how she's doing by the way she swallows her first mouthful of coffee in the morning, the rhythm of her stride on the stairs. In the evenings, we sit on opposite sides of the living room, the rasp of pages from our respective books the faintest of communications. It is a kind of love, and a kind of loss too. I remember when we would have at least told each other what the books were about.

I know I am lucky that even when the dark falls so early in November, I have Gretta to come home to. Tonight, walking down the cooling streets of our tidy little neighbourhood, I just want to be sitting with her on the splintering wicker couch in the sunroom with the shrieks and chortles of primetime in the background for comfort, though I haven't had the TV on since god knows when and I know that there are clothes to be mended draped over the screen. I'd love to watch a rerun with her now, even with all the plastic laughter and blow-dried hair. It would be the next best thing to having a conversation, if we could sit side by side on the couch, laughing at the same pratfalls at the same moments. It becomes easier to slide my hand into hers when she's smiling, even if she's not smiling at me. Just before I walk up the drive-way, that's what I'm hoping for.

But still, when I'm at the foot of the stairs to our front door, I don't go right in. I stop to fiddle with the package of midterm exams I'm carrying, the buckle of my briefcase, the cuff of my jacket. I don't even fully know why I'm stalling. I guess I'm afraid that she'll already be asleep or pretending to be, and we won't talk at all. I'll take out my keys in a moment.

"They found her. Oh, Len, they've found her."

On the second-storey balcony of our townhouse is Gretta, with her hands clasped on the rail, and her hair draped around her face, leaning down to call to me. "Len, that girl, your student. Catherine Reindeer. She was just on the news. She's alive. The police found her." I haven't heard Gretta speak so joyfully in a long time. The light of the bedroom flashes behind her head.

I am on autopilot for a few moments and eventually wind up standing on our hallway hardwood in my dark, heavy shoes. Gretta pads down the hall from the bedroom and pauses halfway down the stairs, looking at me.

"She was—they rescued her? Catherine's okay?"

She presents the story like a gift in a cupped hand—proud and eager. "No. No, she escaped. Some guy on his way home from work found her sitting beside Highway 13, just out beyond the new subdivision. I heard on the radio. She was all bloody . . ."

"And the other one, the kid that disappeared from the high school?"

"No, I don't—well, the news didn't mention him." Gretta's chest bumps against the loose blue fabric of her blouse. "They never did connect those two cases, I don't think."

For so many months, Catherine and Donny were a lucky penny that Gretta and I passed back and forth between us. Her despair at the loss of people she didn't know revealed some of Gretta's softness that I'd forgotten. Every time she brought them up, her cheeks hollowed as her mouth turned down, and she looked the way I felt. A topic on which there was little to say other than *So horrible*, but somehow it was comforting to say it to each other.

"But she's alive? Catherine, she's okay?" I ask.

"I don't really know. The news story was already half over when I tuned in. I never imagined she would still be alive after so long—girls who disappear usually die." Gretta clasps her hand to her mouth, but her voice continues from underneath it. "Some things you can't be rescued from."

I shake my head. "What did you actually hear?"

She drops her hand. "There wasn't much. The guy, the guy who found her, just saw her, and called the cops, and stayed with her." Gretta is already moving past me, into the living room, switching on the television, knocking sweaters onto the floor.

"—now twenty-eight, Reindeer was last seen leaving the restaurant where she worked last March . . ."

Catherine's high-school graduation picture flashes on the screen. Over-the-shoulder smile and yellow-gold tassels. Then a more recent photo, a squished together double-selfie with her husband, their cheerful faces crowding the frame, leaving no hint of the background.

"Police have not issued a statement regarding Reindeer's abductor, nor whether her nearly eight-month ordeal is related to the disappearance of another Iria resident, seventeen-year-old Donny Zimmerman, who went missing on February 17 of this year. Questioning of Ms. Reindeer is expected to lead to further investigation. She was discovered near the Turgrove junction by the side of Highway 13—"

I hate the use of the passive voice at the best of times—it's weak in essays, sloppy in advertising. But it's especially inappropriate to use to describe a young woman who once ran up three flights of stone stairs to return a pen she had borrowed, her thick ponytail bouncing, her breath not the least hastened by the sprint.

On TV, they're showing an old press conference—Catherine's husband, bearded and wild-eyed, making a plea for any information that might lead to his beloved wife's safe return. Those are the words he used. I've seen this clip so many times I feel like I've lived it; his sincerity, his shaking voice, his ugly cardigan. This is a married man, a man in love with his wife. I can feel the sob gathering in the back of my throat.

"—multiple fractures, lacerations, in addition to severe malnutrition and, apparently—"

"Gretta."

"—stabilized, though doctors are unsure—"

"Gretta, let's not watch this right now."

Her eyes are wide and wet. "Sure, they're starting to repeat themselves, anyway. No new information." But she doesn't change the channel and her gaze doesn't stray from my face.

"—unavailable for comment at the time, though a press conference—"

I reach out blindly for the remote and mash my thumb onto the buttons. On the next station, Louis C.K. is eating a doughnut.

After shutting off the ceiling light, I stand propped against the doorway and stare into the bedroom. All I can see of Gretta is her sharp profile, haloed by the green electricity of the alarm-clock display. I watch her nose tilt as she slowly looks toward me, though I know her eyes can't have adjusted to the dark yet, that she can't actually see me.

"Len?"

"I'm here."

"Coming to bed?" A creak of springs—the familiar sound of her rising onto her elbows.

"Of course." I walk to the edge of the bed—I know it's three steps, I have memorized this whole house—sit down beside where I know her hip is. My eyes slowly adjust until her pale face emerges from the shadows for me. Her hand reaches up, brushes along my jawline. Invited in, like a vampire, I finally lie down.

She asks quietly, "Aren't you thrilled? These stories don't usually have a happy ending."

I slide a hand down over her silky skin of her sternum and the rougher rayon of her nightdress. The fabric clings to her, not slinking up like I want it to when I stroke up over her ribs. I could count them, through the thin fabric and her thin skin. This is a summer nightgown; she should be wearing something warmer when the nights are this cold.

"Or you wanted to rescue her yourself, is that it?"

My first thought, the one I don't say, is, "Of course I did." What I actually say is, "It's not the end, that's what's good."

She nods and reaches for the drawstring at my waist, then stops. "Did you hear that?" Her body is tense, drawing away from me, pressing into the mattress.

"Just the wind knocking something." I've managed to slip a hand under her nightgown. Though I can't make out the colour in the dark, I know that the red has faded to peach from too much line-drying in the sun. My palm glides over the cords of muscle in her thigh. "You're fine. Everything's fine."

Her wet eyes shift and skitter, searching the room behind me. "No wind tonight." I try to kiss her but she twists away. "Maybe it was nothing." She's shaking, tears sliding back on her temples, into her ears. She brushes the tears away with her wrist, impatient. I don't know what she's thinking.

"You don't— You don't usually hear things, Gretta." She doesn't usually weep either. I wonder if it's for Catherine, or for whatever has gone so quietly wrong between us. I try to scoop her shoulders up so I can draw off the nightdress, but it takes me a few tries before she understands what I want.

"That poor girl. And the boy—still no one knows what happened to him, or anyway they didn't say . . ."

I can watch her eyes watch me and still not be sure exactly what she can see. "I know. It's all right. I've got you."

Afterwards, Gretta murmurs against my stomach. "She'll be okay. Maybe she'll forget a little bit; she's just a kid."

I don't remind her that Catherine's in her late twenties, or that she has a husband, a house, a future that was more or less already laid out when the worst thing happened. Who knows if she can get that future back? But I don't want to start complicating the conversation now. Gretta, her mouth open against my skin, is falling asleep in my arms like she hasn't in months. It is a relief to hug her to me, to feel the curve of my palm fit perfectly below the curve of her shoulder blade.

I should let this story end the way she wants it to.

At the End of Breath

The shock of the moment welds Grey's feet to the floor, but he can still raise his hand to make his Jean-Paul Belmondo gesture, running his right thumb around the bow of his upper lip and the dip of his lower one. Doing this in front of the cop who brought him to the hospital, Grey feels self-conscious in a way he hasn't in years. Maybe not since he started imitating the gesture with an adolescent fervour the first time he saw the movie *Breathless,* somewhere back in high school. Watching that cheerful thief watch the confusion of Paris and brush his lips in consternation, Grey saw something he could use, something to do when he didn't know what to do. In front of his parents' medicine-cabinet mirror, he trained himself, learning to use the gesture in moments of stress and distress and deep thought. By eighteen, he had finally internalized the motion to the point that he, like that small-time criminal, was scarcely aware of the touch at his mouth, save for the tiny measure of comfort it brought. In the twenty years since, he has traced his mouth in concern and terror and anticipation and barely been conscious of it, but now, in this small, white room, he wishes his hands hung at his sides. Still he can't stop. Webbed with thin blue blankets and IV lines, black thread stitching across the left edge of her jaw, Catherine is breathing.

His left hand is on the doorknob, and even though he's pushed the door to Catherine's room all the way open now, he can't quite let go yet. The metal is smooth and cool in his grip but warming, growing moist with sweat. He watches her breathe. He can't tell if she's unconscious or if her eyes are swollen shut. The yellow-purple flesh around them doesn't twitch at the echoing click when he finally releases the doorknob, drops his hand from his lips, and slides one foot across linoleum and into the room. One step and then another and then she's real.

This moment—Grey standing at the foot of this strange bed—is the best-case scenario. This is what he has prayed for with such repetition and passion that the prayer too has passed into unconscious habit. For the eight months she's been gone, every streetlamp he saw, barking dog he heard, moment of stillness he experienced, has been accompanied by that *please please please please please* that doesn't require will or thought. It just comes; he gives his mind the freedom. And yet, in all that time he has never let himself look too closely at the possibility that Catherine might not be alive anymore. He's never allowed himself the thought of that other Catherine, past-tense Catherine, subterranean and still.

He has pictured this room before. Everything that has happened and is about to happen has already been imagined a thousand times in the darkness of his silent bedroom: the respectful tap on the front door at dinnertime, the cop's heavy face in the window, the gulp of terror at the possibility of the worst news tinged with the lottery-scratchcard hope of *what if?* The semi-hysterical questions he asked in the police car, the many bobbing journalists with their cameras and questions on the plaza in front of the hospital—it was all distressingly like a TV crime drama. The excited, beaming deference of the hospital staff and the bleached whiteness of the hallway, the nurses' station, the door to her room. The narrow barred bed. Except, in his fantasies, the hospital room had a window.

There have been things he didn't imagine—couldn't, or wouldn't. If she wasn't dead and wasn't with him, then she was somewhere else, but he never pictured where or how, any more than he pictured the insides of his eyelids. And he never pictured how she would look in the hospital bed—partly shaved hair, broken dirty fingernails, her tall form so rigidly pinned on her back underneath the white sheets. Catherine could never sleep on her back. He had needed to save his strength for whatever reality would sooner or later deal him; he had no reserves for potential tragedies. Even in the worst of fear—the nightmares where she was bleeding, sobbing, being dragged away by the hair, or the times he watched her mother weep into a cup of tea—it always seemed possible that he could get to this moment. And here it is. This is his new reality, unambiguous, unimagined, sharp as a knife blade: his wife on this white, white bed. His vivid, fidgety wife, who bounced through drugstores and libraries, now a stone sculpture of herself—except for her breathing belly rising small under the sheet. His stomach churns with both relief and revulsion at having her back but not back, alive but broken.

The cop sidles into the room behind him and stops abruptly when he really sees her. An hour ago, standing on Grey's front porch, this man had said the words *good news,* and now seeing the object of that news steals the blood from his face. Grey senses the officer's dismay and pity washing over him and Catherine both. He wants to bring his fingers back to his mouth but doesn't, now too aware of the pathos of his borrowed gesture, perilously close to a thumb in the mouth. They regard this new reality together. This truth is a parody of good news. Grey feels a weighty hand clasp his shoulder.

On some level, ever since he met Catherine, he had known that his happiness couldn't last. That he would spend a birthday alone, sitting in a lawn chair in the rain so as not to hear the wail of the phone inside the house. In retrospect, maybe Catherine had always been just about to set a narrow foot into the mouth of a bear trap, be clonked on her shiny-haired head by an anvil, be snatched away by a wolf. In having her in his life at all, he'd had more luck than he'd earned, and his good fortune had leached away some of hers. The shocking thing was not that she disappeared, but that she had returned. That she could return from hell and make it feel like summer had come again had seemed both possible and preposterous until she did it. He was a man who believed in catastrophe. Perhaps what was truly shocking was that he had been so unprepared for this one.

Once it arrived, though, once she was taken, he'd known almost right away. Almost. He had been waiting for her at a nice restaurant with Evan and Angie, his oldest friends, and the time spent waiting for Catherine passed pleasantly, until it didn't. Evan was telling a story about a local politician's legal troubles when Grey fished out the last slice of olive loaf from the napkin-lined basket, then stared at it in his hand, saying, "We ate the whole basket of bread and Catherine's still not here . . ." Catherine mocked people who thought they were important enough to make their friends wait. Grey let the sentence trail off as if it were an idle thought, before checking his phone again. There were no new messages.

Suddenly the evening that had been spooling out before them like a red carpet—the martinis, the gossip, the warmth of being with old friends—evaporated. He had been picturing Evan the godfather of his and Catherine's someday child, balancing the baby carefully in his awkward hands. Now, seeing the bottom of the breadbasket, he pictured Catherine stepping in front of a speeding minivan, or some other accident he couldn't imagine. He couldn't imagine. Yet he already knew the tone events would take when the waitress set down the second serving of sesame crisps and olive loaf. Nevertheless, he had stood up, politely excused himself from the table, and made the call to nowhere anyway. Her cellphone rang aimlessly, and was later found in a muddy puddle in the parking lot at the restaurant where she worked. Since then, his time and mind have been taken up with prayers and other forms of despair that require no forensic confirmation.

This body in the bed, this Catherine-he-once-knew, she is a confirmation of another kind, but he can't be sure of what. That his luck is suddenly returning? That she always had the strength to survive something far worse than his nightmares? Because this scene—these thick gashes on her concave cheek, that awkward angle of her right arm, the web of tubes tangling from her left wrist to a clear plastic bag—is a nightmare that his mind would not have been able to conjure ten minutes earlier, let alone eight months ago.

When did this become the best-case scenario? Long after the optimistic volunteer searchers in their neon ski jackets and the underfunded police department and the brusquely bored newspaper reporters and even her stoic, sweet-eyed mother gave up hope. He and Sue sat week after week in her apartment eating schnitzel and pot pies and all the things she loved to make for Catherine, talking about Catherine's noisy laugh, her notion that all fruit should be served chilled, her fussiness about organizing bookshelves. But sometime in the summer, Sue stopped meeting Grey's gaze and her tone grew heavier, though she kept telling stories about Catherine's childhood, and the dinners got more elaborate. Or perhaps it was when he almost got rid of his landline—it was getting so expensive—but then he realized that if he did, even if Catherine somehow got to a phone, the first number she would think to call would be out of service. Or the night he slept diagonal on the bed and didn't wake up sweating. Or perhaps it was during that numb period when he'd seen glimpses of a future without her and thought he might live through it, or sometime during the past few months when he scarcely wept at all, and never on the bus.

But he's been proven wrong and, in his error, won everything. Catherine has come back as a living person, not as an eighteen-point headline. These monitors and this narrow bed: this is the longed-for triumph, the victory lap, and grounds for promotion for the cop in the corner. Catherine's mouth is a meaty swell, the colour of raw chicken liver. Her thick dark hair has been razored, not by her captor's cruelty but by the gentle hands of nurses, to get at the wounds underneath. Even the spikes of surgical thread along her jaw are a victory, a better alternative than others.

The white-walled room is tiny—one more step puts him at the shore of the bed. Behind him, the police officer, young beneath his beard, has dropped back against the wall. Grey can hear the man's heavy breathing and knows they are both fighting to continue to *see* her, to accept this celebration. For all his clairvoyance, Grey does not know what comes next. Does he embrace her, wake her, ask her how she is? Can he touch her hand? So many of his memories of Catherine are touches. He can remember her skin against his hands, his chest, his throat. What he sees now is an unrecognizable body—gaunt, fragile— and the wires and tubes contain her like a cage, fencing out his pathetic need to touch. Should he be carrying flowers? How long will it take for this day, all these past days and weeks and months of suspended anima- tion, to become blurred memory? How soon can he forget how it felt to half awaken in the night and nuzzle her empty pillow? Would now be possible, somehow?

Has the cop seen *Breathless*? Part of Grey—the weak part, the part that would hide from his beloved wife—would like to buy the cop a cup of coffee and tell him about the early days of Goddard and the French New Wave, when things were more linear but still so cool that you could get away with not feeling, if you wanted to.

But you can't. Grey can't leave and he can't stop feeling the loss of Catherine's loud laugh, so incongruous with her low, even voice. The loss of that voice too. Can he talk to her? No one has told him what he's allowed to do here. There are things he can't quite bring himself to believe: the blankness of her third left finger; the pillow of bruise under her eyes; the blades of her hips sharp enough to slice through the thin blue blanket—these all hammer at his eyes and mind.

Will this be enough for her? Will this be too much? She was not a woman for whom any sort of pain would be muted. *Is.* She was fearful of many things but she enjoyed her life, or at least he believed that she did. *Does.* She put huge amounts of cilantro in her salads and followed a recipe for Bloody Marys that called for pickle brine. He was constantly finding her socks in the front hallway—she hated to have anything on her feet but believed the laws of conformity required it outside the house. She read constantly, on the bus and during breakfast and especially sprawled on her stomach at home on the couch or in bed or on the lawn. She said her favourite poets were the ones who irritated her slightly, the ones who stopped her from easily sliding her eyes from left to right. Once, she painted the coffee table vermilion and then tripped over it, striping her pyjamas, which she continued to wear for years, even so. They had a bright blue couch to go with the red coffee table; this made sense to her. Once, she went through a Barthes period and wanted to work in advertising. She never drank Guinness, she never shopped in malls. Once, at a summer job, she was able to prove a need for the more expensive kind of paper clips, the coloured ones, to code her files, and Admin ordered them every month in a little box, just for her. She only brushed her hair when it was wet. She laughed and laughed at pratfalls and puns and other things that were marginally funny. She slept on the left side of the bed.

Grey kneels at the left side of her bed. From this ungated side, he can lean across the slippery sheets and place his cheek, pale and gaunt with the killing fire of hope, against the deep curve between those jagged hipbones. As he presses his thick lips to Catherine's cloaked belly, he hears the policeman's sharp inward hiss of breath—Terry, his name is Terry—but he *feels* Catherine's breath. Beneath his unshaven face, her stomach tightens into itself, but then it pushes up again. The disinfected hospital air is sliding inside her, pumping through her and through him and through Terry, a perfect intimacy.

The room is silent. On TV medical shows, there's always a steady beep of some sort of monitor, but Catherine's seems to be off, or on mute. Can the doctors really have such faith that this small, frail heart will keep beating? Grey can't. He keeps his face pressed into his wife's stomach. He has to feel her breathing to be sure. And as he feels the rise and fall of her belly and watches the slight twitch beneath the unrecognizable yellow slit of her eyelids, he is sure. Hair can grow back. Blood can clot. This is nothing like the movies. And in the back of his throat he feels the miserable burn of gratitude.

PART TWO

Sad Stories

The story ended oddly, with all the characters jumping into a previously unmentioned lake. Grey flipped back to the beginning, looking for a mention of water, a dock, unhappiness. He hadn't been skimming: he'd understood the story at least enough to read it aloud to Catherine. Still, he just couldn't fathom why the wedding party had leapt, weeping, into the water. And reading the story from the beginning again, he found no reference to swimming or the shore until the bitter end, and no pages stuck together. Perhaps he wasn't meant to understand, in that way.

He leaned over the bar of her hospital bed and whispered, "Do you know why they went into the water?" If Catherine had been able to answer, she no doubt could've offered him a symbol, a twist, some insight that would have made the story come together in his mind. She had always paid closer attention than he did, to prose and to life. He brought books home from work so she'd read them, talk about them, let him use her ideas and connections to create theme displays for the bookstore chain he worked at. He read everything too, of course—he considered it part of his job—but she read better, deeper. She could live inside a story—sitting on the train beside the characters, eaves-dropping on their conversations, understanding their tones and pauses, their lives and heartbreaks. And she'd come back filled with their insights and ideas, as excited as if she'd spent the time with friends. In those days she always returned to the real world. But now, Grey wasn't sure she'd ever emerge from whatever other world she was lost in.

Now, Catherine was locked inside her own pain, and none of his questions about books or how she was feeling or if she wanted him to bring her another pillow elicited a response. Now, it was difficult to tell when Catherine paid attention and when she didn't. The whole time he was reading the story to her, her gaze had been fixed on the glistening blank of the television screen. She didn't turn toward him when he put his hand on her shoulder, which was still skinny but gaining some soft-ness under the cotton sleeve. Or when he said, "Good night, Catherine." He wanted not to be crushed by this, but he knew that sometimes she did react—there was no reason not to hope—and so every time she ignored his voice or the sound of her own name felt like a rejection. Sometimes she stared right at him, like she could see his scruffy beard and sleep-deprived eyes and hopefulness. Like she loved him. He wouldn't stop longing for that connection, that gram of affection, until he knew for a fact it was impossible. For now, it wasn't.

"Your mom will be here in the morning." She kept watching the still TV as he walked out the door and didn't move when he said, "I love you."

Grey always looked over his shoulder on his way in and out of the hospital—for weeks reporters from the local papers or television stations had been showing up to ask him about his wife's condition. The hospital had security staff, and although Grey rarely saw them, they somehow managed to keep journalists away from the interior corri-dors of the hospital, at least near Catherine's room. But once he stepped outside, he was sometimes accosted in the parking lot. Today, as soon as he stepped off the sidewalk, a young woman in a snug violet coat approached him and asked briskly if she could ask him a few questions regarding his wife.

"She's fine, thanks." That was his usual answer. He never said, "No comment" because even to his own ears that sounded too much like a dodge when he truly just had nothing to say. But he always kept walking. The cops had advised him ages ago not to talk to reporters except in a formal press-conference environment. He strode on now and as usual the reporter followed him to his car. "Do you have any comment on the police activity at a house on the south edge of Turgrove County, where your wife may have been held?" She had more questions, about the house's alleged owner and where that person might be, but when he opened the car door, she held up a small plain business card.

"If you ever want to talk, just call, day or night."

Everyone he knew—his friends, Catherine's mother, the staff at the hospital—seemed to assume he wouldn't want to talk to the media, that he would find it an invasion of privacy. But it was very tempting to talk about the silence in Catherine's room, her endless gaze on the TV whether it was on or off, the yellowing bruises on her arms, to tell it all to this warm-skinned and carefully eyelined young woman. It was her job to hear about the worst things, like the thick purple vines of cut on Catherine's palms, like what was found in the basement of that little brick house out in Turgrove. It was her job to break down the hard stories in a way that people wouldn't turn away from, a version that could be digested in a commercial break. If he told her, the young reporter probably wouldn't even cry.

But instead he took the card for want of anything better to do and got into the car. Then he nodded and said, "I'm fine, thanks" as he pulled out, and away.

Grey meant to reread the previous evening's short story at breakfast. Catherine used to finish the last page and then immediately go back to the first; she said every reading yielded another layer. But he must have left the book on Catherine's bedside table, so he read the Art and Culture section of the newspaper instead. The wordy, gleeful book reviews made his head ache. There wasn't one about the swimming wedding party book, but another sad-sounding book of stories was well praised. Perhaps he'd put together a Sad Stories table display.

He ate a chocolate-chip waffle and microwave bacon. Single-man food. For years, Catherine had made him breakfasts of granola with yogurt or steel-cut oatmeal. Since she'd been gone, Grey had grieved and prayed, thrown his toothbrush, her picture, himself at the walls, but he'd also marched down the frozen food aisle and bought McCain fries, polar bars, 10%-fruit drink—things that used to line his fridge-freezer when he lived alone. He was happy to have those things again, which was something he probably wasn't supposed to feel.

He searched the books section of the paper for a mention of a happier short-story collection, or at least a simpler one. He read Catherine only short stories now, one per evening, filling in the otherwise long silent space between when her mother left for supper and the end of visiting hours with something slightly more intimate than television. While she was gone, he read poetry—a couple of books by the poet from Iria Catherine had been reading right before . . . before. He'd gotten them from the store a few weeks after she disappeared, when he'd still been in the crazy stage of sobbing and phoning the police over and over. By the time he could manage the calm to read anything, it was starting to be spring. Grey read with his back to the window, to block out the robins and chive shoots and snowdrops that Catherine had been waiting for all winter. He found himself drawn to the poems because not only were they something Catherine liked, they were *like Catherine,* so simple and matter of fact. A lot of the shorter ones were about waiting tables, reading books, things Catherine talked about all the time. And he could hear her voice reading them in his head. Catherine used to sprawl on the couch behind him while he played video games on mute, reading some of these same poems aloud to him, and he remembered the lilting up-notes of her voice when she was happy.

Once Catherine returned, he tried reading these to her, but the words were not as vibrant when he read them aloud in the hospital. They were diminished by the beige paint and the lack of windows and the hectic murmuring in the halls; by Catherine's refusal to come out of her bubble of silence. Dr. Durnsville, the therapist, told Grey not to think of it that way, but he couldn't help being frustrated. She was there but not there, present but under glass. He read her the poems he remembered she liked best, even though the words felt strange and cold in his mouth. He struggled to follow the meaning of the poems with her vacant gaze pointed away from him. Poems are so spare, what you build into the silences is as important as the words themselves—Catherine had taught him that. But he could tell she was building nothing in her silence, rendering every poem meaningless.

After a few evenings of this, he thought he would—they would—absorb stories better because they were more like whole worlds, had more to live inside, but it didn't really work out like that. He was often exhausted and distracted, that could have been part of it, but he swore the stories shifted on the page, starting out as one thing before becoming another. He never knew where he stood, what to hope for, which characters were moving forward and why. The only reason he kept reading was his belief that, somewhere deep inside her mind, Catherine understood the stories. Maybe she was listening: her gaze flickered perhaps half a dozen times in the ten days she'd been back. The hope for more was enough to keep him going. That, and the silence when he stopped was too much to bear.

After breakfast, he phoned the hospital and reminded the duty-nurse that he wasn't going to be in that morning. It was the first day he hadn't gone in right after breakfast, but the nurse did not seem interested. Grey hated to leave Catherine alone, but her mother would be there by noon at the latest. Sue, he knew, would bring a portable DVD player and some of Catherine's favourite movies from childhood—*A Bug's Life, The Little Mermaid,* something about a dog that could play basketball. They each had their ways of trying to get through, their own burdensome sacks of nostalgia.

"Yes, Mr. Reindeer. If there's anything, I have your cell number." There were voices in the background, the hum of machines that over the past days should have become familiar.

"Well, I'll be in later. Please tell her."

"Of course, Mr. Reindeer. Be sure I will."

He put a touch of force on the End button and stood staring at the phone a moment. Then he put on his sneakers and coat and went over to Evan and Angie's.

Angie answered the door, her shiny hair pushed behind her ears, her slate-coloured suit sleek against her body except for the untucked blouse over her belly. Disloyal as it was, Grey found her glowing health, her frank and questioning gaze, were such a relief.

"Oh, Angie, you are so beautiful."

"Hey, Grey." She hugged him and in the pullback grazed his ear with her ChapSticky lips. "How's it going?"

"You're not working on a Saturday, are you?"

"Nah, a brunch thing, not work, just work people. It's fun."

"Well, not as much fun as *we're* going to have." This from Evan, from some other room.

"Eat a lot of brunch for me, okay?" Grey patted the curve of his own belly, thinking of how it might feel to touch Angie's. The baby wasn't yet big enough for anyone to feel a kick, but he was looking forward to when he could. Angie was one of the few women he knew wouldn't mind if he asked.

"You know." Angie leaned back against the closed door. "Since this is the first day you've had away from the hospital, shouldn't you just relax? You guys don't really have to do the Christmas shopping."

Evan came into the room buttoning up his shirt, his hair wet to the scalp. "It'll be fine, efficient, very male. Down the list: sweaters, books, toys, chafing dishes, eat at Manchu Wok."

Angie picked up her gleaming leather briefcase—Grey had once seen her polish it. "I can do some of that, Ev. Especially since that's actually not the list at all. Who is getting chafing dishes?"

"I was kidding."

"Grey, you've had some year. You'd be excused if you didn't get everyone *stuff*. . ."

"I do not want to be excused from Christmas." Grey smiled and pointed vaguely at the tree he knew to be on the other side of the living room wall.

Angie went long-faced. "Oh, *no*, of course, no, I didn't mean—"

Evan clapped one hand on Grey's back and another, gentler, on Angie's. "Go to work, Ang."

"Brunch."

"Go to brunch, Ang. We're going to the mall, not the moon. Besides, everything's returnable."

On the highway toward Elk Ridge, the mall on the other side of town, Grey looked at Evan and Evan looked at the traffic, his head tipped back against the headrest, his knobby Adam's apple casting a small shadow in the still-rising sun. They have been friends for a very long time, but Grey knew that over the past year he had become a hard man to talk to. Evan did better than most; he had more material to work from. He had every single morning in high school, the university parties, all the Halloweens, all the New Year's Eves, both their weddings.

Throughout the long quiet months that Catherine was gone, so many people from work, the neighbourhood, his family had brought food and cried on his couch, but outside of Catherine's mom, only Evan and Angie came and stayed. The first days and weeks, when sleep was impossible and the phone never stopped ringing, Evan and Grey had sat up nights playing an old version of *Sonic the Hedgehog* Evan had somehow managed to find a working console for. Grey was sometimes on the phone with the police or some relative, sometimes too angry or terrified to sit still or talk, but Ev kept showing up. And when he had a case that took him to Seoul for a week, that Friday night Angie was at the door with a Bundt cake. "You'll have to teach me to play, okay?" Even though there would always come a moment where he would realize again that Catherine was gone and he didn't know where and no one could find her, Grey had a few moments of normal life when Evan and Angie were there.

"How's Cat? Did that blood pressure thing settle down?"

"Yeah, she's good now." Grey had been so worried when her blood pressure spiked, but once it was fine again he'd forgotten all about it and moved on to the next panic. "The doc didn't know what that was about really. Just a fluke."

"Well, I guess that's still good, though. Any news about what they found when they dug up the yard? Seems like they should've found what they were going to find by now."

"Yeah, yeah." A red Corolla passed on the right, which startled Grey but not Evan. "Well, they told me, but it's not like it's on the news yet . . ."

Evan sucked in a breath. "You don't have to say. I mean, you can tell me whatever you want. I just—"

"I guess . . ." Grey hiccupped and peered out the window at the scrolling industrial parks. "They're pretty sure they found Donny Zimmerman. The high-school kid who disappeared the month before Cat. He hadn't been—been dead that long."

"Shit. His parents must be devastated. I can't imagine."

"I can." Grey closed his eyes against the nausea. "The news isn't official yet, so don't talk about it to, you know, anyone."

"Except Angie?"

"Oh, yeah, sure, except Angie."

"Catherine must have known him, or seen him. God."

Grey nodded, eyes still closed. "That's the part I can't imagine." He concentrated on the sound of the tires on the road, which always reminded him of an endless exhaled breath. Finally he felt like he could open his eyes without vomiting all over his lap. When he did, Evan was gazing at him nervously. "Watch the road, Ev."

"I know how to drive."

Grey smiled weakly and said, "I see no evidence," and Evan finally looked away.

After an appropriate amount of silence, if there was such a thing, Evan asked, "Got a list? Know what you're getting everybody?"

"Sorta. You know the fluffy things that go on pillows?"

Evan shrugged so high he knocked the headrest. "What?"

"Like duvets for pillows?"

"Really? They sell these for money?"

"There's these home-décor magazines in the waiting room at the hospital. Her mom was reading one, cooing over the—"

"Pillow duvets."

"Right. So I'm gonna get her some. You got ideas?"

"I was thinking books, actually. For the other partners, now that I'm one too. It's sort of classy, you know?"

"Lawyers read? Really?"

"Well, with work gifts, it is actually the thought that counts. That I *thought* that they'd read is enough."

"Right."

"Right. Actually, should we stop in?" Evan pointed ahead at the turquoise-roofed bookstore a few intersections ahead. "You can give me your professional advice."

Grey closed his eyes again. "God, no. Going to work on a Saturday, no."

Evan made a *pfft* sound. "You don't actually work in that *store*. It won't be arduous." He got into the right lane, signalled.

There was not a lot of time, a few car lengths, before they'd have to turn for the bookstore. Grey tried to imagine what that girl would say to him in front of Evan. What she might repeat. Something about Catherine—something that would sound like a lie, as if Grey had been lying to strangers. He jabbed Evan's arm with his elbow and said, "I work in *all* the stores in the chain at least sometimes. They know me there, there'd be . . . conversations." He started to raise his hand to his mouth, realized Evan would recognize his anxious gesture, put it back in his lap.

Evan's expression sobered. He nodded once and flicked off the signal. Grey flattened against the velour of the passenger seat, his heart a heavy echo in his ears.

He'd been in that store a week ago, testing the Christmas-wrap plano-gram and doing a surprise inspection. The staff were jumpy as he pointed out asymmetrical displays, incorrect shelving, outdated signs. He couldn't actually fire anyone, just force them to do extra work; still, most store-level staff were bunny-scared of district-office types.

But not her. Sixteen or seventeen, bones still close to the surface. She'd been stomping down the centre aisle with a tower of dirty, festive coffee cups from the in-store café when Grey and the manager found a floor-plan problem. The theme tables—*Creative Cookery, Historical Perspectives,* and *CanLit*—were so close together that they blocked the most obvious path to the restrooms. The manager on duty, a young man with camp-counsellor eagerness, yelled, "Chrissy!"

She didn't startle, or glance at them, just set the cups on the floor and plodded over. Grey was on the point of remarking, "Garbage in the aisle—really?" Then he looked at her face: her eyeliner had been wiped off just recently and not very well, streaks of black kohl fading toward her ears. Her eyes had red streaks, her nostrils were a translucent pink. The manager cocked his head, listening to something in his earpiece for several seconds before announcing, "Chrissy, I need to deal with a situation at cash. Please do whatever Mr. Reindeer says." Leaving Grey to move tables with the teary teenager.

"If you could grab it, see, so—" As often as he had to do it, Grey never felt comfortable straining in his suit, clipboard clenched under his elbow. Grunting and heaving undermined his authority, what little he had.

Chrissy's wrists were blue-veined and bony, but she hefted the table easily enough. They waddled, him forwards, her backwards, like an awk-ward Fred Astaire and Ginger Rogers, to the edge of the coffee shop, before plonking down the table just as his forearms were starting to wrench. "It's all right here, um, Chrissy. But the Creative Cookery table shouldn't have festive-wrap sets on it. Move them over to Gifts, okay?"

She stared at him, her eyes dark. "It's crowded over there too. People are always tripping on the floor baskets."

"Well, is there a rejig you could do to prevent future accidents?"

She thought about it, her gaze settling on the side of his face, but not for very long. "No."

Grey exhaled. No one cared much about merchandising, the vitality of traffic flows, symmetrical displays. "Well, try. And fewer titles on the risers. More than eight, people stop seeing books and just see piles." Grey stooped after some paper on the floor.

Chrissy was still staring, fidgeting with the hem of her vest. Suddenly: "Reindeer—I know that name. From the news. The woman who was killed? Catherine Reindeer?"

The piece of paper was a receipt for three guitar magazines: $18.97. Grey regarded Chrissy from knee height and for a moment he believed her, believed in some magical wireless from the hospital into this sad girl's brain. Catherine was dead. He let the devastation he'd long feared and been waiting for finally come. He would have to give all her clothes away, her little tennis shoes, the closet would be empty on one side and he would be truly alone. He tipped backwards from his crouch to the floor, wrists dangling off his knees, gaze on the waist of her velvet skirt. Then reality slid back in.

"No."

She flushed, wiping the hair out of her eyes. "I'm sorry. I read this thing in the newspaper—but I'm an idiot. I must have remembered wrong."

Grey braced his hands on his knees and stood back up to face her. Standing seemed better, but he still wanted to weep. "No, no, that was her. Us. She's my wife. But she didn't die. She's fine—really great, actually. It was all a misunderstanding."

He could imagine it being true, Catherine truly *really great*, at home reading Nabokov while she waited for the kitchen floor to dry, picking at a bowl of kale chips. He could have that again, someday. Maybe. Despite the books he'd noticed out of order on the lower shelves behind Chrissy's skinny ankles, despite the din of cash registers and cappuccino machines, he felt a shiver of joy to see the salesgirl's stretched smile at this happy ending, no reservations, no doubts. She nodded and whispered, almost to herself, "Oh, oh, that's really good."

He blinked back from the daydream and told the girl she could go now, and Merry Christmas.

Chrissy shrugged shyly and leaned down to pick up the cups she'd left on the floor. He never found out what she'd been crying about, before.

—⚬—

The mall was wild with Christmas: bell-heavy music, glittery jewellery displays accessorized with fake snow, a wispy teenager sobbing into her cellphone, "But it's *only* seventy bucks!" Evan's eyes bugged; he worked constant overtime in a quiet office, and rarely went anywhere besides sombre cocktail lounges where everyone drank scotch. They stood frozen in front of the mall map, staring at all the capitalism.

Evan had once been caught shoplifting in this mall, at fifteen, when Grey hid a scented loofah lotion in his backpack at the Shoppers, then stood at a distance, laughing, as the slender cosmetics clerk chased Evan outside to reclaim it. What else was there to do, all those boring winter weekends of high school, but play pranks, shove each other into the fountain, smoke in the parking lot, eat mountains of popcorn chicken in the food court. It all seemed trivial at the time, but more than twenty years on, the memories seemed sepia-toned, even sweet.

Grey gave Evan a half-hearted punch in the shoulder. "On with it, then." They started toward a store that looked like it might sell pillow duvets.

In the rows of linen softness, Evan asked, "How's work going?"

"Oh, fine." Grey was stroking something navy with a faint nap to it, like felt. "Well. Everyone wants to talk about Catherine. But it's too weird with people who don't even know her, you know?"

"I get that." Evan tugged at a rolled-up tablecloth that unfurled rapidly and lacily, landing at his feet. "Shit."

Together, they crouched to refurl the lace.

"I'll get you the books. At discount, if they're popular stuff. I just don't want to do it today."

"How popular?" Evan shoved the tablecloth back on the shelf, where it did not fit as neatly as before.

"Well, best-sellers, or Recommended Reads."

Evan blinked. "Recommended Reads?"

"That's, like, the sale branding." Grey winced, then pointed and said, "I think I'm gonna get these. They're called 'shams,' it says. Not pillow duvets."

They each took a plastic case of blue shams and walked toward the snaking checkout line.

"As in, *This book is a good read*? That's cute."

"Yeah, it's so we can get the, um, alliteration on the signage . . . signs."

Evan fiddled with a bottle opener shaped like a duck. "Believe it or not, my sister'll love this."

They paid, went back into the mall, walked on.

"Do you read them? The Recommended Reads?"

"Sure."

"They make you?"

"It's *recommended*. Besides, what else do I have to do?"

"You doing okay, man? I mean, the mall is tough on a good day. You got the shammies—we could call it a day and go play *Mario Kart*."

Grey kept walking; it seemed important to move at a fast clip, not to let anything weigh him down. "Shams, not shammies. And I'm good."

Hustling to keep up, Evan clasped his shoulder. "That was some heavy shit you said in the car. You're not ditching Christmas if you don't *shop*. Just get everybody ten scratch tickets and take a nap."

Grey stopped abruptly and leaned against the edge of a pink-and-gold lit fountain. "I can't nap, I can't sleep. I just want to have one normal day out of this fucking wreckage of a year. And you're the most normal guy I know."

Evan nodded slowly. "Aw, Grey, I never knew you felt that way."

Grey rolled his eyes. "Please don't hug me right now."

"Right. Normal guys don't hug." He leaned back next to Grey, then bolted back up and patted the edge of the fountain where he had just been resting. "Grey, this is *wet*. You gotta up your standards."

Slowly righting himself, Grey pointed at the gleaming jewellery display across the way. "For Angie, anything?"

Evan swung the shams gently. "We're supposed to be saving for the house."

"Sure. But a little something to say, hey, way to have my baby, right?" They walked on a few paces, past a woman carrying a toddler whose face had been painted to look like a CareBear. Grey would not be buying any gifts for Catherine at the mall—because how could he know what she wanted, and because he suspected she wanted nothing at all. It was suddenly important that Evan get Angie something perfect. "How about there?" He pointed at the window of Thyme Maternity, all the fat mannequins in sequined evening wear.

"Ah, too early. She doesn't need anything but loose pants and an untucked top so far."

"I say think ahead, buy the biggest nine-months muumuu. Tell her you can't wait."

Evan stared at the disco window display. "I *can't* wait." He clutched the bag, swallowed the jut of his Adam's apple, nodded. "Okay. If you're up for it. It's a foreign land in there."

"I don't mind." And despite the trickle of envy in the back of his skull, he didn't.

They really did go to Manchu Wok, long into the afternoon when the worst of the food-court tide had ebbed. They still had to eat at a counter, looking at each other slantwise. The food was all nostalgia: deep-fried chicken curls in sugar sauce, broccoli beef gluey with cornstarch, sand-coloured fried rice.

In the carb-stuffed haze, Grey took out a receipt and a pen and said, "Well, tell me your list."

Evan stared blankly. He had a grain of rice clinging to his upper lip.

"Book-wise." Grey wiped his own mouth, then nodded at Evan.

Evan mirrored him and brushed off the rice. "Jeez, I really don't know what's out. That's why I wanted you to tell me. Can you tell me?"

Grey shrugged. "I don't know these people."

"Grey, c'mon, I told you, it's about per*cep*tion. It's about cred, not about what book is going to give them the most joy when they're snowed in at O'Hare at 3 a.m. What are *you* reading?"

Grey opened the eggroll sauce and drizzled it onto his empty plate. "Book of short stories. I can read one story to Catherine in a night."

"A Recommended Read?"

"No, no. Short stories mainly aren't, you know."

"Really? Why? Too short?"

"Too obscure, I guess. Too hard to finish and say, 'That was about x, y, and z.'"

"But good? This book you're—you guys are reading?"

"Well." Grey pictured the splash of the bridesmaids jumping into the greenish lakewater, then the bride's long train streaming behind her, catching leaves and minnows and flowers from her bouquet as she breast-stroked. Then he pictured Catherine's still profile, her unseeing gaze—he couldn't help but feel that if the story had been better, she would have turned toward his voice. "Not sure. I don't read with quite my full attention."

"And yet you know more about this shit than anyone I know."

"I don't. My job is spreadsheets, and ordering teenagers to move display tables."

"Pick the books, Grey? Eight good books, no two the same, that's it. It would really help me out."

Grey nodded and, gathering their bags, they set out from the food court. The mall was no more crowded than earlier, but less organized, less polite. A woman in a thick orange cloak shoved past Evan, who grinned. "Ah, Christmas. Where to next?"

"Back to your place, to get my car. I can see Catherine before the nurses' shift-change."

Evan kept his gaze straight ahead, on Santa's Crystal Palace. "I can go with you, and then take you back. I haven't seen Cat in . . . only once since she's been back. And that was weeks ago."

"You don't have to." Grey sped up to hurry through the Body Shop's fake-fruit aura.

"Of course not." There was a snap in Evan's voice. "I'd like to." Gentler.

"All right."

Grey saw the reporter slouched in her car as they pulled into the hospital lot, but she only glanced at Evan's Volvo, then back down at her phone. Arriving in a car she wouldn't recognize felt like a trick, and her bent head looked small and sad through the windshield. Had she been at the hospital all day? He knew about that kind of endless waiting. He raised a hand to point her out to Evan, but then put it down—he didn't even know her name.

Inside, the hospital was bright and calm; someone had put green tinsel along the nurses' station desk in Catherine's section. As soon as he entered her room, Grey's clenched shoulders eased a bit—nothing had changed, she hadn't gone anywhere, she was still quietly watching the air in front of her face.

Grey said, "Hey, Catherine" from the doorway and then immediately felt self-conscious; he scurried to the side of her bed, touched her limp hand. Even after only a day away, he felt like he saw her more clearly: her hair had started growing back, covering some scars he might never know the reason for. Somehow, even on the intravenous diet, the hollows in her face had filled in a bit. But she wasn't looking at anything. When her eyes lit on something, when she really saw and understood, they gained a flickering purpose, became a gaze you could feel on your face. Rare, but a dozen times since she'd returned, Grey had seen her watching him, her warm brown irises shifting to follow his movements in the room. He dropped everything in those moments, the book, the coffee, whatever trivial thing he'd been occupying himself with, and just told her he loved her, that he was waiting whenever she wanted to come back to their lives again, that he would do anything for her. Those were the moments she was most likely to hear him, and he tried to offer her as much as he could to keep her there with him, to prevent her gaze from drifting away again, though it always did.

Evan came confidently into the room, then stopped several paces from the foot of the bed.

Grey glanced quickly at Catherine. She was elsewhere today, not reacting to any sounds or movement in the room—her consciousness locked inside herself, or gone entirely, Grey couldn't be sure.

He glanced back to his friend and saw the tears coating Evan's eyes. "Ev, listen—"

"She's getting beautiful again. She is." A drop caught in his eyelash, then fell down along his cheek, into the glitter of stubble there.

Grey nodded and glanced away, giving Evan a moment. He saw the collection of stories was splayed open on the nightstand just as he'd left it. He was looking forward to reading more, even if he didn't understand some of the stories, even if they seemed grim. They were still stories, with people and events moving forward—something to hold on to. He opened the book at random and started to read aloud, to Evan and Catherine and any medical staff that might come into the room, just in case anyone was listening.

Sometimes Nothing Happens

"It's a weird thing," Daria tells Elliot. She's doing up Stevie's diaper and Elliot is holding the baby's feet so he can't kick. "Catherine came back and nothing happened. Everyone was so happy, watching the same news story over and over. Then some time goes by and you never hear anything anymore."

"Well, she's probably pretty fucked up." Elliot shakes his head and tries to jam Stevie's left foot into the bottom of his sleeper. "What? Did you think she was going to start picking up shifts at the restaurant?"

"Of course not, but I don't know what to do. This isn't, like, usual. Do you think I should keep trying to visit her in the hospital?"

Stevie kicks his father firmly in the jaw and Elliot reels back.

"That hurt?" She shakes out a sleep sack, holding it open and ready for the next step.

"Yeah, some. He should do MMA someday. And you should do whatever you want. She's not really your best friend."

"Still, I want to do the right thing. I called Grey when she was first in the hospital to ask if I could do anything. And I brought him that thing of muffins, remember? So he wouldn't be hungry, sitting around in waiting rooms all the time."

"Oh, yeah. Nice of you." Elliot grins at her over his shoulder as Stevie's right foot finally catches and stays in the sleeper. Then he starts struggling with the snaps along the inside of the leg while Stevie writhes in silent, red-faced fury. Daria knows the screams are coming.

"But I haven't *seen* her. When I went over to the hospital, Grey was like, Oh, thank you for the muffins but now is a bad time. And he looked like he was dying—all pale and sweaty. So I didn't push."

Elliot raises an eyebrow, like *Oh really?* And that's probably what he says but she doesn't hear it because the howling has begun.

Daria swoops down with the sleep sack and stuffs Stevie's flailing legs into it, then catches him under the armpits and pulls him into her arms. His spine is stiff, his head thrown back in rage, and a brilliant sound emanates from his wet pink mouth. Elliot has his back against the wall, trying not to flinch.

"You can go if you want. I've got him."

Elliot widens his eyes, eager, yet hesitating. "You sure?" They are both yelling, and Elliot is fingering something in his breast pocket. Probably a joint. He's kind of a stoner, though Daria told him he has to be straight when he's around Stevie and she thinks he mainly is. Still, it's like he's counting down to when he can smoke up.

"Yeah, it's good. I don't work until four tomorrow, so I can stay up with him. Get on home." The baby is still rigid against her breasts, but Elliot could probably lean across and give her a little peck on the forehead or cheek or whatever. But he doesn't.

Daria watches from the window as Elliot jogs across the parking lot and gets into his car, a weirdly elegant Cadillac from the 1980s that his dad fixed up for him. She jiggles the baby pointlessly as Elliot's headlights flick on and exhaust appears. He backs out and drives away without blinking the lights at her or honking *goodbye*. She holds up Stevie's tiny clenched fist and waves it at the taillights. "Bye, Daddy," she whispers in her high-pitched Stevie voice.

The action startles the baby into a momentary lull in his crying, but he soon picks it up again. Daria cannot fucking stand it when Stevie cries unless he is right against her. Placing him in the valley between her breasts where she always thought her heart should be doesn't really make any difference to the baby, but when the screaming gets too much, it's the only way to comfort herself. As for Stevie, walking is the only thing that soothes him to sleep at this point in the day. Even though she was on her feet at the restaurant for eight hours, pacing the hall in her fuzzy orange slippers is far less exhausting, more peaceful, even with Stevie squalling in her ear.

After he is down, sweaty and limp from all the energy it takes to yell for fifty minutes, she fills a glass halfway with ice cubes and then dumps lemonade over them. The last two inches she fills with white wine out of a box in her fridge. She read online that the best time to drink is right after you nurse because that is as far away as possible from the *next* time, and it gives your body time to process the alcohol. Except Elliot was still here when she finished nursing, so she had to wait for him to go. Not that she thought he'd judge, more that he'd take it as an invitation to settle in for the evening. Guys like Elliot don't have just one drink, and she knew if he stayed she'd wind up watching Jimmy Fallon and making out with him, and then Stevie would wake up and she wouldn't have any clean milk in her to give because she would have been drinking the whole time.

Catherine never seemed to like Elliot very much. She wasn't mean about it, but whenever Daria said something nice about him like, *He's not bad-looking* or *He fixed my toaster in ten minutes,* Catherine would always come back with *But do you like him?* Which is a tough question to answer, in truth. Daria usually responded with some version of *You've never been really on your own. You don't know what it's like out there in Tinderland.* Which is true, and Catherine usually shrugged and backed off. Catherine got really lucky with her first serious boyfriend, and that makes her charmed but also a bit of a sap.

Daria takes a sip of her drink and an ice cube bops her nose. She feels bad for thinking of Catherine as a sap. It's mean and also unfair, since she isn't here to defend herself—as bad as thinking ill of the dead. Now she feels bad for thinking of Catherine as dead. But in Daria's head, Catherine is in the same category as dead people, it's been so long since Daria has seen her. She jiggles the ice around, takes a better sip, and sets the glass down. She digs her iPhone out of her pocket, scrolls through her contacts to Catherine's two entries. The first one is her cell. Everyone in Iria knows about that phone—it was on the news, or a picture of a similar one was. It's a cheap brand Daria hadn't heard of before because Catherine thinks iPhones aren't worth the money. The cops found it the morning after she disappeared, in the parking lot outside DiGiovanni's Ristorante, where she worked. Where Daria works too. She knows that stupid parking lot well—how tricky it is to turn Elliot's truck around in the narrow centre aisle, the way the spot on the end is narrower than the others and practically impossible to back out of if someone is in the spot across. So even though she wasn't there, Daria knows that Catherine's little Chinese cellphone was either in a heap of brown snow along the edge of the lot or else in the gritty slush. If it was in the slush, the police probably had to put it in a bowl of rice to dry it out before they could get any information from it. Or maybe cops have another way of doing that, faster and with less chance of something going wrong—Elliot's Galaxy never came back to life after going through the wash, despite a whole week drying out in the rice. Whatever, she knows the police were able to get all Catherine's texts and call logs and contacts because the news said there were no clues in there. Her last text was to her husband, telling him she was going to meet him in thirty minutes at some French place uptown. Which she didn't do.

Catherine's second number is labelled "Cat Land"—a landline, which Catherine still has since her husband is old and thinks landlines are important. Daria laughed a lot at that, which pissed Catherine right off, which was really hard to do.

"He actually has a cellphone, he isn't a Luddite," Catherine told her. "He just thinks you need both."

"But, just, why? What can a landline do that a cellphone can't?"

"I don't know, okay?" Catherine sighed, rolled her eyes. "What does it matter to you?" But she was blushing a little. Could you be genuinely embarrassed for another person? Daria had never been in love like that.

Daria feels pretty old for twenty-two, but Grey is from another generation entirely—Catherine is twenty-seven and he is ten years older than that. Every time he came into the restaurant, Daria felt like she had an overdue English paper. Actually, Catherine is twenty-eight now. She had her birthday while she was stuck in that torture chamber—Daria's eyes burned when she saw the reminder pop up on Facebook last May. People were writing stupid shit on Catherine's wall about how they loved her and prayed for her and whatever, but Daria just shut the page. She knew Catherine wasn't reading fucking Facebook, wherever she was.

A similar burn flares in Daria's ribcage when she thinks of what must have happened to a girl gone that long against her will. She knows it had to be against her will because Catherine never even called in sick to work. The news reports that Daria sometimes watches hinted at the worst things in the world.

She lets herself poke her finger at "Cat Land" on the screen but quickly hits the red phone icon to cancel the call before it can connect.

Elliot's right: she and Catherine aren't that close. Daria has these numbers in her phone because she has the numbers of every server at the restaurant in case she needs to get someone to cover for her. Even the breakfast guys can sometimes be begged to take a dinner shift. She sets the phone down on the table along with the wine and then stands to convert the couch into the bed. Then she picks up the phone again to make sure her ringer is on—Elliot usually calls before she's asleep. Late at night, Elliot will sometimes say that he loves her, that he imagines them getting married and taking care of Stevie together. Even though she knows he's very stoned by that point, it's still something.

—⁓—

"Did you hear that news about that kid?" Stephanie asks as she and Daria start setting up her first tray of salads.

"Hear what?" Daria doesn't have a lot of time for chat at work—there are tips to be made.

"The kid, Donald Something, who disappeared around the same time as Catherine. He's dead!" With Stephanie, you can really hear the exclamation marks.

"Oh, god. So they found Donny Zimmerman's body?" With the tray perfectly set on her palm, Daria straightens up but then sways a little. It's the word *body* that makes the idea of death real—a human being becoming an object.

"Yeah, like buried in the yard outside the house where Catherine . . . you know. If you're going to murder someone, you should try a little harder to hide the body, don't you think?"

Daria steadies her tray and walks away even though Stephanie has opened her mouth to launch into another sentence. She doesn't want anyone, let alone perfect blond Stephanie, to see how shaken she is over some stranger's death, and if she had said anything at that moment, it would have been obvious. She can't help but think of dirt on Catherine's tan skin, her body crumpled in a hole. She didn't know Donny Zimmerman, doesn't even know if Catherine knew him. She has seen photos of his mom and dad crying in the newspaper but not in a long time—Donny was old news for a while, but now everyone will be talking about him again. His parents seemed so alone, clinging to each other on the front steps of their house. They looked lonely even though they were both there.

Daria hipchecks the door open, thinking about when Donny Zimmerman first disappeared. She remembers sitting on the back stairs while Catherine read an article about him on her phone, her eyes brimming with unshed tears. She talked about going to one of the candlelight vigils at the high school, though Daria can't remember if she ever went. All the fuss Catherine made over some kid she'd never met. Sometimes she thinks it was as if Catherine was writing the script for how to feel once she was gone too.

Daria swallows and takes a deep breath before she strolls into the dining room to deposit the salads and take some garlic-loaf requests. She sometimes feels like Cat is talking to her inside her head because Daria learned so many things from her: the way she set up her trays and order pads, even her polite little lines with the customers. "Enjoy this!" "Can I get you any finishing touches?" "Hope it's perfect!" Catherine was the best of the dinner girls, and DiG's front-of-house staff are mainly girls—young and also attractive. DiG's is a high-endish restaurant with a nice crowd and good tips, so most waitresses, and all the ones that last, put up with knowing they are a bit of a show for the male customers. At least, that's what Daria thinks—she was never sure if Catherine understood that part of the job, or even that she was pretty. And she was pretty, with her heavy dark ponytail and small bright face. Not gorgeous or anything; catalogue, not runway. But still. She definitely didn't flaunt it, for tips or for anything else. When Daria was twitching in the mirror, trying to get her top pulled up above slutty but below sweet, Catherine would wash her hands and say, "You look fine." As if fine were enough.

She and Catherine weren't so much friends as people who worked a lot of the same shifts and had no beef with each other. But during all that time together, they had absorbed little glimpses of each other's personalities. Or Daria had. She never knew what their relationship amounted to in Catherine's eyes, but when she skipped her period the second month in a row, it was Catherine she told. She didn't know why, but it was the right thing to do, because Catherine said, "Do you want a baby?" As if all things were possible; as if she were offering salads from a tray and Daria could pick whichever one she wanted. Was it really that simple in Catherine's mind? But if she hadn't asked her that question, Daria might not have that firm *yes* she said in response to fall back on when Stevie is shrieking or puking on himself and she thinks she hates him.

Daria is startled to see the message icon on her phone when she's on break, but it's just a text, not a missed call. Elliot has a pretty good sense of what's a real emergency.

She waits until she can lock herself in a washroom stall to read the message.

Ell: Did u put kermit doll in the bag
DariA: No sorry 4got hows it going?
Ell: Gud hes asleep now
DariA: Great!!! Wat r u doing?
Ell: DVR UFC
DariA: O right. Back to work.

She puts the phone away, disgusted with herself. Why does she even like this douche? He doesn't ask her one question, doesn't care how her night is going, doesn't even want to talk about Stevie. He is only barely doing his part, and that's because his mom makes him. Maybe Elliot loves the baby—she can't tell. But he probably doesn't love her. Plus, he's a loser, so why does she even care?

She pulls out her phone again.

DariA: Don Z is dead the news said they found body

Ell: Gross who?

Her thumb hovers above the screen for a minute, then another. What can she possibly say? It's entirely likely that Elliot never noticed the news stories about Donny, that he only ever knew about Catherine because Daria told him. How do you tell someone a life they never knew about is lost?

Then her break is over and she's spent the whole of it in the bathroom. Elliot never cares about anything other than what is right in front of his face—he doesn't deserve a text back. The stupid prickle of tears in her eyes is a surprise—she didn't think she could be so upset about the death of a stranger. Maybe she isn't; maybe she's just upset because she's in love with a douche. She jams the phone into her pocket and scurries out into the rest of the evening.

At the end of the night, Daria waits by the restaurant's back door, peering out the chicken-wire window. The hallway is dim and dirty, and the walk-in fridge and freezer, both of which look like dungeons, are right beside her. She's waiting for the punch clock to tick over midnight so she can punch out, dreading the cold black parking lot. She's also waiting for Ashish, one of the busboys, to walk out with her. Outside, the night is dark and thick, cloudy without a moon. Before Stevie was born, Daria could call Elliot for a ride if she didn't want to wait for the bus or walk in the cold or rain or whatever. He would do it without any questions or complaints because he knew she'd come over and he'd get laid or at least a blow job if she was really tired. Daria didn't mind the walk all that much, but she didn't have the energy for both the walk and a fuck—she had to choose. By the time she got knocked up, she was getting a drive home from him after almost every dinner shift.

Of course, he can't come get her now—Stevie's probably conked out in the Pack'n'Play Elliot's mom bought for him and would cry bloody murder if he were woken. Plus Elliot is bad at getting the car seat strapped in properly. It'll take her twenty-five minutes to walk to Elliot and his mom's place to pick up Stevie, and then Elliot will be all affection. Usually she'll be sort of into it but exhausted, and with the Pack'n'Play just a few feet away in Elliot's room the sex isn't that great anymore. But tonight she's feeling pissed enough at his stupid texts that maybe she'll be able to resist and just doze in the beanbag until Stevie wakes up.

The clock finally hits midnight. She scans her card and then Ashish appears from nowhere and does too. He opens the door, then steps back with his arm still bracing it open, and she scurries out, pulling her hood up, tugging her awkward purse over her shoulder. Ever since Catherine went missing, the management's been making sure that staff shifts end when someone else's does, the idea being they'll buddy up, maybe carpool or walk home together, keep each other safe. Which is bullshit. Four steps into the parking lot, Ashish says, "G'night" and gets into his car. He's not even a jerk—he's just sixteen and driving his dad's car and eager to get on with the good part of the night. If she asked, he would probably drive her to Elliot's or at least the cross street. But it hurts her pride too much to ask a fucking kid for a ride. At least he beeps at her on his way out of the lot.

There's not much light in the parking lot, which is blacktop but gritty—installing some extra lights would be more useful than all the parallel shift nonsense. Donny Zimmerman was grabbed from a parking lot too. He stayed late after a basketball practice to work on his free throws. And then someone took him from right outside his school gym.

When Catherine disappeared from just outside the restaurant, it started to feel like parking lots were the problem, like they were dangerous, or cursed. The creepiest thing was that one of the articles about Catherine included a wide shot of DiGiovanni's and its parking lot, taken from the street, and off to the far right was Daria walking to the bus stop.

"It's pretty blurry," Elliot said when she showed him the photo.

Daria had stabbed at the page with her finger: "Anyone who knows me would know the purple purse and spike heels. Anyway, it doesn't matter if anyone realizes it's me. *I* know, and the picture makes it seem like I'm going to be the next victim."

But Elliot had rolled his eyes and said the paper was just trying to show people where something bad had happened, which didn't make her feel any better since it was a place she had to go most days. Plus, it was still fucking creepy to be in a picture headlined "LOCAL WOMAN TAKEN." Daria had been nice to the reporters around the restaurant before that; they seemed sort of glamorous to her. After she saw the photo, she avoided them like death.

Once she's across the parking lot, the sidewalk is at least a little brighter. Daria still has her three-inch heels on, which is dumb—she should wear sensible shoes to work. Elliot calls these her slutty shoes, but the tips are better when she wears them. Even after scrambling around the restaurant for eight hours, she can walk fine in them—she's talented that way. But the one thing she can't do is run.

The walk to Elliot's building is scary because she knows what can happen now. The street is deserted and somehow the icy December wind feels ghoulish. None of it is interesting-scary, like in the movies—there's no echoing footsteps that might be her own, no tricks of the eye or mind, no mysterious strangers just out of view. It's only a long dark walk on streets that don't have many policing eyes—there's almost no one out in this part of town at this hour. It isn't a bad neighbourhood, which is the trouble in a way. People stay out later in a bad neighbourhood.

Her heart squeezes thinking of her Stevie someday being old enough to walk on the street alone, to shoot a free throw, to disappear. She picks up the pace, eager to see his sleepy, snotty face.

She should have taken the bus, she thinks when she's between stops. Waiting is dull and cold, but at least she is at an assigned spot, waiting for a scheduled and populated bus. Walking alone in the dark, she is a checker without a board—anything could happen.

And the thing is, she knows the guy who took Catherine is dead. He can't touch her or anyone anymore, but Daria is still afraid. She did this walk so often while Cat was gone, spent so much time thinking of whoever took her that now an image of a shadowy monster hunts her always. Even though she saw the news report where a lumpy black bag was wheeled out of that nice beige house, Daria still believes someone evil is waiting behind the next mailbox, lamppost, tree. Even if that one man is dead, he made her see that these things can happen, that nothing keeps a girl walking home alone safe and sound except good luck.

And Daria isn't very lucky—not with her parents, who kicked her out when she got pregnant. Not when she fell in stupid love with Elliot, who will always live with his mom and whose hands are always a little dirty. But maybe she got lucky with Stevie, who is perfect and who can clearly pronounce *truck* and *yogurt* even though he's only a year and a half old. Winter is in the wind and her skirt is way too short and she has no plans for what to do with her life when a short skirt no longer makes people want to give her money.

The lights of Elliot's building are coming into view. She's nearly there, nearly safe. Maybe she's been safe the whole way here, but the thing is, you don't know until something happens or it doesn't. Catherine probably never realized the parking lot at work wasn't safe until the worst thing happened. She rescued herself, though—she did what she needed to do to be safe again. Daria can't process the idea of Catherine hurting anyone because she was so gentle. Daria can remember some awful couple trying to get a rise out of her because they found a mushroom in a salad that wasn't supposed to have them. They probably just wanted something for free, or just some sort of sign that they were winners in life. But Catherine was so charming and quiet against their tirade, trotting off to the kitchen for a fresh salad, not at all bothered. She guarded herself so carefully, but in the way of a person who has always known what she is worth, who knows that she matters.

By the time that guy in his SUV noticed Catherine waiting and bleeding beside the road, she had been gone for eight months and who knows what kind of person she had been made to become. The person Daria had known couldn't have killed anyone. She had cried on the bus after reading a poem about a girl who ran over her tomato plant. The news reports are not very detailed, but the guy who owned that house is dead, and Catherine is alive. She must have killed him. It's impossible, and yet it must have happened.

Elliot gave her a fob ages ago so he doesn't know she's there until she walks in the front door of his mother's apartment and smells the sweaty-peaty smell of his weed.

"Were you smoking with the baby in the house?" she demands.

"No, Dary, no." Elliot struggles up from the couch.

Daria drops her bag and marches over to the Pack'n'Play. She wishes she could trust him, but the truth is that Elliot never pays all that much attention to Stevie, and stoned, he could forget about the baby entirely. But Stevie is just dozing, limbs sprawled like a starfish.

Elliot leans over the mesh wall of the playpen and pats Stevie's feathery dark hair. "See, he's fine, right?" His hand is paw-like and sloppy, sliding off Stevie's head, bending the top of his ear. His touch makes the baby squirm in his sleep. Daria sinks slowly down to the floor, staring through the beige mesh at her son's perfect soft triangle of a nose, a whitish-green crispy of snot clinging around the left nostril.

"Yeah, fine. But weed slows you down. Anything could have happened and you would have been out of it."

"I wasn't . . . getting stoned or anything. Just a little toke."

"Sure." She stares up at Elliot from the floor—he looks baggy and enormous from down here, like an elephant in a hoodie. Eventually he sits down beside her on the floor. Jimmy Fallon is talking on the flatscreen, but the sound is off.

"What is even the point of *The Tonight Show* on mute? The only point is the jokes. It's not like Jimmy Fallon is pretty."

Elliot reaches for a bag of Pop chips. "Well, he's all right, for a dude."

The TV goes to a commercial where a little cat follows a big cat around a beautifully furnished home.

"You really think I should go see Catherine?"

Elliot is mainly concentrating on eating chips and watching the cats on screen. "Sure, why not? She's your friend, isn't she?"

"Yeah, but like, we never even went to the movies together. She was just a work friend. Maybe she doesn't want to see me at the worst time in her life." Now the TV is showing *Futurama*. Daria hadn't realized it was so late. "I never knew her that well and now . . . she must be a different person by now."

Elliot keeps his gaze on the TV. "How do you mean?"

"She was raped and beat up and kept in a basement. She murdered someone."

"Well, she didn't have a choice. It's what anyone would have done."

"What anyone would have done? Really? You think you would have it in you, Ell? You'd have to feel something, to kill a human. To kill anything, really."

"Yeah, I would."

She looks for it in his eyes, the moment when he pictures it, what it would take for him to end someone's life, but it's all pot smoke and whatever the cartoon characters are doing on TV—he doesn't really feel it.

"I hope I don't have to find out, is all." He leans in to kiss her, but when she pulls back he just shrugs.

They sit in silence watching Stevie's little lungs pull air in and out, his fuzzy yellow sleeper rising and falling. There's an appliqué duck over the heart and another on the bum that Daria can't see now but knows is there. She likes this sleeper.

Elliot is breathing heavily too. She turns and sees he's asleep tipped against the edge of the couch. She pushes to her feet and when Elliot stirs she pats his head. Pulling Stevie out of the Pack'n'Play will likely wake him and he'll be cranky. But really, if that's the worst thing that happens tonight, she'll be fine.

Youth Must Have Its Day

Kyla didn't know what had been on the news until her parents burst into her room, but she knew there was a problem. She had been up late the night before, waiting for Donny to text her good night like he always did. He didn't, and he didn't answer any of her messages, and he wasn't at school that day, which was weird, since there was no away game and he never got sick. Then her parents threw open her bedroom door without knocking because they never knocked. Kyla was trying to read *The Death of Ivan Ilych* for English class, which would have been depressing on a normal night, even though she actually liked the book. She wanted to tell them to get out, but Dermott sat heavily on her single bed and said, "We've got some sad news for you, sweetie." A lot of what Dermott said was just for the sake of talking, but just in case, she waited to hear what he had to say.

"There's a boy who's gone missing. A boy from your school. We saw on the news just now. I'm not sure if you would know him. It happened last night, doesn't look like a good situation."

Kyla knew Donny had been at basketball practice the night before, but she only nodded, waiting for someone to say more. Her parents didn't know she had a boyfriend. They had forbidden her to date until she turned eighteen, though they insisted it wasn't about repressing her or prizing her virginity or any of that southern U.S. bullcrap (Louise actually said that). It was so she could have time to grow into a thinking, feeling, loving woman without anyone putting pressure on her to be sexual, completely ignoring the fact that *they* were putting pressure on her to *not* be sexual. She figured not telling her parents that she had a boyfriend was a logical violation of an illogical rule. And so they didn't know about the most important person in Kyla's whole world.

Louise was clutching Dermott's shoulder from above, standing angled toward the door, braving it out in Kyla's room, even though they'd had a terrible argument two days ago about whether Kyla could go to a PG-13 movie with Britt. "We don't know for sure that something bad happened. But your father and I wanted to start praying right away for his safe return. We thought you could join us, since this boy was—*is* your schoolmate . . ."

Kyla's gut was vibrating so hard she thought she might actually vomit there on the daisy-patterned quilt, but she managed to ask, "What's his name?"

"Donald Zimmerman," said her mother, her chirpy voice somehow sounding like a box slamming shut. "A Jewish name, I think, but a prayer for a lost child will surely be heard." She knelt on the floor beside Kyla's bed, tucking her skirt around her calves.

Dermott slid off the bed to kneel beside his wife. "Do you know him, Ky?"

"Yeah . . ." She had worked so hard at keeping Donny a secret all fall and winter, but now she had no choice but to tell them the truth. She just couldn't think of the words. Slowly, almost without realizing it, Kyla sank down to the tan-carpeted floor next to her mother.

As Kyla opened her mouth, Louise said, "The poor lamb. When I think of a young one like you out there in this heavy snow, his parents terrified—" She shook her head.

Dermott touched his wife's shoulder then tucked his chin to his chest and shut his eyes. "Let us pray."

And they prayed, truly—even though Kyla hadn't in a long time. There wasn't a lot she could do for Donny, but she could press her face to the quilt her grandma made and send her thoughts straight up to God, or whoever was listening, for Donny's safe return.

Kyla got up at dawn, uncertain whether she'd slept. She couldn't think how to explain why she didn't want to go to school, so she just took the lunch Louise handed her. There was a moment, standing in the kitchen door, when she could have said to her mother's turned back that she was in love with Donny Zimmerman. But then her mother sighed and faced Kyla to say with bright force, "Have a great day at school, darling," and how could you say anything honest to that?

She spent the whole day on the verge of tears because Donny wasn't in Chem or Algebra. Her throat was sore from holding back sobs, and Britt and Siobhan couldn't think of anything to do but keep bringing her Diet Cokes from the vending machine.

Kyla hadn't realized how many people at school knew she was Donny's girlfriend. She'd never kept it a secret—Secord High didn't enforce her parents' "Christian values," but it was easier to stay out of the spotlight. Even with Donny's parents, she had ducked and weaved— not going to their house more often than any of his other friends, not leaning on his arm or touching his hand in front of them, never saying the words *girlfriend* or *boyfriend*. The Zimmermans trusted Donny to have a girl in his room with the door closed, or maybe they just never noticed the door, the girl. Kyla had begged Donny not to say anything about the two of them to his mom and dad. Dermott and Louise didn't socialize much, but she didn't want to take the chance that they'd hear about her and Donny through some sort of parent grapevine.

But it turned out that everyone at school knew. People kept coming up to her in the hall, patting her on the shoulder or arm, some even trying to hug her—tragedy seemed to involve a lot of touching—and telling her they were so sorry about Donny. She heard a lot of theories, but pretty much everyone agreed that something bad must have happened because Donny was too responsible to just take off. *And he loves me, so he would never have left without telling me,* Kyla wanted to say but didn't. Then she did say it, to Donny's best friend, Beaker, sitting on the rad in the drafty front foyer, eating their sad cafeteria poutine. "Yeah, I know, right?" said Beaker, and for a minute it made her feel a little better, knowing that Donny must have told Beaker that he loved her. Then she pictured a slimy hand reaching out of the earth to grab Donny and pull him down because nothing else could have kept him away.

Two women from the police department were interviewing kids from the basketball team in one of the French classrooms. Kyla knew she'd get called down eventually and she was terrified, but she didn't know why. She had done nothing wrong, and nothing could be worse than what she was imagining. But when they finally brought her into Madame Bernadette's room and she saw the two nice ladies in pastel blouses, both of them drinking coffee and taking notes, she felt better than she had staring out the window in Chem. At least she was doing something to help. Some tiny thing.

"So you are good friends with Donny?" said Pink Blouse too cheerfully.

"Yeah."

"Some friends of his thought you two were dating?" said Lavender Blouse more seriously.

"Well, I guess, sorta."

"You're his girlfriend?" asked Lavender.

"No, I mean, we hung around together . . . You know how it is." She shrugged and attempted a smile.

"Do you know where he is?" said Pink.

Kyla did not expect her to be so abrupt and straightforward. She wasn't sure why, but she'd assumed there'd be more beating around the bush, some working up to this question—accusation? She didn't think anyone would outright accuse her of helping Donny disappear. "No, I—He was supposed to text me two nights ago, but he didn't. I wrote to him like ten times, but he didn't text back. I haven't heard from him since that afternoon."

"Was he unhappy about anything? Did he ever talk about being angry or depressed?"

"No, he was fine. He was excited about the new team jerseys, and this movie he saw on TV over the weekend." She trailed off, then saw they were still staring at her, waiting to hear what movie it was. It was then she realized they knew nothing, had no theories or leads or suspects, and genuinely thought she might be about to provide them with a clue. She had assumed the police knew things she didn't; and they had assumed the same of her.

The women kept asking questions—about their relationship, about Donny's friends and grades, how the basketball team was doing, his parents, whether he got into his first-choice university, how much he liked to drink on the weekends, whether he tried any drugs, which drugs, who he got them from. She knew most of the answers, and, taken together, she supposed they formed the picture of her boyfriend that everyone else knew too: a tall, handsome guy who was popular and athletic, but also sweet and friendly, and good at school, or the subjects with essays anyway. He had nearly failed Algebra and Geometry, and he liked to get drunk with his teammates after an important game—those were the worst things Kyla knew about Donny, and she had tried to learn everything about him. The pastel-bloused women flicked their pencils aimlessly over their clipboards and didn't write much down, but they thanked her for her help and sent her back to class, though they said there might be more questions later.

All that afternoon, she kept waiting for Donny to come jogging into class in an Under Armour shirt and tearaways from an away game that somehow she and his parents and everyone at school had forgotten about. She kept picturing the pissy look on Mrs. O'Leary's face, the happy backslaps from his friends, the slippery joy in her own chest. But the day ended without any of that happening, and Kyla was crying as she walked carefully up the long, icy driveway to her door. She couldn't help it. All those months of keeping silent, when she wanted to tell everyone about riding doubles on Donny's bike down the big hill at the waterfront, or watching some silly Woody Allen film at the Paris movie theatre snuggled inside Donny's coat because it's always freezing there. She'd held back, kept her secrets to herself. And now it turned out that almost everyone knew anyway and who cared if her parents found out in the long run? They already thought she was headed in a bad direction with all her doubts, her sarcasm, her secrecy—why not confirm it?

And really, Kyla was strikingly *good* by Secord High standards. She and Donny had talked about it for months before she even let him put a hand in her panties, and they probably weren't going to lose their virginities on prom night, although now that Donny was gone, she regretted not having said yes to that too. Everything was so fleeting—she had to grab whatever happiness she could. Donny was going to graduate that spring, and there was always the chance that he might break up with her once he was in university. Or maybe she would break up with him when she graduated in a year and a half, or something else could end their romance. Anything could happen. Maybe had already happened.

She dried her face with the edge of the itchy brown scarf Louise had knitted for her and climbed the front step, which was just a cement block, carved away on the underside by ice. Inside, everything was just like she knew it would be, just like it was every night: Louise in the kitchen, making soup, chatting along with the grim-sounding woman on her German *Rosetta Stone* CD. Kyla's sister, Jaycee, playing on the floor with dolls that were not as sexualized as Barbies but still pretty. Somewhere in town, Dermott was packing up his lunchbox from his locker in the warehouse, along with a bunch of broken cookies from the bin beside the packing line, and heading home.

When she saw Kyla, Jaycee dropped her doll and pretended she was a horse. She galloped around the living room, turned, and trotted right into Kyla's side, gave her a kiss on the ribcage. Funny little kid. It was so stupid that Donny hadn't met Jaycee. Everything was stupid.

Louise said, "How was school today?" before she fully turned from the steaming, meat-scented stove and saw Kyla in tears. "Oh, honey." She swept over in her long beige dress and wrapped Kyla and Jaycee both in a warm beige hug. "I was listening to the radio all day and there's no good news yet for that boy. But oh, I've been praying so hard."

Kyla felt weak and small in her mother's arms, but the sobs she'd been keeping in started jerking out of her throat and there was nothing she could do. The past six months' worth of arguments with her mother—over her one lipgloss, her desire to be a journalist, her stay-ing out after school until dinner or even later, her disrespect for God—still burned. She was becoming something her mother had been raised to fear and, despite the hippie skirts and the freedom from "organized religion," still did. But Louise couldn't stop nurturing, even when she was afraid, and the hug was what Kyla needed. She burrowed in.

Jaycee squirmed free after a moment, but Kyla kept her wet face pressed against Louise's rounded shoulder, her small pointed breasts squashed against her mother's large soft ones. It was humiliating, childish, but also the only thing she could do. She knew if she opened her mouth right at that moment, the whole story, the whole useless lie of the fall and winter, would come tumbling out. She'd get yelled at, sentenced to days of prayer and "introspection," and what would be the point? She now realized, buried in her mother's soft arms, that if she'd braved all the anger and talk of sin earlier, maybe there could have been a way through and out the other side, with Donny sitting awkward at their dining room table, calling her father "sir," being sent home by nine at the latest. But now there was no Donny, and no possible chicken dinner, and no point to angering her mother when she needed her so much. She let Louise pull her down to the couch.

"I didn't know that this would affect you so much. This boy, Donald, did you know him well? In class?" It sounded like Louise was goading her. They had been arguing about what was *appropriate socializing* for a while—Louise seemed almost ashamed to admit it, but she didn't want Kyla talking to boys one on one at all. Kyla figured the town her parents had come from was so full of religion that even when Louise and Dermott "broke free," they didn't really know what freedom was. But this time, Louise's grey eyes were wide, her warm, heavy arm a halo.

"A little. He's a good . . . student. He's funny. Everyone likes him."

"We just have to trust that our heavenly Father is guiding him safely home."

Kyla leaned forward, reached for her bookbag, and dumped everything out onto the floor: the hefty algebra textbook, a couple spiral notebooks, a history text with a picture of a castle on it, and finally the slender novella she had to read for English class. She stacked them neatly on the coffee table just as her mother snapped up the top book.

Louise waved *The Death of Ivan Ilych* toward Kyla's face. "Tolstoy! What a wonderful assignment." She flipped the book over; the back cover was curiously blank.

"You like Tolstoy?" Kyla muttered, staring at the green-grey shag rug. Donny was obsessed with Shakespeare, and could recite swaths of *Hamlet*. Kyla wasn't a big reader, so she'd been proud of feeling like she understood Ivan Ilych, could relate to him even. It sort of diminished the accomplishment if Louise, who read mainly the Bible and the grocery store flyers, liked it too.

"Don't look so surprised." Louise smiled, then leaned in closer, as if confiding a secret. "He was a great Christian thinker, you know."

Jaycee had opened one of Kyla's notebooks and started to scribble on the pages with a highlighter, but it took Kyla a second to notice. "No, that's not right," she said, snatching the highlighter away from her sister. "He was a writer. A novelist."

"People can be more than one thing." Louise kept on smiling purposefully. "I don't know a lot about him, but wouldn't that be an interesting angle for your paper—Tolstoy's Christianity? Something I bet a lot of people don't think about."

"Well, what was he, like, Russian Orthodox? I don't know anything about that."

"You'll have to do your research, but I'm pretty sure he was just like us. He believed people should come to God in their own way, outside of silly rules and fancy buildings."

"Just like us?" Kyla's voice was faint.

Louise shrugged and grinned, her signal for "Figure it out."

Jaycee threw her cookie plate on the floor and bellowed, "Someone's gotta pay attention to me!"

Dermott stomped in. "Family!" Louise stood up daintily and Dermott hugged her, then Kyla, then Jaycee. Then he plonked down in the corner of the couch and tossed his feet on the coffee table. "How have you ladies been today?"

Louise guided his gaze toward Kyla with her own. "Kyla's had a rough one, dealing with the disappearance of that young man at her school."

"Zimmerman, yeah. I heard a search party is going out tonight to comb the bush behind the school. Good to see the community getting involved. You can't always trust the police."

Louise stood. "Do you think you ought to go, Dermott? I can have dinner on the table in ten minutes."

"I might. I do feel the Lord wants me to aid this boy and his family however I can. Perhaps this is the way. Or one way."

Kyla felt like screaming at her parents, "You don't even know him." But then again, Dermott had found a way to help while she just wanted to stay at home and cry.

"Can I go, Daddy?" Kyla hated to buy into anything her father suggested, but she knew she'd also hate to stay alone in her room, worrying and reading, not even trying to help. Her throat felt tight and hot. "I don't have any homework tonight."

Dermott raised his furry eyebrows. "Has the Lord called you to help too, Ky?"

She was silent a moment. It was silly to continue lying, but if she told the truth now she'd be grounded for weeks, and no one would comfort her anymore. *If Donny comes back, I'll tell them,* she thought to herself. *When he comes back. Then it'll be worth it, worth the punishment for lying.*

"By works faith was made perfect."

He beamed. "James 2:22. Very nice, Ky. But still, after such a horror for the Zimmermans, I worry about you out in those woods."

"Well, you'll be with me, right? You'll protect me . . ."

She saw Louise turn to Dermott, shrug, then look away. Her mother didn't like Kyla being out after dark, and although being with her father should have been theoretically some sort of shield against catastrophe, clearly Louise wasn't convinced. Suddenly, Kyla wasn't convinced herself. Maybe the person who had taken Donny was still out in those woods. The news hadn't said *taken*, but what else would keep him away? The bush behind Secord High loomed before her, vast and terrifying.

"Okay, Kyla, honey. We'll go right after dinner."

The drive over to her school was miserable because the heater in Dermott's truck didn't work, because Kyla didn't want to talk and Dermott never shut up, because the only words in her mouth were her love for Donny and she couldn't bear the interrogation that would come from that, because they were joining an attempt to find something that —in those woods, after so many hours—could only be bad. *You miss all the shots you don't take*, whispered Donny in her mind. He was always quoting his coach's terrible basketball clichés. He said they honestly helped him, but she couldn't imagine how. And yet that was what she heard in her head right then.

Donny's parents were there to see the searchers off at the beginning. The police gave the volunteers directions on how to space themselves out, how to sweep the beams of their flashlights, what a useful clue or piece of evidence might look like. Then Mr. and Mrs. Zimmerman stepped forward at the edge of the parking lot, clutching each other's arms as if they might be blown over. "Thank you!" they yelled into the wind. "Please, do everything you can—and thank you." Their faces were wet, their eyes scrunched shut.

As everyone started moving toward the woods, the Zimmermans shuffled toward their car, arms still locked around each other. Kyla tried to step back behind Dermott in case they recognized her, but she wasn't quick enough, and they both clearly knew who she was.

"Oh, hello, Kyla," Mrs. Zimmerman called. Her voice sounded faint and fading, as if she might weep. "Thank you so much for being here."

Kyla felt she had no choice but to walk over, Dermott trailing behind her. Halfway there, she realized Donny's mother was rummaging in her purse, his dad staring into the trees. They were trying to be polite, but clearly they didn't care about her, didn't think she knew anything special about their son. And really she didn't, not for the purpose of finding him anyway. Still, she wanted to talk to them, wanted to stand and be counted with them, among the people who loved Donny, whom Donny loved.

She didn't do that, though. She just kept walking and when she reached him, Donny's dad took her hand in his heavy leather glove. "Yes, thank you. We really appreciate it." Mr. Zimmerman looked older than she remembered, deep creases under his eyes and around his mouth. He had probably been up all night as she had been, imagining all the same terrible scenarios she had imagined, and they couldn't even talk about it. He glanced over her shoulder and nodded to Dermott. "Thank you."

When the Zimmermans were gone, Dermott stared at her hard, but Kyla couldn't muster a lie. Instead, a spark of bravery lit her words: "I met them when Donny and I did a French project together. At his place." Expressly against the rules, but Dermott just nodded and led her by the arm toward the woods. Did he not want to hear the truth, or was he not really listening? Either was possible with him.

It was a long, cold evening stumbling over tree roots and trying to keep snow from blowing down their collars or falling into the tops of their boots. Kyla tried to fill her head with memories of Donny—the sweaty collar of his T-shirt when he took off his big hoodie, the grip of his hand on her waist when he tried to teach her to ride his giant bike, the way he always smelled like Axe shampoo and Sprite. The times they had studied together, thigh to thigh on a bench in the cafeteria or at the library. Once, Kyla was drawing a Punnett square and Donny started teasing her. He didn't know anything about phenotypes, but he thought it was funny that she was allowed to study fruit-fly sex when her parents wouldn't even let her watch prime-time television.

"Well, they're not, like, ignorant. They want me to be smart at school and go to university."

Donny chuckled, his face pressed into her ear, his breath on her neck. "I just think it's sad that this is the closest you get to an R-rated movie."

"Do you want me to, like, sext you? Gross."

"Nah, I like you fine, even G-rated."

Kyla leaned forward and brushed her lips across his before turning back to her book as the librarian stoically approached. She whispered, "I want to be at least PG-13."

As Mrs. Rajiv passed, Kyla felt Donny squeeze her hand under the table and she squeezed back.

The search went on for three freezing hours before they were given one last round of tea and Timbits and told to go home. No one found anything useful, or not that Kyla heard about. It was hard to tell exactly what was going on with everyone spread out in the trees and dark like that.

In Dermott's truck on the way home, he hummed a few bars of "Amazing Grace," but when she didn't join in, he quit and tapped her knee with his big hand.

"It'll be okay, Ky. Our heavenly Father is watching."

She pictured God lying on his couch, watching all their suffering on a flat-screen TV, and didn't understand why that was supposed to make her feel better.

After the night of the search party, Kyla came home right after school the rest of the week. It didn't feel safe to be out alone. Everyone was tense, darting eyes and locked car doors all over Iria. Even if she walked to Starbucks at lunch with Britt, they moved quickly, didn't linger out front with the other kids, and checked over their shoulders.

So Kyla stayed home, read *Ivan Ilych* over again, and took notes while Jaycee practised her awful piano downstairs. The picture on the front of the skinny book was of an old man, some artist's idea of how Ivan looked. Ivan, at the end of his life, seemed sad and exhausted, but that wasn't the interesting part of the book or the character to Kyla. She thought about poor Ivan as basically a decent person who worked hard but didn't really know what was important in life or how to find out. The scary part was that he could live his whole life and not even be interested in love or being loved, and die that way.

—⚮—

On Sunday mornings, Kyla's family ate Louise's sausage casserole, then went to what Dermott called "the green church," which was the woods on the east side of town, by her school. Her parents thought churches were constrictive, created by power-mad humans who obscured God's creation with their own lesser processes, rules, and stained-glass windows. Louise and Dermott had grown up with that sort of church, learning prayers and Bible passages off by heart so they wouldn't get hit, but they got hit anyway. Louise talked about having to cover her hair, never getting to play sports. Dermott said he got yelled at when he asked questions, was told to know his place, accept gospel as it was written. They both wanted something else for Kyla and Jaycee.

They said the best place to worship was among the Lord's own creation of trees and sky and wind and grass—the green church, the great
outdoors. Of course, things were only green in summer, but they
always went outside on Sunday mornings, whatever the weather, and
hiked until they found a place so beautiful that whoever's turn it was to
pick could "feel God closer." Dermott always chose the top of hills,
Kyla preferred to be by springs or ponds, Louise liked rocks, but that
was mainly because she didn't want to sit on the ground, and it was
hard to tell why Jaycee did anything.

The first Sunday after Donny had disappeared, Kyla's eyes were
burning from insomnia. The family let her pick her church even though
it was really Louise's turn, and so she followed the path back to the area
where she had tramped through earlier in the week as part of the line
of searchers. Now there was no one but Kyla in her long skirt and tidy
bun, Jaycee in her kilt, Louise and Dermott leaning against each other's
shoulders, everyone in the heavy grey parkas from the army surplus
and wearing tough, scuffed hiking boots. They held hands by the
cracked blue ice of the creek and prayed. Kyla didn't want to be there,
didn't want to hold Dermott's work glove or Jaycee's tiny pink mitt,
but when she began to pray, to ask desperately for what she did want,
something stopped buzzing in her head that she hadn't even known was
there, and she felt a little whisper of peace. Kyla had grown up praying—at meals, before bed, whenever she was sad or scared—but it had
been more than a year since she'd started thinking it was as useful as
reading her horoscope in the paper. Now the woods seemed to quiet as
she thought the words *Dear God*.

After that, Kyla was surprised at how strong the impulse to pray
became, how genuinely she felt herself speaking to God. And how quickly
she fell back into the habit. They prayed again at home over dinner, and
then at bedtime—each time, Kyla's prayers were mainly Donny's name.

She wasn't sure it was possible to hand God her problems, her fears, her hopes—or that God was even there to receive them—but it was the only thing that calmed her. It helped so much that she went back to her childhood habit of praying at random. She found herself wandering around in the blowing snow after school, avoiding her friends and forgetting to pick up the milk so she could pray. As she walked, her brain chanted in circles: *Just let him be okay. Even if he can't be my boyfriend anymore, just bring him back and that will be my sacrifice. I won't see him, I'll make myself forget if I have to. Just let him be okay. Just let him be okay.*

—∞—

Ivan died at the beginning of the book, then the story flashed back and went through his whole life: lots of quick general descriptions when he was young, getting into day-to-day details only when he got older, and then sick. By the end, the pace was almost minute by minute.

Kyla tried to avoid imagining where Donny might be, but rereading the section with poor old Ivan lying on his couch, his tongue coated with a gross flavour and pain radiating from his side, conjured what she was most afraid of. She sat facing forward on her own couch, her legs sprawled on the coffee table, just to feel less like him. A lot of kids were saying that maybe Donny had somehow wandered off in the parking lot and frozen to death. Kyla couldn't imagine how that would have happened. But still, that's one way to die. It had been really cold out, even for February—cold enough to kill someone.

". . . all the while here is death! Can it really be death?" Again terror seized him and he gasped for breath. Kyla shut the book and pulled her mom's laptop over to start typing—she didn't have any ideas for her paper, but she couldn't read anymore. Kyla was scaring herself with the way she'd started thinking of Donny in the past tense, as if she was getting close to

accepting that he wasn't coming back. Something terrible had to have happened, even if he wasn't dead. She was always praying that he wasn't, but he had left with no car or money or anything, so where could he go?

Dermott came wandering into the living room then, trying to seem casual, before pulling a book out from behind his back and thrusting it at Kyla. Jaycee glanced up long enough to realize it wasn't for her, then went back to playing pickup sticks by herself.

"*Tolstoy's Shorter Works*? Great," muttered Kyla.

"I couldn't find the same edition of *Ivan Ilych* as you have, but it's in here too."

"I finished reading it. I'm already working on the paper. It's really short."

"I did too, so we can talk about it at pizza dinner."

From the floor Jaycee said, "Oh, no! I *hate* pizza."

"You don't have to do that. I'm doing fine with the essay." Kyla shifted her legs on the coffee table and glared at her sister. "No, you don't."

"Don't devalue your sister's feelings, Ky. And I think the book could be interesting to all of us."

"Yeah, I know what Louise thinks, but I think he wrote it after he lost his faith."

Dermott stared at the cover. "I didn't get that from reading it."

"Well, it seemed pretty hopeless at the end. Ivan actually thinks to himself—" she reached for her sticky-noted paperback and flicked to find the page but couldn't. "Well, he thought everything was worse after he saw the priest. He thought it helped, but then he felt worse."

"What about the light, Ky? The light he sees at the bottom of the dark hole?"

Jaycee looked up and cocked her head to the side. "I maybe don't hate pizza anymore."

Kyla could not ignore the fact that the worst thing that ever happened to her was what made her the daughter her parents had always wanted. She was home right after school, with no Donny to hang out with at Starbucks, wasting her babysitting money. She was home every night, doing homework, praying with her family, watching the news. And somewhere along the line, she had lost interest in arguing, in telling Louise to read the newspaper and Dermott that she could join the hockey league if she wanted to. And what did she know anyway? The world was turning out to be so much worse than she'd ever imagined.

Someone else disappeared, a girl from the university. A woman, in her late twenties—someone with a husband, a house, which seemed odd for a university student. Kyla hoped she would be much further along in her own life by that age, although she didn't know what exactly she wanted to do yet. The woman's husband was on *Live at Five*, along with Donny's parents. This guy had lost his beloved, same as Kyla, but he was a grown-up. Did that help him? she wondered. Was it better to lose someone after you had lived with them, had sex, held each other all night? Or was it worse—was there just more to lose? Did this man, with the funny name *Grey Reindeer*, wake up dizzy, convinced everything was somehow all his fault, fumbling in his bed for something from a dream, an answer that he could never remember? Did he lie there, trying to breathe evenly before anyone else was awake, wondering how it felt to be missing, if the missing one was scared or in pain, and how would he ever know? This man on the news was the only person in town who could possibly feel what Kyla felt. She would have loved to talk to him. He looked like a nice guy. Louise started adding Catherine and Grey Reindeer into their evening prayers, and though Kyla felt she had nothing more to give, she reluctantly did too.

Everyone in Iria was scurrying to their cars, hurrying home, locking their doors. A few times a cop even came to talk to some random person who walked by the school one too many times. Britt and Siobhan didn't want to hang out downtown or go to the mall anymore. Which was fine. Kyla didn't want to go out either. Easier to stay at home and wash the dishes. Have dolly tea parties with her baby sister, pray herself to sleep. When the weather got nicer, she did her homework in the fenced-in yard, watching Jaycee run in circles and jump off the swings. She could almost accept that this was her life now—no boyfriend, no social life, just homework and prayers and family. But then the pre-grad events started at school: the grad breakfast, grad skip day, all the things Donny should have been doing, that she should have been hearing about all lunch hour, every night when he texted her. There was a black-and-white page in the yearbook with a scattering of shots of him on the basketball court with his teammates, a poem some grade ten he didn't know had written, lots of pen-and-ink drawings of flowers. Kyla went back to crying herself to sleep and was so glad when it was summer.

By the time the cool sunny fall rolled around, she was calm again and finding it easier to keep it together at school, even if people did want to talk about Donny. She'd spent too many nights staring at her dark and silent phone, watched too many news reports that were only about forest fires and the price of gas. She was giving up, or she thought she was.

Then in November the university girl was found staggering by the side of a country road. There she was, but where was Donny? Kyla and her parents sat in front of the ten o'clock news after Jaycee went to bed, and after that, Kyla stayed up and Louise kept clicking refresh on the news websites. Surely this Catherine girl knew where Donny was, could help the police find him, Kyla was certain, but the square-jawed guy behind the anchor desk said nothing, moving on to a story about a jack-knifed tractor-trailer on the 414 as if there were no other people missing in the city, in the world.

Life started back up again, but this time Kyla couldn't face it. She kept staring at every door she saw, feeling almost certain that Donny would be coming through it, or maybe flying through a window, maybe a ghost. Everyone was sure some clue would be forthcoming, some hint of Donny's fate, but she didn't know if the news would be good. After nine months of prayers, going back to being terrified was like falling into ice water—she had grown comfortable in her silent misery. All the evenings she spent pouring out her heart to God, or quite possibly just her bedroom ceiling, she had never gotten a response. Sometimes she felt better and thought that feeling might be Jesus' hand in hers, but sometimes she didn't, and what then?

Kyla just drifted as the days and weeks went on—family dinners, the green church, handing in her *Obasan* paper. She read all the time now, was finally starting to get why Donny loved English class—all these other worlds to slip into, other people's problems to swim in, then climb out of.

There was a hard calc test. Louise made a meatloaf. Christmas was coming but of course they didn't buy a tree. Then one night the first story on the news was a cop at a press conference saying they had found Donny's body buried in a backyard in Turgrove, the yard of a house where the owner had recently been found dead as well, and where Catherine Reindeer was believed to have been held. There was some boring video of a small brick house with a big lawn and people milling around the side of it, none of it giving any hint of the violence that had occurred inside, followed by a short interview with the police chief, who was jowly and grave. Then a note that funeral arrangements had not yet been announced, and the Zimmerman family had requested privacy at this time.

Kyla sat very still. Donny was dead. She could still feel how his fingers felt grasped in hers. The tiny bit of bristle above his mouth when he kissed her. He couldn't be dead because it wasn't possible in this beige living room, with the sports and weather coming right after this commercial break, with her mother's crisp skirt spread out on the couch beside her and Dermott's glass of apple juice leaving a wet mark on the particleboard end table.

Kyla muttered *Fuck* right there in the family room—no matter how often she heard kids from school say it, that word still sounded like the worst thing. She started sobbing and it was as if she'd broken the spell because both Louise and Dermott began to weep too. They leaned over to hug her, but Kyla shook their hands off because *fuck* that shit. They thought there was *light* at the bottom of a hole when there was nothing, just Donny's beautiful hazel eyes and pointed chin buried in dirt. Either God was cruel or God allowed cruelty or God didn't exist, Kyla didn't know which. But she didn't care either.

Louise snuffled into her wrist and put her hand on Kyla's shoulder again. "Oh, my darling, you feel so much for these people. I know it is tragic, but try to be strong. We have to pray for the family, for the people who were closest to him."

"*I* was closest to Donny," shouted Kyla, standing up from the couch. "*I* knew him better than anyone. He loved me, and I loved him. *Love him.* Who is going to be strong for me?"

Her parents were gaping at her, Louise reaching out from the couch, her mouth open in a question that was just taking shape.

The rage carried Kyla up the stairs to her room, the stupid hypocrisy of how hard they had all prayed for Donny, how desperately they had wanted him to be safe, and then her parents wanted to turn around and say it was all God's will that he was dead. Dead and buried under scraggly sumac that were really just sticks because it was December and everything was dying.

Kyla wanted to lie flat on her bed and sob, but her tears were gone. She'd used them all up. She rolled over, catching her arm on the bedside lamp, letting it crash to the floor though she could have probably caught it. Her phone tumbled too, but she snatched it up, though she never wanted to speak to anyone again. No one but Donny.

Somehow she fell asleep, fetal, clutching her phone to her sternum. In the morning, she lay on her stomach, her head aching and her eyes sticky, and peered down into the gap between her bed and the nightstand. There were shards of the lamp base down there and somehow also her copy of *Ivan Ilych*. Her teacher had made her pay $15 when she lost her school copy last winter. And there he was—Ivan, bland and unhappy on the front of her floppy little book full of typos. She got a B on the paper; the red writing in the margin said it was well-written but she needed a few more supporting points for her argument. She'd been doing better in English ever since then—mainly As lately. She almost wished she could go back and write a better paper on Ivan, something about the way he mourned for his life while he was still alive. Like everybody does. And then the memory of last night's news slammed into her, along with a new wave of grief.

Screen time was tightly policed at home, but at school Britt handed Kyla her iPad without hesitating. Most people at school would have given Kyla anything at that point so they didn't have to look at her red, swollen eyes and matted hair. She was like a pathetic celebrity. Kyla couldn't find a current picture of Catherine Reindeer—she hadn't been out in public much, or no one was taking photos of her, or both. But in the older photos, stuff from her Facebook account that the news used, she was laughing and picking apples, petting a cat, hugging a man that Kyla knew from TV was her husband. She looked average—not especially blessed or lucky. Ponytail, cutoff shorts, big stupid smile. Donny was more handsome, and he did volunteer work at the seniors' home. Why did this girl live and Donny die?

At home that evening, Louise and Dermott were for once staying clear of Kyla, too baffled to argue or reproach. The night before, they had extracted from her that Donny was her boyfriend and that she had lied and hidden things from them. She didn't apologize, and they quickly stopped asking her any more questions. So when she paused in the front hall with her boots on, her parents agreed that Kyla could go to the candlelight vigil. What she didn't expect was for them to get up, summon Jaycee, and put their boots and coats on too. At the vigil, they all stood in the mushy wet leaves at the edge of the school parking lot, cupping their candles in their palms. It was only a few weeks until Christmas, and all those hundreds of people around the football field with their little yellow flames in their hands looked festive, or something like it. Kyla was cold, and her tears kept freezing to her cheeks until her mother gave her a wadded-up tissue from her purse. Kyla managed to say thank you but didn't look up. Jaycee kept singing Christmas carols under her breath, and when kids from school came up and hugged Kyla, she sang louder, as if she were trying to block them out.

If there was some comfort in the crowds and candles and cold, some righteousness, some secular prayer, Kyla couldn't feel it. Donny's parents told the crowd at the vigil they were touched by the support, but they looked like they were falling down as they spoke. Donny was an only child—what could his parents do now but fall down?

For days afterwards, Kyla felt she owed them the thousand things she knew about Donny—the little kitten he had drawn on the sole of his left sneaker; the way he couldn't grow a real beard, just fuzzy patches with blanks in between; that time he gagged on a Sriracha peanut and couldn't stop coughing all day. Who cared about those things? Maybe only Kyla.

Or maybe also anyone who loved Donny. But she was too exhausted, too miserable and angry, and in the end she didn't call.

The person she really wanted to talk to was Catherine Reindeer. Catherine, who had survived when Donny didn't. Kyla wanted to know whether Catherine and Donny had been together all that time, and what they had talked about. If he ever mentioned her? If Catherine was there when he died? She was a stranger, but maybe she was kind. Anything was better than thinking of Donny dying alone. Donny never liked being alone. Sometimes he would get Kyla on the phone and then set it on the pillow beside him while he fell asleep.

One day on Christmas break, by some miracle, Kyla was by herself in the house. No one had gone very far: Dermott and Louise were shovelling the driveway and Jaycee was building a snowman in the yard. Kyla was lying on the couch, the side of her face squished into a throw pillow. She focused vaguely on the other side of the room, the bookcase, the heavy books on the bottom shelf. Then she got down on the floor, scuttled across, and pulled out the big Iria phone book from the shelf. Only Dermott and Louise would even have that sort of thing anymore. The spine said 2014, but that didn't matter—no one in Iria moved around much.

There was only one listing for *Reindeer*, of course. It was a weird name.

What could she possibly say to this woman who had been through the worst with Donny, who maybe now knew more about the boy Kyla loved than she ever would?

She picked up the phone, keeping her index finger on the number on the page, pressing so hard she felt a spark of pain.

Long Live Home

There are problems all over the house. Grey keeps things acceptable, more or less, but dirty shirts lurk on the closet floor and the kitchen table is still covered with all the canned goods and toilet paper and bread he dumped there when he got back from the grocery store two days ago. At least he put the meat away. There's nothing guests would notice, or at least comment on, but Grey keeps finding things are broken or askew everywhere. During the months Catherine was gone he didn't notice. Of course, back then he had other things on his mind besides housekeeping and home organization. But with Catherine under this roof again, damaged but alive, *here,* he feels he has let her down. He should not have let the house revert to this bachelor state.

The house—*their* house, which she loved so much—should be perfect for her, for the miracle of her return, especially since she doesn't leave it much. They had both been shocked at their audacity when they bought it, such a precarious and amazing thing to purchase a home all their own. They struggled with the mortgage; every month was a victory. Catherine planned each little improvement like a royal wedding—a new shelf in the entryway where they put hats and keys, yellow tulips planted out front in groups of three, cleared eaves-troughs after a day spent on a ladder with Grey shouting caution from below. Even when she was gone, their house held the halo of her, from the sky-blue runner she chose for the stairs to the memory of the heart-squeezing excitement and fear they'd both felt, standing with their shoulders pressed together on the sidewalk out front when she whispered to the realtor that they wanted it.

Now that she's back, though, her presence is overwhelming; he feels it from the driveway, golden and sad. He loves her so much that some-times he has to force himself to walk up the front steps, open the door, and see her wounded face. When she was gone, he came into the house with leisurely dread—little hope but no expectations either. He could sit quietly on her beloved blue couch—he always found it too bright, and narrow—doling himself out a maximum of two beers per evening through episode after episode of *Orange Is the New Black* or *Game of Thrones*. Sometimes he teared up thinking about all the plot points he knew that Catherine didn't know, how confusing it would be for her to catch up when she came back. Or if she came back.

But she did return, though she was struggling like a scuba diver who'd surfaced too quickly. At first, every time Grey entered her hos-pital room he would find her watching whatever station he'd had the TV on the last time. No, not watching, just staring in the direction of the light and noise. After about ten days of that unnerving stillness, punctuated by a sudden violent flail if he touched her unexpectedly, she started to respond to voices; to nod, to respond to instructions, to engage with what was said. He could tell she was listening, but for another few weeks she was still beyond words herself. Then he came into the room on the day after Christmas and she was furrowing the blankets with her fingers—the most motion he'd seen her initiate.

"Hey, Catherine. How are you?"

And she looked up, right at his face, and said his name. "Hi. Grey. I'm . . . fine." He'd been listening to her voice trapped in the outgoing message on their phone for so long, he'd forgotten how it sounded without the metallic echo of the recording. It was gravelly, soft, alto. His response was Pavlovian—he wanted to talk to her about everything in his head, tell her about his day and how he was feeling at that moment. But he knew better than to overwhelm her with his terror and joy. He sat down on the bed beside her, gazed at her face, and when he touched her hand, she didn't flinch.

A few days later, she wandered to the bathroom and back into bed on her own, without being led, without anyone urging her along. Grey watched her pale, scarred legs below the hem of the peasoup-green hospital gown. From then on, she followed the nurses obediently to various exam rooms, to a therapist's office, but she didn't say much— couldn't or wouldn't, it was difficult even for the therapists to be sure. Grey still didn't really know much about her time in hell, but at least now she looked at him when he was in the room.

A few days into the new year, Grey carefully guided his wife through an alley door, avoiding the reporters who were gathered out front of the hospital, always waiting for a chance to "chat," and brought her home. He watched as she climbed into their bed with the aubergine sheets she'd picked out for their wedding registry. He'd washed them and made the bed before she came home, thinking of her hair growing back, her reading aloud to him in bed, her squatting beside him while he played the newest *Grand Theft Auto*. He'd struggled with the hospital corners, trying to get the sheets wrapped tight and smooth as a gift. For months he had let the sheets hang slack. He didn't like to be pinned down by the covers in bed and hospital corners were a lot of extra work, but Catherine didn't like the sheets floppy, and so he folded and tucked for her.

When Catherine was safely in bed, the phone rang—not his cell, which is what the hospital and the cops and his family called—but the landline, left mainly to telemarketers and pizza-order confirmations and crazies who found his number in the phonebook. The crazy people wanted to tell him theories about how Catherine had been taken by aliens or angels or their neighbours with the weird moustaches, but he'd kept picking up the damn thing because what if someone actually knew something. The cops even put a wiretap on the line for a while, so obviously they agreed with him that it was possible. Now that Catherine was back, he intended to cancel the landline—she used to call it his pointless homage to 1992—but he kept picking up out of habit.

"Hello?"

There was the silence of breath; this was always how the crazies started. But Grey was patient, listening, in deference to his former hoping self. These calls had been all the hope he had for a long time. He waited.

Finally: "Is there someone there?" A small soft voice, a woman or possibly a child.

"Yes, I'm here."

"Um, is, um, Catherine there? Catherine Reindeer? The woman who got kidnapped and, um, came back?"

"May I ask who is calling?" He usually denied that it was even her number because the thing with delusional people who called to "help" was that sometimes they meant the opposite. But the girl on the other end sounded so gentle and tired.

"She knew my boyfriend. Before he died. I thought maybe she could . . . I don't know, tell me things he said, before he died. I don't know." Her voice trembled, on the verge of tears or maybe hiccups.

It took Grey a long moment before he realized who she might mean. "Donny? Was Donny Zimmerman your boyfriend?"

A cough, or perhaps a whimper. "Yeah."

"I don't know if Catherine can talk to you for a while. She's not been . . . well."

"I know, I mean, I guessed. But if—"

"Give me your number and if she can call, I know she will. Let me get a pen."

The girl dictated her number carefully, and Grey repeated it back.

"And please, please don't tell anyone else, anyone besides Catherine that I called."

Grey nodded, then remembered he was on the phone. "Okay," he said at last. He had no idea why the secrecy was necessary, but he understood so little at this point in his life, he didn't think to ask. Instead he said what everyone probably said to her, but how could he not? "I'm so sorry about Donny, so sorry for your loss. I met his parents—such good people. They loved him a lot. Love him."

"Thank you." She was definitely crying now.

"Listen, I don't know what you're going through, but I'm probably the closest . . . I mean, I've thought a lot about your situation. I—"

He knew he was failing but still winced when he heard the dial tone.

—⁂—

There was no TV in the bedroom—years ago, she had said, "Screens in the bedroom are a marriage-killer." She got the idea from a book, but it wasn't the worst rule. She even insisted they charge their cellphones in the kitchen, so the bedroom stayed a quiet, dreamy place. Now, without conversation, the silence was total. When Catherine was in bed, she stared out the window at birds, wind-ruffled maple leaves, and, he suspected, largely nothing at all.

He found it impossible to climb under the pretty purple sheets with her that first night. She had been raped. He knew this because the doctor had told him about *abrasions,* because her therapist had warned him Catherine might react strongly to having her personal space infringed upon, and because he had stayed up late too many nights reading terrifying memoirs about other women who had been held for long periods. As much as he longed to sleep beside her and take in her smell, her warmth, he knew she didn't like to be—couldn't be— touched without warning. And once unconscious, he couldn't promise that he wouldn't brush against her, perhaps even try to hold her in his sleep. The way her body spasmed when someone caught her offguard was the worst thing he'd ever seen, all the more terrifying since he knew she'd seen so much worse. As he came into the bedroom that first night, she was curled into a tight, tendoned ball, eyes shut, but he could tell by her breathing that she was awake.

"It's me, it's Grey, Catherine, it's okay, it's just me," he said too fast, all one word. He came around her side of the bed, and when she opened her eyes the look of frozen horror was like nothing he'd seen before when she was his smart, serene wife. He had no idea what she was remembering—and he was too weak to ask. She turned her face to the ceiling and then, a few moments later, toward him again. "I'm sorry. I'm fine." He had no idea what that meant either.

He slept on the guest-room futon that night, but as the weekend went on, she was okay as long as she saw him coming. He read to her, made her toast and tea, and watched her eat and drink, downloaded stupid movies to watch with her on his laptop, of course in violation of her rule. But she didn't enforce it, and seemed to pay attention to the movies, though she didn't laugh at any of the jokes. Who could blame her? Grey sat next to her for hours with the books, the food, the movies, and Catherine seemed calm. So after a few nights, he emerged from the bathroom, minty and damp-faced. She watched him pull back the duvet with as much interest as she watched clouds roll across the sky or Keanu Reeves dart across a screen. When he lay down beside her and said, "Good night," she even parroted it back to him. And when he sank down onto the pillow, she did too—monkey see, monkey do. He closed his eyes. When he opened them again a few minutes later, Catherine was staring out the window.

—m—

Sue has been struggling, breaking into sobs far too often—when Grey is reading aloud and Catherine doesn't react to a funny bit, or when Catherine fumbles or drops things, which is constant. She stares in silent wonder through her tears at Catherine, this new person, so changed from the daughter she knew. But Sue promises to be strong and spend a whole day with Catherine on her eleventh day home. Grey has to return to work because it's been a long year and there is only so much understanding the merch department could have. But Sue can trade a weekday shift for a Saturday one at the bank sometimes. So he goes in, does some work, and leaves seconds after his boss does. When he gets home, he finds Sue sitting on the couch, legs neatly crossed at the ankle, reading a book with a sunset on the cover.

"Hey, Sue. How is she?"

She closes the book, not marking her place, and shrugs. "I don't know. All right, I guess. She spent the day in bed, only ate half a sandwich, didn't really talk to me. I mean, she's *fine,* but she isn't . . . her." Sue begins to weep.

Grey sits down next to her on the couch, palm hovering over her back for a moment before he remembers that he can touch her. His chest releases a tension he hadn't known he was holding when Sue leans into him, actually accepts his comfort. After a few quiet sobs, she murmurs, "I wanted her to come back so badly, but I didn't think it would be like this."

He bows his face into her hair, stiff against his jaw. "I know. I missed her so much—I thought if I had her back, I would never ask for anything else." The smell of hairspray burns his throat. "But she's back, and I still miss her."

Sue takes a tissue from her sleeve. "I'm sorry, Grey, I didn't want to upset you. I know these things take time and she's a strong girl. But it's hard to wait, when we've already done so much of that. And I don't know how to help her."

"I hope we are, somehow. I think she's working on it, in her head, getting better."

Her smile is kind, but Grey sees a terrifying hopelessness there. The tears are gone. "There's a pot of soup on the stove—just bean and bacon, nothing fancy, but I figured you wouldn't feel like cooking." She stands, picks up her book.

"Thanks, Sue. Will you stay and eat?"

She shakes her head. "It's been a long day. I'll be back in the morning, though. They're letting me take a few more Saturday shifts."

So Grey climbs the stairs alone. Through the doorway, in the dusk light that flickers through the branches outside the window, he can see Catherine is still in bed, watching the shadows move. He rustles his jacket in the doorway until she turns toward him.

"Hey, Catherine. How was your day?"

"It was okay. I slept a lot."

"Do you want dinner? Your mom made soup." The banality of the conversation makes his eyes sting, but as much as he wants to say something inspiring or at least kind, he has nothing to offer but soup.

She nods slowly, her chin tipping down into the stretched-out neck of her T-shirt. His T-shirt, he realizes—one of his old worn gym shirts. A kind of proxy embrace.

Downstairs he reheats soup, listening for a sound from above that doesn't come. He stands in the dining room, a bowl of soup in his hand. Would she come down if he called her? It's what they've always done since moving into the house. They had many conversations through walls, up stairs, around corners. Catherine always seemed to like that, to chuckle at some private joke as she asked him questions through the bathroom door, the kitchen wall. He realizes he should have asked her long ago what that was all about.

He slides a spoon into each bowl and takes both up the stairs

Together, Grey and Sue manage a version of this plan with other meals on Tuesday, Wednesday, and Thursday. Sue strengthens her resolve, no more tears that week, but she's worn out. She greets Grey at the door with the news she persuaded Catherine to play a game of Go Fish, momentarily cheered, but then she shakes her head in disgust. "In a house full of poetry, in a city full of friends, all my daughter can rise to is asking if I have any sevens."

The bank Sue works at is having a staff meeting on Friday afternoon and Grey encourages her to go. She, too, is running out of other people's patience. Besides, when he asks Catherine if she minds spending the day alone, she shakes her head without moving her gaze from the snow-crusted branches out the window.

Friday night, Grey works nearly an hour late—some new specs came in at the last moment, and a whole display has to be rethought—but the truth is he can't face the idea of cooking her some soggy pasta to eat on their aubergine sheets.

Catherine has always been a better cook than him, which didn't matter when she wasn't there. His own standards are low, his palate unrefined—he prepared mushes of vegetables and meats he was happy to call stew or curry or stir-fry depending on the seasonings. It's more depressing to serve them to her. He can remember her up at dawn, in the kitchen kneading butter on a chilled marble board—it took until the next day for the croissants to be ready, but they were filled with light and air and butter.

He comes home with Swiss Chalet and flowers—purple tulips that must have come from very far away to be so vibrant in the depths of winter. When Grey arrives, the house is silent. He wanders past the kitchen, the scraps of breakfast toast he left in the sink, the book he left folded over on the dining room table—all of it undisturbed for the last ten hours. At the foot of the stairs, he already knows that Catherine is staring at the blood-orange sunset. Her hair smells like the curry he'd made for dinner three nights ago because she hasn't showered yet this week; he knows this too. And that, when she sees him, her expression will be faintly pleased but largely—nothing. Largely nothing at all.

When he realizes they don't have a vase, he puts the flowers in a juice pitcher of water and carries that and the sack of chicken up the stairs. Be grateful, he tells himself. He has her back in real life now, as well as the images of her he keeps in his head: the one of her laughing and hopping on one foot outside a locked park bathroom, snow in her hair; the one of her resting her head on his stomach, knees curled in, reading a book; so many more. Does she ever think of that ghost of herself, he wonders, and her old simple life full of work and books and food and love, before everything bad came raining down?

He reminds himself of Donny Zimmerman, found buried in the yard of the house where she was kept. It could have been Grey instead of Donny's parents weeping at the memorial on TV, him instead of that poor young girl on the phone. He is grateful to have his wife back, he is. He just wants a *little* more.

Catherine's gaze comes directly to the door as he enters—a good sign, maybe. "These are for you." The tulips flop in her direction. A droplet of water sloshes onto the rug. The mustard-coloured rug, he notices suddenly, is ugly.

"Thank you," she says.

He sets the vase on the nightstand, the bag on the bed beside her knees. "Quarter-chicken dinners, one with salad, one fries, just like always!" He cringes at his own tone: too close to that of a host on a children's TV show. He unwraps the meal, being careful not to get grease on the duvet, and hands Catherine her plastic oval takeout container, fries jammed around the chicken like packing peanuts. She holds it out for him to take a fistful of the fries, which he dumps on his chicken. Then he takes some salad, still using his fingers, and drops it into her oval. "Bon appetit!"

They chew for a few moments in silence. He watches her fine jaw working under her olive skin, now pale and striated with tiny red veins. Capillaries?

"Catherine?" He says her name mainly to see if she'll turn toward the sound. Sometimes she does, sometimes she doesn't. This time she does.

He swallows a fatty bit too quickly and feels it slither down his throat. "I know you're not, you don't have to be . . . *okay*. I don't want to push you. Like Dr. Durnsville said, you can take all the time you need."

She looks at him—he feels it. This is one thing that hasn't changed; Catherine's intense gaze. Forget the way novelists talk of haunted eyes, eyes with a depth of worry—Catherine and Grey both think that sort of description is crap. Eyes are wet live cells, and when they watch you, you feel it.

"But I don't think this is good. I think it might help you to . . . start some routines. Maybe you could . . . get out of bed, at least. It might help you and . . ." A prick, a selfish prick—how could his discomfort matter in the face of her genuine suffering, the scars on her palms and forearms?

Her gaze drops as she pokes one slightly burnt fry with another. Eventually she eats that fry, and a few others, and the wing part of her chicken. She gets up to pee and to brush her teeth, but then sinks back into bed beside him. "Goodnight," she says blandly but unprompted.

"I love you, Catherine," he whispers. He feel like he says this a thousand times a day, but he's not sure if it's ever out loud.

He waits a long minute, and when it comes it's very quiet, but eventually she says, "I love you" back.

They have a very quiet weekend too, but Catherine is out of bed a few hours each day. She wanders from room to room, exploring as if for the first time. She stares out all the windows, studies the spines of the books on the shelves, opens closets and cupboards and gazes at what she finds inside. But she's exhausted by even a half-hour of moving through her old life, especially if she has to speak, and keeps returning to the soft duveted kingdom of the bedroom. When he spots her in the den, gingerly touching her pretty blue couch, he asks if she wants to watch TV and she nods, sits down beside him. He had been planning on *Orange Is the New Black* but that doesn't seem right. He opens up Netflix and scrolls through. "Whatever you want is fine. See anything you like?"

Catherine cocks her head, taps his hand when she wants him to stop so she can read a description. Which is exactly what she used to do. Which is unnerving, because they really don't do anything they used to do anymore. They end up watching a sitcom about attractive young people running around a bar trying to find true love. It's impossible to take their gossip and sex seriously, but Catherine gives it her full attention, her hands on her knees.

On Monday when he comes home from work, she is in the kitchen, and her hair is damply clean. Her clothes are from her past life as his cheerful wife, an undergrad, a waitress, a sweet nerd. These clothes were waiting for her in the closet, but now the jeans are so loose she has folded the waistband down over the pockets, and the cuffs of her favourite dark blue blouse are rolled back while she grates a carrot on the counter.

Grey has brought her a cake but she probably actually needs something else. After what she's been through, who can imagine what she needs? He hasn't brought her flowers again; they looked stupid in the juice pitcher. Maybe she needs a vase. Maybe a better grater. Half the kitchen is sprinkled with flecks of orange.

She scrapes carrot off the grater, the cutting board, and her hands into the salad bowl. Without glancing up, she asks, "Did you have a good day?"

"Fine. You?" He toes off his shoes and kicks them onto the mat. He gives her a beat to respond, but when she doesn't he's ready with, "Hey, I brought dessert." He raises the cake box at her. Her smile is small, bitten. He winces at her effort, his weak contribution. The torrents of conversation he used to receive, in those pre-trauma days, when he'd come in the door to Catherine studying for exams or writing papers and full of italicsy commentary—they seem like fables now, or memories of another woman. Her dark hair is just getting long enough to hang into her face. When she brushes it out of her eyes with the back of her hand, she reminds him of a silly young girl he once knew, someone he rarely sees these days. He has always known her with long smooth hair falling down her spine, with a book in her hand, with a frank, affectionate gaze. Without these accessories, she looks like a stranger. Almost a stranger.

She plucks a beer from the fridge, opens it, and hands it to him. The gesture is familiar, and comforting. He knows she's really trying; he just wishes she would say more than two words to him at a time.

She opens the oven door and pulls out a pan with the pork roast that had been in the back of the freezer, about to succumb to freezer burn. She turns toward him with the brown lump of meat on the pan framed by her oven-mitted hands—Christmas-patterned ones, though Christmas is over. She must have noticed that the everyday ones were covered in burn marks because he is an idiot and left them too near a burner one dinnertime rush. He doesn't know where she found these; Grey hasn't seen them in years. All the time she was gone, the house hid secrets from him.

"It's good to see you . . . up and about."

She nods, though she seems a little unsteady, unsure. Still she's moving, active. As she crosses the kitchen, he reaches out to touch her, only to have her pull away from him toward the stove. Grey freezes, wounded, tears suddenly hot in his eyelashes. All those nights in bed, her warm shoulder centimetres from his own, he hadn't dared touch her despite his longing—picturing her startling away from him, cringing toward the far edge of the bed. He'd thought it was his imagination. Apparently not.

When she faces him again, empty-handed, he is still standing with his hand frozen outstretched.

Her wet eyes flicker in the kitchen light. "The pan was *hot*. I had to put it down."

"Oh . . ."

She reaches out, taps the back of his hand. "I made dinner for you."

He lets his arm drop limp at his side. "Thank you." This is what he dreamt of when she was gone; he needs to be more grateful. "Thank you so much." When the tears have cleared from his eyes, he gathers the cutlery from the drawer and begins setting the table.

—⁂—

The weeks flow by and Grey has noticed that Catherine assigns herself new tasks each day. Doing the laundry, cleaning out the junk drawer, scrubbing a mysterious ink stain from a wall in the hallway. She asks him about his day and follows up on what he says, wanting to know how plans and worries at work are going.

But there are many things Catherine doesn't do now—read, make phone calls, engage easily in conversation, give hugs, focus on anything for longer than the length of a sitcom. Sue has tried all the DVDs she saved from Catherine's childhood, Disney classics and zany adventures, but Catherine gets up and wanders off about half an hour in.

She also doesn't go anywhere unless someone asks her to. She doesn't have a problem with leaving the house, but she doesn't initiate it. In her previous life, she was never a socialite, but she liked the library, her mom's place, her own yard—places that now, when Grey suggests them, she shakes her head at. Grey, Sue, and Dr. Durnsville, have all urged walks to the park, down the street, even around the yard, but Catherine always demurs politely, her eyes canted away.

Her only excursions are to see her doctors and therapists several times a week. For those appointments, he comes home from work early and often finds her already waiting by the door with her shoes on. Totally normal, except she doesn't have a book or a magazine with her—and Catherine used to read when she was on an escalator or in line at the grocery store. Instead she just stares at a blank space beside the door where they'd always meant to hang a picture or at least a mirror. He doesn't like to think about how long she's been sitting there.

She was trapped for so long. He's seen the basement now, in grainy newsprint colour beneath a dull headline. Staring at the photo, obsessing over not the bloodstains on the floor but the tiny window set flush with the ground on the outside. Eight months. How did she keep opening her eyes when there was so little to see? And how can she stay indoors day after day, still confined, although now by her own walls?

If he can't ask, who can? When they were first together, he asked her a million questions about her life, her childhood, her parents and friends and jobs and school. After they started sleeping together, he queried the exact sensations in her clitoris, nipples, and vagina during sex, trying to make her come. What couldn't he ask her, his wife?

So, en route to the therapist's office, driving through the sleety streets downtown, he asks, "Are you scared? Scared to go out?"

That shrug again. She meets his gaze, though. "Fine. I'm fine."

"But—I mean, you don't go out unless I'm with you."

A chubby woman with a stroller crosses slowly against the light. He presses the brake as a new thought strikes him. "I'm worried you might be getting, what's the word? Agra-something."

The old Catherine would have quickly filled in the blank, and in fact Grey has asked prematurely—the word slides into his mind a beat later: *agoraphobia*.

This new Catherine stares at him while he pulls into the clinic parking lot. "I don't have that. I just . . . I don't know. My bus pass expired ages ago. I don't have any money, and I haven't talked to most of my friends. I can't even remember my email password." She seems to collapse back against the seat from the effort of having said so much, the most he's heard her say in one go since she came back.

He pulls into a spot right by the door and twists the key before speaking again. "I didn't think . . . I should've helped you more, I just—"

"You are helping me. You are." But her head dips low, examining the floorboard with its crumpled receipts and salt stains. Finally she returns her gaze to him, a rare treat and a challenge. "I just don't know how to help myself."

He leans forward but catches against his forgotten seatbelt. "If you need me to take another leave from work or if you need to move away from here—I would do anything for you. You know that, right?"

"Of course I know that." She unbuckles her seatbelt and slides forward, presses her palm onto the back of his hand, the most she has touched him in nearly a year. "You're the whole point."

Dr. Durnsville is both rote and kind. *How are you, Catherine? How are you sleeping? Are you eating much? How do you feel in the mornings? What do you do when you are sad?* The doctor rubs her hands down her thighs a lot. Grey suspects she's never had a client who has been in the newspapers before. She mentions the calls from journalists often enough that Grey can tell it bothers her.

Has your mother been to visit again? How do you feel about that? Have you been writing in your journal very much? Do you feel comfortable sharing anything from your journal?

Catherine's answers are precise, clinically helpful.

I feel okay, thank you. I try not to sleep more than nine hours or so, but I get tired. Every morning I feel good, but then the day wears on me. When I'm sad, I look out the window. She seems comfortable in the first half of the sessions, comfortable enough in the time they spend together in this white sofa-ed room, chatting about the banalities of insomnia, iron intake, trauma. *When my mother visits, we watch movies, and she tries not to cry. I don't write in the journal very much, mainly recipes or ideas for what I want to cook.*

Grey is only there for the first half of each session, something Dr. Durnsville suggested. There had been an explanation the first time she asked him to leave, but Grey had waved it off—he has always given Catherine her space, let her have her secrets, even back when the stakes were so much lower. Of course, that doesn't mean he doesn't want to know what happens once he's gone, not when Catherine so often returns to the waiting area red-eyed and shaky. Her words in the car this afternoon make Grey realize how little he knows, still, about what she is feeling. Perhaps he has left her too much space, given her more privacy than she wants. Or maybe there's just no way out but through the worst of it.

Sitting across from Dr. D and beside his wife on the expensive white-leather couch, Grey suddenly wants to ask the hard questions. In the midst of the rundown of meals eaten, he asks, "Do you think about him a lot?"

The expression on the therapist's face is tense, watchful, but she doesn't intervene.

"Who? Dex?"

This is the first time he's heard Catherine say this name. By the time she felt up to answering questions, the police had located the house where she'd been held, found the body of the man who held her captive. Once they found Donny Zimmerman's body buried in the backyard, there was nothing left to investigate. The cops said the cuts on her hands were consistent with the shattered fluorescent tube that cut the veins in Dex's neck and face. Catherine had killed him, or at least helped him die. The paperwork was filed, of course, but for the most part Catherine was spared much questioning.

"I try not to. But of course I think about him. He did a lot of damage." He nods slowly. "I think about him too."

She scrutinizes him, really seeing his exhausted face. "You shouldn't. He was—like a tidal wave, like a hurricane. All that pain, and for no . . . for no reason." Her voice is shaking slightly. "But he's dead now. Right?"

The therapist murmurs, "Yes, he's dead and buried. But it is still okay to be angry."

Chin jerking from side to side, Catherine says, "*No.* He's gone. It's done. There's nothing, no one to be angry at."

Dr. D's bony hand darts out, as if to touch her, but she pulls back before making contact. "That's good moving on, Catherine, but it is understandable to feel some anger, some rage. If not for yourself, and it would be completely natural, then perhaps for—"

"Donny." Her voice is a stone dropped in water.

By the time Grey stands to leave at his appointed time, Catherine has said little more but she is crying, which is not surprising. The surprise happens when she sees him get up: she eases to her feet too and makes a move to follow him.

Grey glances at Durnsville before saying to Catherine, "You have another half-hour, Catherine—you can stay. I'm just gonna wait for you in the other room, okay?"

"No." She shakes her head and her hair flops over her cheeks, finally long enough to move. "I'm ready to go now." She walks to the door and nods at Dr. D, who gets as far as "Take a moment to transition and—" before Catherine darts out, as if fearful of being caught.

The new Catherine does what she is told, or she does nothing at all— this initiative is a first. Grey shrugs at the doctor and follows her out. By the time he gets his coat on, he has to catch up to her in the parking lot.

—◊◊◊—

Perhaps a good compromise would be a new chair in front of the window, or a loveseat—there's room. That way, Grey thinks, Catherine could stare out the window without lying in bed, and maybe sometimes he could sit with her. Not too long ago, they'd had an uncomfortable olive-green chair in that spot, which no one ever sat in. They used it for clothes worn once, not yet dirty though not clean enough to go back in the bureau. During Catherine's long absence—during the time, Grey supposes, when she was getting beaten and raped daily— the improperly sealed bedroom window leaked during a west-driven rain and drenched the chair. It didn't dry properly, even in front of the radiator, and after a week it started to smell. Now there is a blank spot by the window where Catherine stares sometimes. As he chews a bite of ham steak, Grey realizes Catherine hasn't asked about the missing chair, but surely she has noticed that it is gone?

They have started eating dinner at the dining room table every night, which is nice. It's easier to talk when he is not trying to balance a plate of stir-fry over the sheets. The heavy blond wood table with carefully lathed legs was one of Catherine's favourite things they bought for the house—she loved it almost as much as the blue living-room sofa.

Catherine lasts through the meal and more of the cleanup every night. Now as he tells her about work, she carefully lathers and rinses their dishes and cutlery while he dries. Still, he senses her scripting, struggling for scraps of their past conversations. Their old normal, with all its relaxed banter and literary criticism and puns, is like a movie he saw a long time ago.

"Did you go to the lunch? With those American sales guys?"

"Yeah, I did. It was really good. They're sharp but not pushy. You know?"

Catherine runs a fork under the tap, places it in the rack, then pulls a steak knife out of the soapy water. Her face is pale and tight—there is still no slack in her cheeks. "Great."

He isn't sure it is—she would probably have said *great* to anything while she was trying to balance a knife under the spray. He has noticed her care with potential weapons.

There isn't enough to say about his day, and she says nothing about her own. Jokes that would have made her laugh until she couldn't breathe in the old days make no sense now, but he doesn't know what kind of jokes this new Catherine would like. He wants to be the charming sweetheart she fell in love with, but increasingly he feels bogus, an imposter.

"Do you want any books? I'll get you whatever you want from work.

Discount still in effect." He says it an advertising-y voice, then shakes his head.

She shrugs, carefully sudsing the traces of gravy from a flat white plate. There is the quiet of water trickling into more water, the whirr of the furnace below their feet. It's the coldest part of winter. "Maybe a cookbook, if you see something nice."

He nods and leans toward her. She has been trying—clearly trying—to say enough to make him happy, to interact in ways that seem normal. But her attempt is always only, "This episode of *30 Rock* is funny." Never, "Remember when Alan Alda played Jack's dad on *30 Rock* and I laughed until I got the hiccups?" Always normal, never who she used to be.

But Catherine was never a recipe cook, preferring to guess and experiment, to do things her own way. This is new.

"A cookbook? What kind—I mean, what kind of food do you want to cook?"

She shrugs again. "Whatever. And maybe some new pots, with lids that match. It would be nice to have something shiny and new."

There's a rust-tinged saucepan lid in his hand, and the old dented grater on the counter beside him. It's amazing to Grey that after all his resignation and doubt, they still want the same things, a little bit.

The store is crowded even on a weeknight, but with fewer manic children than on the weekend. The rubberized steps in the main entrance are wet from tracked snow and far too wide for everyone to have access to a railing. Grey takes Catherine's hand, which is cold and damp—they had to park so far away. It takes him several seconds to realize this is a move from the old playbook. Catherine has shied from his touch since she returned, sometimes with such fearfulness that he has learned to keep his hands away. But he hasn't come up with a new way of being near her yet, so sometimes he forgets, like now. Perhaps, for a tiny moment, Catherine has forgotten too, because her hand stays quietly in his. Or perhaps she is just frightened of the crowd.

The second floor is windowless but tastefully lit. Shoppers are surrounded by a honeycomb of small rooms, each stuffed with furniture draped with throws, shams, and sheers, everything freestanding burdened with accessories. They have come here to find the things that they need.

Grey picks up a folded blue blanket wrapped in paper from a wire bin full of identical blankets. It has the density and heft of a teddy bear. He gives it a hug—it feels right—then passes it to Catherine. "For the back of the couch? For while we're watching TV?"

Catherine wraps her arms around the bundle and squeezes. "Okay."

The stroll through the designer rooms is aimless. Even though the chair he wants will go in the bedroom, it isn't thematically "bedroom" and Grey knows they won't find it in this section. He regains Catherine's hand and this time it is dry; he suspects she has wiped it on the blanket.

By the time Grey saw the photo of the basement where Catherine was held, things had probably been moved around or hauled into other parts of the house. He tried to imagine her living there—sleeping, watching the old tube TV in the corner—but it was impossible. He just kept picturing her in her waitressing uniform with that ridiculous apron that covered nothing, bouncing around his car and drumming on the dash, listening to something angry by Sinead O'Connor. He'd known her so well for so long, and then she just disappeared. How was that even possible?

"What was Donny like?" He had sat in a lot of overheated uncomfortable rooms next to the Zimmermans, nervous and quiet, but bonded in their shared misery. He felt as though he'd met Donny many times through their stories, the pictures they carried in their pockets like passports. "You must think about him a lot. *I* think about him a lot."

She does not answer immediately. As they walk past a teenager's room with thick blue blankets draped artfully on a loft bed, Catherine pulls her hand back from Grey and begins to stroke their blanket as if it were a puppy.

They are in a large, loud room filled with couches now, the walls rimmed with chairs. A child zips past their knees, ponytail streaming. Still stroking the blanket, she says, "He used to tell me stories. We both did. There wasn't much else to do. We were friends."

"Can you tell me one? One of Donny's stories?"

She is standing beside an angular red couch when her knees seem to just drop out from under her, and suddenly she is sitting down. He sits down beside her.

"Well, I don't know. He had this plan for prom. He wanted to take his girlfriend on his bike. Like riding doubles, you know? He said they rode like that the first time he took her out for coffee after school. It sounded romantic, but I was worried about her dress . . . I guess it doesn't matter now." She dips her head, swallows wetly.

For a moment his palm hovers over her shaking back, hesitating, before he finally lets it rest between her shoulder blades, feel the warmth of her living body. She doesn't flinch. "I'm sorry. It must've been terrible to lose him."

She strokes the bright red canvas of the couch cushion between them—Grey remembers the furniture in this place being nicer. "Yeah. He was a sweet kid. He helped me." A tear plops on the upholstery.

"His parents gave me their number in case you wanted to talk to them. His girlfriend too."

She shakes her head. "I want to be kind. I know they—they must be so sad. But I'm not—"

"It's fine to wait." He taps the back of her hand. "They know you've been through a lot."

"I'm alive though." She sighs and looks away, her gaze resting on a bin of cellophane-wrapped tins beyond the arm of the couch. She reaches across him without standing, picks one up and holds it out to him. "This is so perfect. See, it's a grater that catches the cheese."

He runs his fingers over the surface, the sharp-edged holes dulled by the cellophane. "Yes, perfect. Let's buy it."

Catherine smiles, a trickle of tear sliding beside her nose. She stands and goes over to the sales desk to get a vinyl shopping bag and drops the blanket in. When she returns and holds the bag open to him, he adds the grater. Once he's up from the couch, he takes the straps from her and slings it over his shoulder.

Will they always live in quiet now? Slow sentences instead of constant chatter, long silences? But perhaps eventually, someday, the feeling will be the same as it always was—the feeling that she is the only person who really hears what he is saying, and that he can be that for her too, as long as he listens very closely.

Standing beside him, her fingers touch his and then she clasps his hand. They start to walk again, surfing through the crowd of other shoppers. They move faster now than they did before, maybe because the few items they have found show them how much more they need.

Sometimes the Door Sticks

First-person books have always been my favourite. Novels, short stories, memoir, poetry, anything with an "I" in there somewhere. I love the idea that the characters own the book, that the story is lived-in, intimate. It's always nice to slip into someone else's skull and leave my own behind. Before, when I closed a book, real life used to drape slowly back over me: Oh yeah, I'm Catherine. I need to get off the bus, go to work, do my CanLit paper. Now the shock is sharper. When the story ends abruptly or the book falls shut or my attention wanders—and suddenly I'm me again, feeling the rug where my T-shirt's rucked up—it's a blast of cold water, a kick in the back of the knee.

I've lost interest in me—and that's all anyone wants to talk about now, it seems. I prefer not to be in my own head if I can avoid it. During my therapy sessions, Dr. D asks me a lot about what *I* feel and what the experience has done to *me*. The short answer is that it's turned me into a person who lies on the floor all day reading instead of going to work or school or the grocery store, but therapists never want the short answer and I don't usually have the strength to elaborate.

Everybody tells me that I'm "doing so much better." And it's true, I guess. When I first came back, I couldn't concentrate enough to read a line, couldn't even follow along when Grey was reading to me. The effort of just staying conscious, of not going back in my mind to the worst things, kept the stories out; my own life loomed so huge that I couldn't imagine anyone else's. Later, I had to focus on the basics of taking enough steps to get across a room, of looking back at people looking at me, saying hi. These normal things take so much concentration when you've gotten out of the habit. Washing my hair and putting on clothes feel like putting a ballgown on a cat—so much effort and what was the point? I'm trying to get back the autopilot I used to have. When I watch movies with my mom, I try to anticipate the moments when I'm supposed to laugh. It's hard, but her shoulders relax when I react like I'm normal. Sometimes I wish I were a robot, feeling nothing, able to follow a program and glide through the day on a series of commands I don't even have to think about. Then there are days when I feel like I already am one, ignoring everything good and beautiful in my life, just clonking forward, and I have to fight to not be a robot. Every day is exhausting.

At least I can read again. My mind wanders and I often have to flip back to remember what I've read, but I'm getting to the point of living with the characters again and forgetting who I am for a little while. So far I've been reading mainly short stories, just because Grey bought so many collections for me when I was in the hospital. I like the brief glimpses into the lives of people I'll never know. The stories feel like a good primer on how life works, how families and lovers and jobs and friendships are. All the inexplicable things that I used to be able to deal with.

I don't think I'm ready for poetry yet. I'm not ready to fill in all those ellipses with my own mind, but eventually I want to go back to Julianna's poems. I found one of her books in the living room. It wasn't my copy; there were none of my careful notes in the margins. The weird thing was, I was too scared to read any of the poems—I just flipped through the pages but wouldn't let my eyes focus on any stanzas or individual words; it all blurred together. I recited her poems so many times while I was in the basement, especially the one about prying a stuck door open with a butter knife, that they started to feel like prayers. Will reading them now make me feel like I'm back there again, with all the doors stuck? Did I even remember them right or understand what she was trying to say at all?

I can't read the poems I like, I can't go outside alone. I can't even lie on the blue couch that I've missed so much. Perched on the stiff cushions, I feel awkward and exposed, unsafe. If Grey is sitting there beside me, I grit my teeth and sit up straight, but otherwise I go back to sprawling on the floor, the way Donny and I always did. It's safer—you can't be knocked down. And sometimes it feels like he is still with me down there.

The front door creaks and jingles, then swings open into the hall. Grey shuffles in, his rain jacket drooping around him like a broken tent. "Hello," he says quietly, voice directed nowhere in particular, before he looks around the doorjamb and sees me there on the floor. "Catherine. Are you okay?"

Catherine is all he ever calls me now. I guess *Cat* feels too familiar, considering how little we know each other anymore. Slowly, I sit up, then tip to my hands and knees and at last coil and stretch up to standing. "Fine. How was your day?"

"Bit slow, but I got a lot of little things done." He has wandered into the kitchen, where the roast chicken and potatoes should be nearly done. "Smells good in here."

Small things are all I can do for Grey. It's for him I get out of bed, wash my hair, put on pants, shirts, underwear. Roast a chicken and potatoes. We met in an emergency room when I was twenty. I would never have met him anywhere else; he's ten years older than me and I would've thought him nerdy and fat if I'd met him in high school. But late at night eight years ago, with a dishcloth on my scalded arm, I saw that he was sweet and smart and would remember not only my birthday but my mother's too, would buy me books for my commute that were exactly what I wanted to read, would eat in my restaurant and compliment me on how well I handled rude customers instead of how cute I looked in my uniform. He was so charming. He probably still is charming, but I don't seem to be capable of enjoying it anymore. Every interaction is only draining.

Grey used to make me feel warm and relaxed, eager to tell him everything I thought or felt. I dreamed of him every day I was gone— him hugging me to his chest, reading me stories in bed, telling me I'm beautiful. Now that I'm actually back, I feel like a ghost of my old self, haunting my life but not a part of it. I can touch him but not really. There are days now when Grey is the only person I see.

Because Grey is a good husband, he starts setting the table without even going upstairs to change his clothes or check his email. I get the chicken out of the oven. It takes me a while to assemble the meal—I do everything slowly now—but eventually we sit at the dining-room table and fork chicken and salad into our mouths. "It's warm out, for March," says Grey. "Feels like spring, almost."

He won't go quite so far as to suggest a walk after dinner: he knows that I am still afraid of our polite quiet street, the neighbours with their dogs and babies, their Honda Civics and snow shovels. He knows that everything is overwhelming to me, but he wants to pretend otherwise, so he doesn't ask me to do anything extra.

"Would you like some barbecue sauce?" I don't know where this housewifely side is coming from, nor Grey's grim masculinity—just one sharp nod, a zip of the chin, to indicate assent. Who is this person? I'm tired of silence, but I don't have anything to say. I used to talk so much—about school, about work, about things I wanted to do or read or buy. We would both read the same book and then talk about the characters as if they were friends of ours. Now the barbecue sauce is all I have to offer.

I zone out for a bit, staring at the blinking clock over the stove. I know how to fix it, but I haven't. The blinking 12:00 is calming, as if time isn't moving forward. As if I have as much time as I need to patch all the holes Dex left in me. I'm not sure how long I watch the clock, but when I tune back into the dining room, the meal is nearly done, the last few bites ready to be scooped up and chewed. And then the dishes, and then I can start to wander toward the bedroom and the joy of unconsciousness.

—m—

Grey has never been hit in the face with violent intent; a few accidental pokes during street-hockey games, maybe, but that's it. I can't think of anyone I know who's been hit hard in the face, and I used to know a lot of people. Most problems just aren't handled violently these days, not in the places I would go anyway. Not at the restaurant, no matter how drunk or pissy a patron might get over the wrong salad dressing. Not at school either, where everyone would talk about privilege and voice and try so hard not to trample on anyone else's thoughts, or seem to. Besides, these days there are so many easier ways to mess someone up. Steal their credit card, hack into their Facebook account, tell them they're bad in bed and boring out of it. Before Dex, I had never really imagined a life that included being hit, even though I read about it in books of course, heard about it on the news, watched it happen in movies, a crisp thwack of flesh on flesh, knocking the hero backwards but leaving no permanent mark.

That was the thing that happened to me most at Dex's house—a lot of things happened there, but always interspersed with the blows, the fear of blows, the huddled crying after. Donny and I were always hurting from the last time, and steeling ourselves against the next.

When I saw Dex's hand looming toward me the first time, I closed my eyes, the way you do for a kiss. The punch felt more like a wall smashing into my cheekbone instead of a fist. I couldn't make out the individual knuckles against my flesh, or even the shape of a hand—it was just a thud of pain at the side of my face, throwing me back, stinging my nose and eyes. I staggered but stayed standing, wobbling at the foot of the basement stairs. I was still coming out from whatever he drugged me with. Donny told me later that he was in the corner watching, terrified for me, terrified for himself. But I didn't know Donny yet. I think if I had, I would have felt better knowing he was there, but since he was a stranger, his dark shape across the room just added to the fear. He could have done anything to me; Dex did.

—◦◦◦—

Grey runs all the errands so I try to at least keep the dust off the bookshelves, cook nice meals, lug the heavy laundry basket down to the basement. I don't like the basement, even though we had it finished years ago, with bright yellow walls and pine-coloured laminate flooring, soft corduroy furniture. It's a den, a playroom for the children we haven't had yet—nothing like Dex's cinderblock cellar where I thought I would die every day. But something about the light slanting in from the high windows, the faintest damp . . . I don't like being down there.

Sometimes I think I should go out shopping on my own—buy new shoes, a package of dishcloths, be a little more independent instead of waiting for Grey to come home and do things for me. That's when I find myself standing outside on the front lawn. The sidewalk is a hem, an end to our property, our home—I can't seem to cross over without Grey being right there to ward off evil. Pathetic. The lawn isn't really any safer than the curb. Dex took me from a parking lot, and it was scarcely dusk. Even with a restaurant full of people on the other side of the lot, it turned out I had no defences.

But I used to leave the house every day and for years nothing terrible happened to me, until one day it did. So I could do it again. I could stride past men strong enough to throw me down, I could talk to strangers. I could go back to school. I think about the number of people I used to sit beside in class or at the library or chat with in the caf, who never tried to do anything to my body, never hurt me. And I convince myself to go outside.

The first breath of fresh air is always a jolt—cold and clean and alive with wind. I walk down the three shallow cement steps and onto the lawn. The problem is all the space. I should like things being open, bright, so unlike the clammy closeness of the basement. But the yard is so exposed and empty, someone could come at me from any direction. The ground is soft and brown from being hidden under snow all winter. Spring is coming early, and all the melt has gone into the lawn. I can feel it seeping through my tennis shoes as I walk over to what's left of our flowerbed. Mostly it's all wet black twigs and leaves on their way to mulch, but there are stalks and twisted yellow leaves in the spongy dirt, and I see a few dead flowers still standing up straight. Grey grew flowers the summer I was gone. I crouch down to look closer.

I'm still there when Grey's navy Corolla rolls into the driveway. I watch him get out, lock the car, then turn to see me. I want him to be pleased—he's been encouraging me to go out more, but he probably didn't mean crouching in the flowerbed. He touches his lip nervously as he strides over—not pleased to find me outside. Worried.

He comes to stand beside me. "Hey, Catherine. You okay?"

That's all he ever asks me. Maybe the problem is that I'm not but always say I am. I wish he'd stop asking—it's easier to pretend if he doesn't keep asking. Just once, I want to have a conversation where I am not a damaged person fumbling with life. Just to be the old Catherine, for a while—smart but not that smart, kind of pretty, a good waitress, married to Grey—that would be so nice. Even though I'm huddled on my sodden lawn like a crazy person, I want that normalcy.

So I try: "Sure. How was your day?"

"Good. Good day. I went out at lunch and got you a cellphone." He rummages in his briefcase and pulls out a flat white box. "I got another Android, 'cause I know you don't like the fancy ones."

"I don't *not* like them. I just don't see the point." That sounds like such a normal thing for me to say that Grey stares as if he's seen a ghost. "Thank you."

He bends down and hands me the box. "The number's on a card inside. I already put it in my contacts, and I put my number in yours."

I guess he's waiting for me to stand, but I don't. "Did you plant flowers last spring? While I was away?"

"What flowers?"

I point and he leans over to peer into the dead weeds and sumac. "Those are tulips, Catherine."

I say, "Oh" like the word *tulip* means something to me, but it doesn't.

He shakes his head, eyebrows pressing low. He looks ridiculous from this vantage, peering down over the curve of his tummy. "They're perennials—*you* planted them, when we moved in. They just come up every year on their own. Remember?"

"Oh," I say for real this time. The past has retreated to the blue line of the horizon. If I planted tulips once, or knew how to cross the street without my heart becoming a pulsing beat in my chest, it was a lifetime ago. I clutch the phone box in my hand, the corners digging into the soft pads of my fingers. "Of course I do."

—ɷ—

The time before Dex took me seems like a thousand years ago now. Everything blurs together. Most of the classes I was in at the university blend into the ones from the year before or after, all the way back into high school. Professor Altaris's class stands out, maybe because it was my favourite, or maybe just the most recent. And waitressing doesn't change that much over time—the customers and the dinner specials might change, but what happens every day is always the same. And Grey has always been Grey.

If I try, I can remember specific things, get beyond that general sense of *before*. We used to touch a lot, Grey and I. Probably most young marrieds do. But not just a kiss at the door and a snuggle in bed, I mean hugging while we did the dishes, leaning over to kiss each other across the table in restaurants, his hand on my thigh in the car. It wasn't anything I really thought about unless someone pointed it out—he was just always close by and I liked to touch him. Donny and I were always touching too. We'd hug each other so tightly for warmth and comfort, the hard brass button of his denim jacket would dig into my soft upper arms. When he was dying I stroked his face, the small soft patches of beard mixed with the scruff of stubble—he wasn't old enough to grow a proper beard. Now I never touch anyone on purpose, and something in me almost leaps out my throat if someone puts a hand on my back when I don't see it coming.

Everything comes back to Dex, those months when he devoured me, when I was nothing. Dr. D wants me to keep thinking back further, to my real life. And I do try. I remember sex with Grey. We were together eight years, long enough to have our own sexual vocabulary: making love on a Sunday morning versus fucking on a Saturday night. I imagine every couple is like that, but I don't really know. I was so young when we first got together; my teenage romances hardly count. I remember my breasts against his hairy chest, his rough fingers rubbing up my spine, but over-top these memories is a closed-off feeling, as if I were watching my past through a sheet of plastic wrap. Sometimes it's like déjà vu looking at him across the table or the couch or the pillows. We are the same people in the same space, yet all the ways we used to be together are warped and corrupted now. I want to tell Grey I'll come back to him eventually, really back, but I don't know if it's true.

I remember other things, from before, some of them not as sealed off—I feel like I could go back to certain places if I were just brave enough. The semester Dex took me, I was reading *Sometimes the Door Sticks* for Professor Altaris's class. That was how I found out about Julianna; her book wasn't the sort of thing I would have chosen for myself. At first, all the poems seemed too familiar, rusty car doors and greasy hair—I didn't go to school for more of what I already knew. I liked reading for the way it took me away from myself, even before there was so much I needed to get away from.

Right before I was taken, I was working on my final essay and trying to figure out how she made her poems sing when the words were so ordinary. Then I was trapped and hurt and terrified, and I realized that everything ordinary was what I loved. And so I tried to escape in my mind back to those ordinary things by remembering her poems. When I really concentrated I could recall whole stanzas, whole poems, even though they kept changing over time. I kept telling Donny that one about the beige dishcloth—the poet didn't know if it was beige to start with or had faded from a brighter colour—but the lines were a little different every time. I wanted to write it down, make the words stay still, but in the basement we didn't have anything to write with, so the poem skittered around in my mind and wouldn't leave me alone.

When he was in front of the class, Professor Altaris moved like he had just beamed in from another planet and was testing the gravity, afraid to crash through the floor or float away. He would have made an awful waiter: always dropping things, striding into the projector beam and blocking the picture. A bad server but a good professor— I liked him anyway. I wish I could remember more of his lecture on Julianna's poems. I don't think we covered many of them in class, actually; the lecture was mainly about her murder. He thought it was tragic that she was deprived of the chance to keep writing and develop into an even better poet, tragic that we will never read those later poems. He sounded like he was a little in love with her, really, which I think everyone in the class found embarrassing. Of course it was sad she died, but we were studying literature, not history. Besides, what I suspected then I now know is true—a lot of the worst things happen for no reason. Life isn't written by an author who is carefully considering her words. Sometimes there is no hidden meaning, or meaning at all. The poems, though, we could read and maybe someday understand.

During my last class (though I didn't know it would be at the time), I went down to the lectern afterwards to ask Professor Altaris about my essay topic, and he seemed so delighted to be talking to a student I felt sorry for him. He kept losing track of the things he was trying to put in his briefcase because he never took his eyes off my face.

"So what intrigued you about Ohlin's work?" He was shuffling papers into folders. A few drifted to the floor. "If you start with what you find most compelling, you can often find a thesis there and then expand out to some of the other poems."

"I don't know if I'm intrigued." I shrugged, which made my heavy backpack drag up my spine. "I just feel like I could write a good essay about some of the poems. I think I understand them because—"

He crouched for the papers, still looking up at me. "Are you sure that's wise? Your final paper is an awful lot of brain space to devote to something that you don't really enjoy."

"Her poems are like my actual life—she writes about waitressing and I'm a waitress, she writes about plugged sinks and so is mine."

"So you can relate?"

"No, I don't care about that. What the poems are actually *about* is boring. It's the voice that I like. I like seeing where she keeps her distance and where she is closer to the reader. Sometimes she seems to be right there inside the poem, you know?"

Clearly that wasn't the right answer—Professor Altaris looked even more oxygenless and gulpy than usual. Thinking back, I wish I had asked him more about the poems line by line: Why was the *goldfish flag of the mailbox* so easy to see in the mind even though it didn't really make sense? What did *the red wail of last call* mean? Did he think describing the *men too tired to be kind* implied anger, or just sadness? Even still, despite my nonsense question, he tried to answer with something useful.

"Well, don't forget that the poet chooses her subjects." The papers were a messy fan in his hands as he rose toward me. "I feel like there's romance there too—in the voice, sure, but in the action too. That hope that after the dishes are done there will be something more. The actual words she uses *are* her subject in a way. The beauty of the language imbues the object, don't you think? Kitchen-sink realism but also . . . more?"

I wasn't sure about the question marks. Was he really asking me? I paused to think. I was doing well in the course; I thought I could say something intelligent, if I tried. I shrugged again. It wasn't like I didn't find my own kitchen sink—double-sided and stainless steel, with the dishcloth Grey's mom had crocheted draped over the centre—romantic. I loved it passionately because it was ours, in the home we'd bought together. But that sink was too personal, not intimate exactly, but only ours. I didn't care about other people's sinks. And yet I could see Julianna's kitchen clearly in my mind, and when the poem described "a foamy baptism" I knew just how she felt, tired and scrubbing but not at all unhappy. How did she do that— import her vision into mine? But I didn't say any of this to Professor Altaris.

"Maybe come back to them in a couple years, when you're a bit older and—"

"I'm a mature student. I'm already much older than most of the kids here. You can't get me on an age technicality . . ."

He tried tapping the edge of the papers against the lectern to get them to line up but they buckled and slid. He wound up just stuffing them into his briefcase, crumpling and folding to get them to fit. "And how old are you, exactly?"

"I'm twenty-seven."

"Ha!" The crack of laughter echoed in the empty room. "You're not old enough to have perspective on how old you are." The briefcase finally clasped shut and he appeared prepared to leave, but he didn't. "You could mature yet. Some do, some don't, at this point."

"And what makes it happen—maturing?" I wasn't flirting, I don't think.

He tipped his head left all the way to his shoulder, like he was stretching his neck. "Well, life. Any move forward is good, right?"

Now I know that isn't true. Some experiences aren't worth learning from.

"Julianna was twenty-seven too," I reminded him. "She had some wisdom." I believed that, but I wasn't sure if I could prove it. Maybe you can never prove wisdom.

He gave a wobbly nod, like he was not 100 per cent convinced. "Yes, she did."

"I wonder how she found the words, found the poems. I mean, how do you know where to start, what will make sense to people?"

"Catherine, I'd give a lot to know the answer to that. It's that gift that the poets have and the rest of us try to learn." He shrugged, his jacket crumpling around his neck. "I think maybe you just start, and then keep going after that."

—⁓—

When I was ten, my mother gave me a copy of *Our Bodies, Ourselves,* which I read quickly and then gave back. I wasn't happy to learn that sex existed. Of course I'd heard rumours: at recess, out toward the farthest soccer field that no one played on, boys would yell, "Do you want to HUMP?" and then run off punching each other. But until I read the book I didn't know about the mechanics of sexuality and it turned out that was how I preferred it. I gave the book back, but I couldn't stop seeing those diagrams of bodies inserting themselves into each other. Once you know, you can't unknow. What a penis looked like and how one could shoot goo into you. How people apparently did this a lot—even people I knew. Even if not recently, most grown-ups had done it at some point.

It was too much information, and that information imprinted itself in some very active part of my brain. Every time I saw an adult or semi-adult—my parents, my friends' parents, our neighbours, my babysitter—the thought would balloon before I could stop it: *You had sex. You, Stephanie, forbidding me to eat Cheetos and sending me into the yard to play, you opened your pale legs and let your boyfriend shove a pink elephant trunk into your hole and pump up and down until he squirted clear snot.* Everyone became only their ugly hairy parts and icky urges.

I learned to like sex around the time the teen movies think you're supposed to, sixteen, seventeen. Sex with Grey was my favourite, which is also what a screenwriter would want. Partly it was being in love and partly we learned each other's bodies as well as our own. I loved his hands, his chest, running my fingers through the soft hair at the nape of his neck while he went down on me. I loved the pressure of his body on top of me, the smile against my neck after. I had had sex before Grey, but I hadn't had time to get it right. But I knew from the start Grey and I were going to give each other all the time in the world.

Even though I knew from my grade-school health classes that someone could use sex to hurt me, I never saw it happening in my mind like I did with all those grown-ups humping away that one summer. Now it's an image I can't stop seeing. It's always possible. Any man could make me feel small and useless and like a bag of skin to be tossed down and fucked. Any man—the cops that took me in, the doctors, my cousin standing weeping in the doorway of my hospital room, even my husband. Those big hands with the long wiry hairs above the knuckles could always grip my shoulder, wrench back and down, make me fall to the floor, sprawl. It isn't a thought, that's the problem; it isn't something that comes from the part of the brain I can control. It's just a flash, a twitch of being pushed down, forced open. With all I learned in my twenties about loving sex—the pleasure of my husband and the softness of his touch and the warmth of it all—that scared-kid disgust at the nakedness, the spurt of mucus, it all came back the first time Dex knocked me down and opened me up.

—m—

To catch the bus to the university, I used to go out the front door, down the driveway, turn right, and walk about two blocks. It was pretty quick no matter what time of day I had a class. For the bus to work and to my mom's, I had to walk about six blocks, then turn left and walk a block more—way more hassle, and that route was infrequent too. Those were the three main places I used to go. All are safely familiar, in that way my therapist singsongs it: "SAYflea faMILyar!" But my mom is so close to tears every time I see her that I can't be near her for too long. And the restaurant, filled with people who know me but not well, who would want to talk but wouldn't know what to say, seems too miserable to bear.

The university campus is big enough that no one notices you if you don't want to be noticed, and I loved it there. Loved the library, loved the sprawling green fields, loved the nineteen-year-olds in their sport sandals and hoodies, the poetry readings, the profs with their briefcases rushing through crowds of students. I loved all my classes, even the ones that weren't actually that great. My favourite idea of myself is sitting on the steps of the Humanities building, reading and eating a sandwich, occasionally saying hi to people I knew from class as they drift by.

I've been thinking about going there all week. If I told Grey or my therapist that I had a plan to go somewhere, anywhere, they'd be delighted, tell me I'm "making progress," but somehow that makes me not want to tell them. Sometimes I like to pretend, just for a minute, I'm a normal person who might run out to the mall because she wants new gloves, or go to campus to see a friend or grab a book from the library. Someone who whenever she feels like going for a walk would just go. Put on her shoes, drop her phone and keys in her bag, stride down the chipping cement stairs out front. Like I did one thousand times before—more. That old Catherine, relaxed and cheerful, seems like a dreamgirl—impossible. I want to be her again, but I feel a choking tightness in my throat as I stuff my keys and my new phone and $5 from Grey's change-cup in my pocket. (I miss my Kate Spade purse, lost in the slush in DiGiovanni's parking lot.) My hands shake doing up my sneakers and the bows are floppy and lopsided. But I force myself to march to the door, down the stairs, and then, the hard part, over the edge of the blacktop driveway and onto the sidewalk.

All my good plans fall apart at the bus stop. I feel so exposed just standing there, not moving, nowhere to go. My shirt sleeves flutter in the breeze. A white top, an old one now too large. The whole thing flutters on me. Why didn't I think to wear a jacket in March? Goddamnit, I'm not even wearing a bra.

I wrap my arms tightly around my chest so my nipples don't press against the fabric. The money for my fare jingles in my pocket. Two teenaged boys come up to the stop, snickering and punching each other. They stop when they see me shivering in my self-straitjacket. The one boy is pale and freckled, the other one black with an upturned nose; both about seventeen. Donny was a seventeen-year-old boy just like them. I don't know if he had freckles because it was too dark in the basement to tell. I was never afraid of Donny, maybe because everything bad that happened to me happened to him too. When you live through the worst with someone, you have to love that person—or at least I did. There wasn't any other way to survive. Donny loved me too, but he didn't survive. These are the sweetest-looking boys, but with their large hands, fleshed shoulders and thighs—they could do anything to me here. I'm sure Dex looked sweet to someone too, once. In a flash, I could be thrown to the ground or into a van. There is no van. They are staring at me. I weigh my options: I could call Grey on my phone, the number is in there, I checked and rechecked. But to unlock the phone, open contacts, touch his name—that would take time, time when I wouldn't be looking out for myself. Anything could happen. I finally fling myself into motion, feet pounding down the street, arms pumping, nipples to the wind. I know it is cowardly to run home, but as my feet thud on the pavement, it seems like the opposite: I feel so strong.

When Grey gets home later that day, I am standing at the edge of the lawn again. But this time I'm doing much better. I've got a bra on, tights and shoes, a coat. I've brushed my hair, and it's clean. The car sighs as Grey turns it off. Before he even opens the door his eyes catch on me. I wonder if he notices I'm wearing my nice green dress, the one he used to like. The tidy hem sits exactly in the middle of my kneecaps.

Every time Grey comes home, I remember again that I love him. Alone in the house all day with all these books about other people, I keep forgetting that feeling. When I was away, Grey was a magical concept, this mythical being of love and kindness and rescue, ready to wrap me in some sort of endless perfect hug. Every time Dex made me suck his dick or I was too hurt to move, I thought about when Grey gently kissed me goodnight on my eyelid or gave me his sweater, the bright blue couch he let me buy even though he thought it was uncomfortable, and how I fell asleep holding his hand so many times that if I closed my eyes I could still feel his fingers in mine.

Grey didn't rescue me, which I guess I was expecting because that's how it goes in stories about men who love women when bad things happen to the women. Probably I was still expecting it even when I started trying to rescue myself.

He walks across the lawn until he is standing a few feet away from me. The yard is not that wide. We always thought we'd get a bigger place someday with room for kids to run around, when I finally finished school and got a real job. It suddenly jolts into my brain that Grey has carried more responsibilities in the past year than I've realized. He kept our old life going, holding open this little space for me to fall back into.

"Thank you for paying the mortgage all these months."

"What?"

I close my eyes and everything spins. "And the hydro bills and the garbage fees and all that. Oh god, did you send my taxes in April? They were almost done . . ."

I hear Grey shift his feet in the squishy wet grass. I open my eyes, and his hand is above my shoulder, waiting to rest once I've seen it, been forewarned. "It's okay, I took care of it. I would do anything for you, Catherine, you know that. Your taxes . . . it's not that much."

"Thank you," I tell him, tears dribbling down my face. I can't believe I can fall apart so quickly, even in my pretty dress.

"I wish I could do, could have done more."

I look at him, finally. The crisp beard, trimmed around his square jaw, the warm dark eyes, the broad shoulders obvious even under his bulky jacket.

"I wish you could too." I sniff, trying to stop myself from crying. I feel like I'm always crying. "But it doesn't work that way. I have to do it, mainly."

"But what, though? What do you have to do? I mean, I under—"

"Remember my life. And forget this year. I don't know how I can keep remembering Dex and just walk around."

Grey shifts his briefcase from one hand to the other. "I don't know either. But you're doing it."

I shake my head and my hair whips into my eyes. "My life was stolen. Remember when we used to actually have sex sometimes and it was amazing and easy, and now I can barely let you hug me? Remember how I was never shy about talking to strangers because waitressing kills shyness? Remember how good my tips used to be because people liked me? You liked me."

"I love you," Grey says loudly, his eyes panicked. He tries to reach out for me, but he's still holding the briefcase. We both look down, so he opens it and holds out a thick clothbound book. "It's fairy tales—the old-school ones, by the Brothers Grimm. I thought you might like something simpler, more straightforward. Wicked witches, the occasional wolf. It's a little violent, but not too bad. Don't read too much into it."

"It shouldn't need to be simple. Remember how good my essays were? Professor Altaris said my midterm paper was *witty*. But now I can't do anything. Now I'm just—" I flop my hands at my sides, standing in the cold on my wet lawn with cars slipping by in both directions, our neighbours heading home, glancing curiously in our direction. "I have nothing left."

Grey closes his eyes for a long moment and then opens them. "It's late. Do you want to go inside?"

"I dream about Donny all the time, and then I wake up and it's like he's died all over again. No one rescued him. We were together every day for so long, and then he was just gone. I keep feeling like he's next to me."

Grey nods slowly and swallows. "I know a little about how that feels." He means me, but I can't think about that—all my losses crowd out his. Suddenly he looks smaller, weaker, his jacket too long in the arms, the cuffs hanging over his hands. "Do you want to tell me about it? Let's go inside and sit down."

"I do not want to go back into the house. It took me half the day just to get here."

"Ok. I'm sorry—"

"What are *you* sorry for?"

"Nothing, I—"

Suddenly I feel a million degrees, sweating and frazzled and furious. "Dex buried him in the backyard, but I heard the police found the body and took him somewhere. I don't know where." I stop, almost choking on my own breath.

"You must miss him a lot."

I close my eyes, keeping the tears in. "Of course I do. He was all I had for a long time. And then Dex——"

"You must have hated Dex."

"I hated him, sure, but I'd hate a wave if I were drowning too."

"It's okay to be angry. There's nothing you can't say to me."

My eyes spring open and Grey is still there, nervous and sad, waiting for me to say something. "Of course I'm angry—all I am is angry. Everyone keeps saying it's fine, it's normal to have this rage, but they don't say what to do with it. And I've already done so much. Nobody rescued me, no one came to help Donny, and I have to live the rest of my life without him." I hunch my shoulders, wrap my arms around myself—the only hug I can bear. My armpits and collar are soaked with sweat. "Everything was supposed to go back to being easy and perfect when I came back—the way I didn't even know it was before. But Dex is still everywhere, and everything is tainted. Now I can't touch you, and I can't read the poems I love or see any of my friends. It isn't fair, and there's no one left to be angry at, and there's no one here to fix it but me." A sob catches in my throat but I push it down—I'm so sick of crying, of losing my voice, of letting it all overwhelm me.

Grey is crying too, which is even worse. "I'm here. I can't fix any-thing, but I am here." A tear plops on the collar of his jacket.

"I don't want you to cry," I tell him. "I want you to be okay. Someone has to be."

"Yeah," he says breathlessly, "all right." He wipes his cheek on his biceps. "I'll try." He looks down at the book in his hand. "This is a stupid gift, I'm sorry. I know you're not able to read much these days and I just thought . . . something simple . . ."

"It's okay. I think we actually have this one. My mom gave it to us, ages ago."

"Oh, well, fuck it." He's quiet for a moment, then he holds the book out to me again. "Do you want to tear the pages out?"

"What? No, you can just bring it back."

"You could rip it up, if you want. Maybe it would be cathartic—give you something to do with your feelings."

I finally take it from him. The cloth binding is rough against my fingertips. I open the book and tear out one page—it makes a good solid ripping noise, but it's only a blank endpaper. I try to toss it onto the lawn to pick up later, but the wind tumbles it over the dead grass and into the street where a Civic smushes it into a puddle. Satisfyingly destroyed—it's just brown wet mush when the car drives away. I grasp the title page and pull that out too, then crumple the page into a tight ball in my fist before dropping it to the dead grass at my feet. I tear out and crunch another page, and another. Grey cocks his head and bites his lips as he watches me. I flip to the first page of an actual story, but as I slide my fingers and start to tear, I read the words *Once upon a time.* I almost forget what I'm doing, it's so natural to read a story when I see those words. I stop with only a tiny ragged rip at the top of the page. Then I close the book and hand it to him.

"No?"

I shake my head. "It was worth a shot. Maybe I'll tear some blank paper later. I like books too much."

He clutches the book to his chest. "At least that hasn't changed."

"That's true."

"If you change your mind, let me know. I get these at a discount, you know."

A quiet laugh blurts out of my throat. "I'm not crying anymore."

"Me neither." His eyes are still wet though, and red around the edges. Probably mine are too. I can tell he feels awkward standing out here from the way he keeps angling his body toward the front porch, but he's trying.

"Do you know where Donny is? I mean, his grave?"

"I don't know, but I can find out."

"I'd like to meet his girlfriend sometime. Kyla. Donny told me a lot about her."

"She called, remember, while you were still in the hospital."

I nod, swallow, rub my wet cheek with the back of my hand. "What did she—does she know that I haven't really been—"

"It's okay, she seemed to understand. I have her number, you can call whenever you're ready."

"Of course." Grey is watching me closely, waiting to see if I will say more. "Sometime soon, I do want to call her. She loved him and I loved him too, but we knew different parts of him. I can tell her what I know."

"I'm glad, Cat. I know I'd want that, if it was—" he breathes deeply "—Donny who survived."

I decide then that I can take his hand, that we can go inside and eat something for dinner and that the evening will go on. Grey's free hand looks warm and strong. When I slide my cold fingers into his, I feel the pads are calloused. Then I bite my lip and carefully tip my body against his, like a tree falling in slow motion. For a moment he doesn't respond, is still as a statue, but then he draws his arm around my waist, presses his mouth into my hair. My heart is pounding, but I think it will quiet down soon. His embrace is loose, and I know I could break away if I needed to.

What the Dead Remember

Before she died, Julianna didn't consider herself a very interesting person. On her days off, she sometimes went to a bar with her boyfriend, Sean, or to the movies with her best friend, Carly. She had a cat named Archie, and she wrote poems at the breakfast table in her pyjamas. A publisher was going to put out a book of them in the spring. Her poems were the most interesting thing about her when she was alive, but they seem less important now, even though she knows they're the only real thing left of her in the world.

Julianna is still too wrapped up in what the living are doing to be worried about how they will remember her. She always imagined that the world would fade from her view when she died, but it hasn't, so how can she turn away? She floats in the middle of the restaurant kitchen, watching it all swirl. Drew training the sprayer on a crooked castle of saucepans, Ayesha counting her tips and jamming them into her apron pockets, Gav chasing up and down the grill with a flipper in hand. It's negative degrees outside but this white-tile room is all steam and smoke. There's a wash of colour and noise, but it's only early evening so the chefs' whites are still white, the stainless steel still glossy.

Carly hefts a tray of first-course orders onto her shoulder, wrist straining—somehow she is heavy-armed but not very strong, which always struck Julianna as unfair—then strides toward the swinging doors with the tray above her head. Julianna drifts behind, watching her swing her bum to push open the out-door into the back hallway, then cross over the dirty hall carpet to the proper green rug and good lighting and a new kind of noise and rush. She dodges around a running child, grins at a man miming a signature in the air, zips around a parka on the back of a chair, and reaches the table that ordered all that salad. Julianna loves watching her be so good at her job.

"'Kay, I got the two salads, I did 'em separate so you could have the dressing on the side but you don't have to." She plonks the bowls down, then the stack of chilled plates. Julianna always liked how they felt on her palm, icy and dry. "Would you like cheese on your salads?" Carly takes the rotary grater off her tray and waves it like a pompom. "Or pepper? Anyone for pepper?" Everyone takes cheese, no one pepper, which is standard. Julianna isn't crazy about black pepper on anything, the way the sharp grits sit on her tongue without dissolving. But now, with the world and all its flavours about to leave her behind, it bothers her that she can't recall the exact taste of pepper, beyond sharp and gritty.

It's so strange what slips away and what stays.

The bright fireworks pattern of yellow and orange on the industrial carpeting, the metallic smell of bottled tomatoes, the shriek of a child who has just dumped a glass of ice cubes onto his lap—these everyday memories outshine moments she thought would burn so bright from her life on earth: her first kiss; her father lifting her up a moment before the neighbour's dog would have bitten her; the first time some-one—the librarian at Secord High—read one of her poems and said it was good. And she does treasure all those big, important moments. It's just that the aimless boring nights at the restaurant, those nights where nothing happened but everything smelled like oregano and Windex— for some reason they cling the hardest.

When she was alive, Julianna would have tried to write this all down, make the Windex and the wind slipping through the cracks under the kitchen door and Gav's voice yelling orders come together in a few perfect lines she could keep, and share. Over the years, she's written so many poems about penne pasta, flat shoes, and pleated shorts, the bun clamped to the back of her head in the damp and grease of the kitchen that wouldn't come down even when she took the pins out. The way sometimes she was so tired, she'd slump sideways on the bus, and let Carly take the pins out for her. Sometimes she wrote less narrative, more feeling—about how it felt to fall in love or the colour of the sky ten seconds after the sun set—but it was all of a piece. She was trying to make moments—things that had happened, ways she had felt—stay with her in a way she could come back to whenever she needed to.

When Julianna looks around again, Carly is coming back into the kitchen at a trot.

Ayesha yells from the salad station, "What time is the visitation?"

Carly fumbles trying to clip her order up above the hot table because her head is turned toward Ayesha. "It's seven 'til ten, but you don't have to go for the entire time. We could just get off an hour early and go for nine."

"What? No, Carly," Ayesha says, pausing to count out her croutons—once a lady yelled at her because she didn't get enough. She puts four more on a Caesar salad, then returns to the conversation. "We don't walk into the church while it's going on. That's disrespectful."

"No, it's not—it's not at a *church*. This isn't the funeral. It's the visitation."

"Are you talking about the thing for Juli? Where is it?" This is Gav, from the line. Half a dozen other voices join in from around the room—a line cook, the kid on potatoes, the new dish guy struggling to load a rack of glasses—all calling out questions about the logistics of the visitation.

"The obituary said it's tomorrow at the funeral home. It's like—like an open house."

Sheila, the dining-room manager, comes in and sees all the eyes trained on Carly. She nods sharply and begins to pull folded napkins from the shelf to restock the wait-station. Carly joins her and takes an armload into the dining room. When Sheila follows, the little pause ends and everyone gets back to work.

Gav swipes his forearm across his sweaty face and dumps rigatoni into a bowl. "You got the obituary, Drew? My old man threw out our paper 'fore I could clip it."

"Yeah, I got it."

"Could I see it? I just wanted to see her picture, is all. I don't think I got any of her, ever. If we go to the funeral and you can see her, I wanna be able to remember the real girl. She didn't talk a lot, but she was pretty alive, you know."

Julianna twitches, or feels like she does, when they talk about her. These were her friends. They spent hours together every shift, so they were intimate with one another's moods and rhythms, parents and partners. She never met Drew's girlfriend, but she saw the little packets of cookies she made for him. Gav and Ayesha flirted and fought, flirted and fought, until Julianna didn't know what to hope for, but they were entertaining to listen to. She and Carly would throw croutons when things between them got too snarky or too mushy. When Julianna submitted her book for publication, she brought all the envelopes she got back to the restaurant before she opened them. Whenever there was a rejection, Gav would say, "They don't know shit," even though he never read her poems, or any poems. Carly and Ayesha would hug her, and Drew would find a way to get at least a couple pieces of cake off the high-strung, nearly silent pastry chef before the end of the night.

Then one day she opened the envelope and her eyes swam over the words "Delighted by the inventiveness of the language and the formal ease." It took her a few moments to make sense of the most pivotal sentence: "We would be honoured to publish your collection."

She remembers Carly hopping from foot to foot. "I knew it! They want it—I knew it! You're amazing, girl!" And then she clutched her in a hug before Julianna could finish reading the letter. She felt another set of arms embrace her and Carly both, and then everyone was cheering. Everyone else was delighted, but Julianna couldn't make the news real in her own mind at all. When she got home, Sean asked how much the publisher was going to pay her and then snorted at the number; he thought she should hold out for more. When she said the money wasn't the point, he ignored her the rest of the evening.

Back in what she supposes is the present, Drew stares down at the bedraggled basil leaves he's scattering on a spaghetti plate. "I don't think, I don't think they're gonna have the body there. So you can see her, I mean."

"Oh. I guess 'cause—yeah, they wouldn't," Gav says. "She always was kind of a private person."

"Yeah." Drew slides the spaghetti onto the pickup shelf and starts plating some chicken in a creamy sauce. "You can ride with me if you want. My girlfriend'll lend us her car for that."

"Thanks, man." The oven screeches as Gav opens it and slips the paddle in to yank out a just-done lasagna, dripping over its ramekin. "I can't even process it. Remember in September when she cried about Princess Diana dying. She took it so damn hard, a stranger across the ocean. Kept saying how she was too young and never got to do what she wanted. And now fuckin' this. Like she knew."

"I know it, man, don't I?" Drew claps his palm on Gav's shoulder and nods toward Carly, who counts a dollar in dimes into her palm, then pauses, wipes tears from her eye with a closed fistful of coins, counts again. "Everyone knows it."

After work Carly, Ayesha, Gav, and Drew go to a bar, as usual. As a concession to their jobs, no one asks the waitress for anything to eat. At the end of the evening, they will tip far more than any of them can afford. Julianna only joined them a few times, but she remembers well how it felt to watch them go off together laughing and punching each other's shoulders while she scurried toward the bus stop. She remembers the times Sean let her go, how fine and easy it felt to sit on a high stool without someone holding on to her arm, drinking a beer, her only responsibilities to talk and laugh.

These were Juli's best friends. *Are*, she thinks. She loves them still. At the table, though, no one seems to be feeling the love that Julianna is sending. Drew sits with his mouth open for a moment before putting beer into it. Everyone sits in grim silence, thinking of her, and there's nothing she can do to make them feel better.

"What do we wear? You guys know?" Gav asks, picking delicately at his beer-bottle label. "I don't know if I got nice-enough shoes. You think I should buy shoes?"

Ayesha squeezes his hand. "Aw, Juli never cared about your shoes. She won't care now, neither."

"Hey, will her book still get published?" Drew gestures with his beer. "I really wanted to read it. Finally find out what she was always writing about."

Carly sighs. "Yeah, sure it will. Why wouldn't it—it's a book. Doesn't have anything to do with her, necessarily, once it's done."

"But it's not just *her*, right, for the funeral?" Gav slurps foam, swallows. "There'll be people there—her folks and, like, uncles and shit. Maybe Sheila'll go, even. I oughta look respectful, you know."

Drew flattens his palm onto the wood grain of the table. "Sean will be there."

"Well, yeah. He's her boyfriend," says Ayesha.

"Fuckin' asshole," says Carly, looking at the copper-wire hairs on the back of Drew's hand. "You know, whatever happened to her, it had to have been his fucking fault. I told that to the police when they interviewed me and they were like, yeah, obviously."

Ayesha twists toward her. "I don't know about that. He loved her."

"We both saw him knock her purse out of her hand in the parking lot that time. He was mad because she couldn't find some goddamn *thing* he wanted, cigarettes or something." Carly is shredding her cardboard coaster. "It was open—shit went everywhere and he didn't help her pick it up. It was snowing." She shakes her head and, when a thick curl falls into her mouth, sucks on it for a moment before spitting it out.

"That's a shitty thing to do," Drew says, "but it's not leaving a body in a field."

"She always had bruises on her arms, her legs. You saw her move around the restaurant—she wasn't clumsy. He had a parole officer— Juli ever tell you that? He couldn't control his temper, got into a bunch of fights at work, broke some guy's jaw one time—she told me. Something must have happened because she didn't usually talk about bad stuff. She was really upset on the bus home one night, half asleep, almost crying. The cops better be checking up on him."

Julianna doesn't want that—she doesn't want anyone to go after Sean. Even though she is angry at him, she's sorry Carly hates him so much. They're still linked, Julianna and Sean. Just imagining his narrow, weather-raw face, the dry creases in the palm of his hand, the low *thunk* of his bottle-opener keychain against the door as he unlocks it—she feels herself drifting toward him.

He's in the living room, in their low-ceilinged basement apartment, on the sprung couch swathed in a thick, colourful quilt in that northern way that no one in this city can understand. He is sunk all the way in the corner of the couch, clutching the wood-grain armrest, watching on TV as the puck bounces off the side of a skate and out of harm's way. His hoarse grunt is a cheer. She knows this because she knows everything about him, because that is the only way she can love someone. Almost everything about him.

She used to literally wring her hands like a fretful Victorian maid when she was nervous or upset. Carly made fun of her for twisting her fingers into knots at bus stops, in front of angry customers, over her notebooks, when her cat was sick. Now that she is bodyless, Julianna finds she misses the hand wringing. The clutching, containing, if only of herself, was comforting when there was nothing else she could do. Now she has nothing at all.

Sean sits in front of the TV, drinking, yelling for the good plays, and then when the game pauses for commercials, he weeps during the ads for bleach and popcorn. The apartment looks the same as it did when she was alive, except messier. There's only a tiny bit of kibble in Archie's dish, and she can't see him anywhere. Sean always talked about how they should let the cat "go wild" and now that she's not there to tell him that cats can't be wild in the city, just hit by cars, she figures that's what's happened. If she still could, she'd probably cry. Archie only ever had her to take care of him; now he has no one. Of course, the same is true for Sean.

She drifts into the kitchen, which is a swamp of old food and dirty paper towels clumped on the counter. The sink, which she liked enough to write a poem about even though the hot water was inconsistent and it was small and shallow, is filled to the brim with plates and mugs. The low ceiling and lack of windows always made the kitchen a sad room, but she liked to write at the narrow beige breakfast bar, because Sean mainly left her alone there, and it was far enough away from the TV that she wouldn't be distracted. It's an ugly room, but she bought bright orange tea towels and potholders to make up for the lack of sunshine. Now she sees that the towels are sopping and browning, and the potholders have fallen behind the stove. Some of her notebooks are still on the counter, though—her imaginary fingers twitch to write in them, or at least flip through the pages.

She drifts back out to the living room, watching Sean watch his terrible, most beloved Leafs lose again. It's like it always was: him rooted on the corner of the couch, her drifting around—tidying, nibbling, reading a page, scribbling a note. Except now, she doesn't have any of those actions left to her, except the drift, and not even really that. She can't move because she isn't anywhere. Just there. Useless.

—⁂—

The world is starting to feel fuzzy to Julianna—streets and intersections she used to walk to without conscious thought now have vague locations on her mental map. Now, she can't even picture where Fenderson's Funeral Home is in relation to her apartment. She just *is* there, in front of the pretty old brick building, and then inside the quiet rooms.

In the anteroom, the gang from the restaurant is standing around, waiting to be told where to sit. Carly is silent and calm, but Julianna can sense her anger. Normally when Carly gets upset, her curls bounce and her eyes light up, her hands dancing as she tries to make her point. "You're such a cutie when you're mad," Julianna used to tease her. "You should try to go on all your dates when you're really enraged—brings a nice colour to your cheeks." Carly would roll her eyes at that, but the teasing jostled her out of her mood more often than not. She's in a black jersey dress with a drooping sash, her chapped plump hand clutching the arm of the corduroy blazer Gav borrowed from his father—only Julianna sees the tendons stand out around her knuckles, the tension in her rigid shoulders, lines curving around her mouth. The others are distracted, looking around at the other mourners.

The object of Carly's blue glare is Sean, slouched against a tasteful cream wall by the tasteful polished side table with the coffee and tea. "He's not even fucking—he's not even fucking paying attention. He was the person she loved most and he's not even—"

Suddenly Julianna's parents loom into view at the other end of the room, blond and miserable, pulled tightly in on themselves. She drifts closer toward them—she hasn't seen them in over a year, money too tight for visits. They are murmuring to each other, clutching each other's hands and arms. Someone comes up to them and offers coffees and they nod as one. She has not been close to her parents in a long time—they never forgave her for moving away, for Sean—but the unity in their movements, the tenderness with which they speak to each other is how she always understood love to be when she was a child, before she got old enough to find her own version of it. They are united against the world, a world that sometimes included Julianna and her rash, sad decisions. Even though they are grieving now, they still have each other, always.

Julianna used to be part of a pair—not like her parents, but in their own way, when things were good, she and Sean moved through the world side by side too. She remembers a wedding back home in Iria, eight or nine years ago, when she was still living with her parents and trying to go to school and he was making furniture for his uncle, and nothing had happened to them yet. When he told her in the car on the way to the church that her dress was pretty, she had blushed, even though he wasn't looking at her. "It's Shelley's—I didn't get a new dress or anything." They were saving up to get a place together. Her parents weren't in favour of it, but she was working on them, having Sean over to dinners on Sundays. She thought they were coming around.

The wedding was for a guy Sean used to hang around with, and it was a simple event—the bride's dress a frilly eyelet thing her mother had done up. The church was unfamiliar, over-warm and without stained glass. The reception was in the grey-walled basement. Sean held her hand as they walked slowly between groups of relatives and friends, sipping punch. Some of the guys seemed to be going out back to drink something harder—she saw Sean get a couple winks—but he stayed with her all night. Julianna loved being beside him when all his friends greeted him and nodded at her—she felt official, acknow-ledged. Sometimes Sean even had his arm around her, or held her hand, and she let herself imagine her own little white dress.

She rubbed her bare shoulder against his suit jacket. "I was so hot in the church but it's cool down here."

"Basements are always cooler, cause of the damp." He picked up a shish kabob from the buffet and stood staring at it a moment. "Do I just . . . bite it off?"

She drew her hand away from his and rubbed her cool arm. Perhaps Sean would give her his jacket as the evening wore on and got less formal—he didn't like wearing it anyway. "Sure, why not?"

"I just don't want . . . you know, etiquette." He glanced around and then bit some meat off the skewer, pulling it off the end with his teeth.

"I guess there's no good way to eat those, so don't worry about it. I think people just think they look nice and figure how you'd actually eat it isn't their problem."

"Exactly. You always get me, Juli."

She leaned against his arm, cuddled into his warmth. He never did offer her his jacket.

There were so many disappointments in the years after that, so many stupid fights about Sean imagining she was disloyal or not paying as much attention to him as she should have, but she knows he really believed that she understood him, always. She could go far on a compliment like that, and she did.

Remembering her past with Sean draws her to him in the present. His tight face is tucked over his shoulder, trying to see the back of his shirt. The right shoulder blade is smudged with something. The outfit itself is all right—nothing too formal, but he'd managed a white shirt and dark pants. She notices flattened wrinkles where he tried to iron. Maybe the iron being dirty caused the smudge. She couldn't remember the last time anyone used it. If she were alive, she would've seen the mark before they left the house. If she were alive, she would've done the ironing for him. If she were alive, well, they wouldn't be here.

Sean twists one more time and then leaves the room, just as a tall thin woman in a velvet dress starts ushering everyone into another room where rows of cushioned folding chairs wait. It actually hurts to see him go, even though no part of Julianna can physically hurt anymore. But he just walks away, out of the room and into the day outside the funeral home, knowing he won't ever see her again.

Gav stares out the door after Sean. "That fuck, he *left*. He didn't even say anything to her parents. I was watching, he didn't."

Ayesha fiddles with her shoulder strap as she asks, "Should we go and sit down?"

"Of course he *left*." Carly is red-faced with fury. "I was shocked he even came. He was fucking abusive. You know he was. Everyone knew."

Gav won't meet Carly's eyes as she speaks. Drew shuffles his feet, starts to touch her arm, then stops.

Carly catches each friend's gaze in turn, trying to give her words force. "She never came out for drinks after work, always had to go straight home. She'd get so nervous if she missed the bus she told him she was getting. One time when I was picking her up from her place, I saw him kick her Archie—she loved that cat. The sore ribs—remember how Drew tried to hug her last Christmas and she jerked away like he was fire? And that time she was off work for ages and never really said why? I couldn't even get Sheila to tell me."

Gav startles. "You asked Sheila about her?"

"You think Sheila would have let anyone else miss that much work and not fire their ass? Anyway, I was worried about her. I knew she was trying to work a lot, save up for her own car, and then she was just gone. And you guys didn't know and Sheila wouldn't say anything. So I went over to her place, just to see how she was doing."

Gav, Drew, and Ayesha widen their eyes. Julianna is surprised too.

"She'd been gone, like, a couple weeks already, and I knew she couldn't afford it, and she wasn't answering her phone. Sean came to the door, so I told him I brought her a feel-better cake. I was really nice about it, acted like I just thought she had the flu or something."

Gav leans forward slightly. "So did you see her?"

"No. He was totally psycho about it. There are ways to say, *She's not feeling up to guests.* But he just lost it. *Who told you to come here, I don't recall inviting no dumb-bitch girl over here.* He knocked the cake out of my hands—it splattered all over the back stoop. He tried to grab my arm, but I slipped away. He was screaming at me as I ran to my car, all kinds of horrible names."

Gav raises a palm. "That's a crazy thing to do, I get it. But—"

"That doesn't mean anything necessarily," Drew says slowly.

Carly whirls to face Ayesha, who has taken her keys out of her bag, just to have something to play with. "You remember that day Drew knocked all that marinara onto Juli, and I had to lend her a top?"

Ayesha shakes her head but says, "Yeah. But that wasn't because of— she said she *fell*."

"Her whole back was one giant bruise. Where did she fall from, the sky?"

Ayesha whispers, "It was yellow and green and purple. I never saw a bruise like that before. She didn't hear us, didn't know we'd come into the locker room."

Carly looked hard at Ayesha, who was letting the tears fall down her face. "He did that, he did it to her."

"Okay," Gav says. "Okay, he was abusive, he hurt her. But that doesn't prove anything, it doesn't make him a murderer."

"Except that she's dead." Carly bites her lip hard enough to draw blood. "But you think some *other* crazy guy jumped out of a bush and killed her?"

Gav's gaze tilts away to the floor, the soft beige carpet.

Julianna never knew that Carly had come to see her. Sean never said anything. He had been so gentle and kind during that awful period, carefully changing the dressings on her cuts, sitting with her while she read to just gaze at her face, even cooking simple little dinners. When she went back to work after the worst damage had healed, she had been so concerned with deflecting questions about where she had been, she didn't realize Carly's questions were different—more pointed, sharper, but also frightened. Julianna needed to protect Sean, and herself, from the judgment of people who didn't understand. He had hurt her, a lot, but he loved her, and had learned from his mistakes. Or so she'd thought. Now she doesn't know what to think.

"I read in the paper that her face was all busted up, her hands . . ."
Drew stammered. "He loved her."

"I don't doubt he loved her. It's just that he didn't do anything good
with it."

—⁑—

She can conjure the icy tiles and the sharp wind under the door, the
thick wool socks she was wearing, the cat rubbing against her ankle,
and the grit of sleep in her eyes with mascara overtop, but what does
it all mean, really? That the day was Tuesday, so her shift started at four.
That Sean's temper was worse in winter, when there wasn't much con-
struction work. That she had her heavy bag over her shoulder and her
boots were by the door at the top of the stairs. That they'd never been
lucky, either together or on their own.

Things are never as clear as you want them to be.

She had been napping. The previous evening's shift had been endless,
and she spent the morning cleaning the apartment, so after lunch she
fell asleep under the green duvet. When she woke up, Sean was lying
next to her, watching TV in bed, his legs in baggy sweats crossing over
hers, his hand on her thigh. *Don't get up yet, not yet, please.* His bedroom
voice: sexy, sad. Pleading. *Stay with me, just another minute. You're so sweet,
I just want to hold you a little longer.*

But Sheila had been serious: "Julianna, this is the last time you're late
for a shift because next time, you won't have a shift to be late for."

She needed the job; Sean had bought a used van for work and now
they were eating hot dogs every other night. Julianna got up, twisted
away, and rolled out of bed.

Hey, baby, don't go.

I have to go to work, Sean.

Ah, fuck that. You just go where you goddamned want to. You just—

You know I don't want *to serve ravioli to people for eight hours, I need the job.*

What was that? You think you shouldn't have to work, you think I oughta support you so you would just have a life of luxury around here? Is that what you think?

She scurried out into the hallway, ducking as if his words were things he threw at her, went up the cold steps to the landing where her tall faux-suede boots stood knock-kneed beside the door, below her puffy grey parka hanging from a bent nail. The cat started to follow but stopped at the bottom of the stairs—the cement steps must have been too cold for him. She can't remember how mad she really was at that point. Every time she goes back to the memory, she understands it less. She had her coat on but not done up, her purse on the floor by the door. She remembers she pulled fuzzy pink socks over her tights for the long cold walk to the bus stop, but not where her book proofs were—on the kitchen counter or her bedside table? She didn't take them with her, but she can't recall if that was because she was rushing or because she didn't want to face Sean again if she went back downstairs.

She knows she wanted to take the proofs. She was nearly done reading through, one more look on the bus would've done it. The book would be out in the spring, actually printed and on shelves waiting to be read. Impossible; astounding. She could hear Sean grunting and rummaging in the bedroom. Part of her wanted to hug him goodbye, to leave on a good note, but a larger part knew it wouldn't go that way—they'd just wind up continuing the argument. She could work on new poems on the bus instead of the proofs. There were always more poems to write. The ideas that churned in her brain used to be such a joy, a feeling of plenty even when she was broke. That's something she misses in this strange afterlife—poems don't come to her anymore.

She bent down to tug on her left boot, but the zipper caught on the fuzz of her pink sock. Sean came up the stairs as she attempted to jam her heel down into the boot but it wouldn't budge—she had to pull her foot out and tear the sock a bit. Sean started talking about how hard he worked, how she didn't appreciate him, how disrespectful she was. She was yanked around by her elbow—*Sean, that's not what I said*—up against the wall at the top of the stairs. *C'mon, Sean, let me go. I gotta go to work or Sheila will—*

He pushed her down the stairs. No, that's not what happened. He pushed her away while she had her boot awkwardly half-on and she slipped. No, he grabbed her arm and she jerked away, then tumbled. No, she stepped back from his angry face and tripped. He shook her shoulders and pushed her back, too far. He only meant to cuff her gently to get her under control but didn't know his own strength.

No matter how many times she replays the scene, she doesn't know exactly what happened at that crucial moment. She can see herself staggering back and tumbling, thudding into the wall and then half somersaulting down the narrow staircase, her head whacking the edge of a step, then again on the grey concrete pad at the bottom. After enough replays she thinks she can see the instant when her neck jerks and snaps against the side of the third-last stair. But was she still alive when she hit the landing, her coat rucked over her face, her hair a tangle of milkweed? If she was, she'd been knocked unconscious and doesn't remember. She must have been breathing when she stopped falling—but for how long afterwards? She can't say for sure: her old bulky winter coat keeps her from seeing the parts of her body that breathe. Breathed. Shouldn't she know? Shouldn't there be something inside her that tells her, that speaks from her former body to her dead self now? Why doesn't she know?

She remembers the fear fluttering in her belly when Sean came up the stairs behind her. Not terror—she knew him, she loved him—but fear that he would get rough, get difficult, make her late, maybe hurt her. She remembers the weight of his feet on the creaky plywood, the huff of his breathing. She remembers the ache behind her eyes as she realized he wasn't going to let go of her arm, how her jaw and shoulders clenched, her disappointment that he never gave her the hug goodbye she craved. Sean always refused to see how much she loved him, always doubted her—that is the hardest thing to accept, even with the knowledge she has now, that she'd end up crumpled at the bottom of the stairs, dying. Or dead. She honestly doesn't know.

The thing is, even though she can't quite examine the details or explain the exact physics of how her left foot skidded on the avocado-coloured linoleum of the landing, she can see Sean's face and almost hear his thoughts, the way she can't hear her own. She can see the horror, the tenderness, the yearning for that time when she was in grade eleven and they spent hours making that disgusting banana ice cream, both of them ending up collapsed on the kitchen floor, laughing and spooning runny slimy ice cream into each other's mouths. They were the only two people on Earth who knew that story, and there were so many more like it. On those stairs, she was watching the last one.

All this—the tenderness, the memories, the love—does not obscure the fact that after a minute, after two, after watching her neck turn so strangely, Sean didn't come down the stairs to see what was damaged under Julianna's heavy coat. After five minutes, he was still standing at the top of the stairs, white-knuckling the banister with tears in his eyes, but they didn't fall and he didn't go to her. Not after ten minutes. Not after twenty. She loses track of the minutes. Whether she was breathing when she hit the bottom, she was not by the time he plodded down the steps— carefully, he was still in his socks—and pulled her arm and coat and hair away from her face. Her arm fell back and thudded to the floor like a tire. She was no longer alive, no longer the person Sean loved and resented and sometimes knocked around. The book, the job, the cat—there were too many things she was doing lately that he didn't control, and he wanted this victory, or had wanted it in the moment. He wanted her to fall, but didn't want to admit he made it happen, not even to himself. He hated her. They loved each other.

He stared at her face, the bruises ripening on her pale cheeks, a cut across the thin-skinned bridge of her nose. He touched the side of her neck, put his fingers in front of her mouth and nose. He stared at the person he once loved for a minute, for five, for ten, and then he went and got the laundry sack to take her body around back to his van.

—⟋⟍—

Julianna had thought all that was the end of her and Sean, but it wasn't. She is still here, a week after the memorial, floating, worrying, remembering.

Gav, Drew, Carly, and Ayesha are driving slowly along Avison Street in Drew's girlfriend's car, one block west of where Julianna used to live, when she lived. They turn into the lane between the streets, where the alleys end and the light is wavering yellow in the gritty snow. Drew parks two houses away from Julianna's basement apartment and they all sit staring forward through the black windows. It looks like Sean's not there yet, but it's getting dark. He'll be home soon.

"What are we even doing here?" asks Drew, still watching the windows. He draws the emergency brake up, then pushes it back down with a creak. "The cops already interviewed him. You saw in the paper. Seven hours of questioning, and then the next day too—and they let him go. What are we going to say to him? Why would he talk to us, even? We aren't the cops, we aren't the goddamned Scooby-Doo gang."

Carly puts her palm on her purse on the back seat beside her. "The cops didn't know her, they don't care. Remember how hard she worked on her poems? Remember how she'd repeat a line over and over if she thought no one was listening? A whole shift, just going back and forth between 'The yellow-orange ball of the sun' and 'orange-yellow.' Now she'll never see her book in print. She was going to do a reading just for us—I wanted to hear her read. It isn't fair."

Carly is shaking with rage. Julianna is startled by her passion. They were always good friends, but Juli had her books, her difficult boyfriend, her long commute. Carly lived alone in the attic apartment of a family whose baby was always waking her up. When she went to a movie or shopping with Juli, that was the best thing in Carly's week—otherwise, she watched network TV with her landlord's aerial and worked extra shifts. The emotion that is radiating from Carly is love.

"We have to send a message," she says, pulling down the thick gold zipper on her little purse. "The police aren't doing anything."

In the front passenger seat, Gav twists to see Carly's face but mainly sees the gun inside her purse—her brother's gun, silver and black and shiny. He immediately reaches for the bag. Carly snatches it back, like a child with candy.

"I'm not going to shoot anybody—I just want to scare him. He can't kill someone and think nothing's going to happen. That there'd be no repercussions."

Ayesha is calm beside her. Ayesha, who has been crying for a week, is suddenly dry-eyed. "If he never hurt Julianna, then you're threatening someone innocent—you're acting crazy. And if he did, then you're taking a deadly weapon to someone who already killed one person—that's crazy too."

"It isn't loaded, but he doesn't know that. If I can make him think I'm serious, maybe we can get him to confess."

"Carls," Drew says gently, leaning as far as he can into the back seat. "We're all really sad. Juli was our friend. We loved her too. But this isn't a good plan."

"You want him to be fine? You want him to go on drinking beers, sitting in bars ogling the waitress? You want him to get another *girlfriend?*"

Gav stares down at his hand in his lap as if it were wounded. "No, I don't."

Drew pats Gav's knee and Ayesha puts her hand on Carly's shoulder and together all four of them look at the gun. Ayesha says slowly, "The police'll get him. I mean, if he did it. Or his conscience will."

"Who else would want to kill Juli except her motherfucking boyfriend?"

Julianna is outside the car but inside it too. And inside the apartment downstairs, watching Sean sitting on the toilet reading one of her books—a collection of Emily Dickinson's poetry. How much of the way he treated her—the mocking laughter, the dismissal of everything good she accomplished except being pretty, the swats, the slaps, the punches and kicks—was the fear that he wouldn't be able to keep her in his life and how much was just a need to keep her in line?

He loved her. He pushed her down the stairs and then he watched her die. She knows both these things are true but can't comprehend how they can be. Maybe she didn't really understand him after all. And in the end he didn't understand her, didn't understand how much she loved him, and he hurt her for it. But she did. And he didn't understand that her poems were just a way to cling to the life she had, not a gateway to a new one.

She knows she was a good poet—perhaps too awkward with punctuation, too slow to revise, too quick to sacrifice the stanza for the line—and now she'll never know if she could have become a great one. She knows she died on a cold dirty floor that she'd forgotten to sweep that morning when she did the rest of the apartment. She knows she wasn't alone when she died, but something worse than alone. And that's her last memory of life on Earth. But she wants to do one more thing.

She draws closer to Carly, whom she loved the way she thinks she would have loved a sister if she had one. Even without the blood bond, Julianna was closer to Carly than almost anyone—she didn't have many friends as an adult because of Sean. Work was the loophole Carly could pass through, the legitimate excuse for two happy females to sit counting tips and drinking vodka gingers—which wasn't even a real drink—snuck from the bar. Carly's invitations to go shopping or to the movies were usually thwarted because Sean didn't want his girlfriend out "partying" without him. Julianna had to make excuses, and watch Carly try hard not to judge. Carly had her own problems, really just needed a fucking friend, and Sean had taken that away from her.

Julianna's friend is holding her brother's gun loosely in both hands, eyes closed. She has heard Carly describe her brother as a thug and an idiot. She's positive Carly has never held the gun before and has no real plan, just wants desperately for the story to end happily. But that is impossible now. Julianna will just aim for an ending that can be a beginning too. She leans in close and whispers, "Remember when I got my period early and you were coming off-shift so you lent me your work shorts and went home with two sweaters tied around your waist? Remember when our old supervisor called me Carly and you Julianna for months and we swapped nametags and cheques and just went with it? Remember that bus driver who was in love with you, and you made him let me ride for free too? Remember I kept writing that same poem about the butter knife and the door over and over, and you read every version?" With her bodyless mouth on Carly's ear, Julianna remembers Carly's shoulder jiggling against hers with helpless laugher the one time Julianna had gone over to her apartment while Sean was on a fishing weekend. They had watched *Melrose Place* and ordered pizza and sprawled around in plaid flannel pyjamas—it turned out they both had the same set. "You were a good friend—the best. We had fun and when you read my poems, sometimes I felt like you were breathing them in, like they were becoming part of you. That's how I want you to remember me. Let that be what we remember."

Down in the basement apartment, Sean stands up, flushes, and as he reaches for his pants knocks the book into the sink. When he picks it up, there are rivulets of wet on the blue-grey cover, the edges of the pages. Water trails down the margins when he opens it again. Julianna knows he's in pain, mourning, regretful, but she has only one thing left to do and it's for Carly.

In the car Julianna whispers, "I love you, but I'm almost gone." She doesn't know if she can touch anyone anymore but she tries, dipping her invisible shoulder against Carly's warm solid one, pressed firm, the way they always did when they sat together. They weren't huggers, either of them, but they didn't need to be. They were always so close to each other. "Don't make this the big moment in your life, Carly. Don't let him hurt you. Live your own life."

Carly bites her lip again, and Julianna can smell the orange blossom perfume she always wears, and almost see the future Carly wants for herself: the serious job and pretty clothes, the nice man and sweet children. Julianna wants it for her too. She wants her to go forward into this future without something terrible happening tonight. And Carly does it: she opens her eyes, closes her purse, and says to Drew, "Let's go the fuck home."

Catherine Reindeer

Spring helps. Not as much as I was hoping, but having the windows open reminds me that there's not all that much difference between inside and out, and the green grass and silver-budded trees make leaving the house more attractive than it was a month ago. I'm also feeling stronger, better able to deal with real life—or maybe just used to how easily overwhelmed I am now. Perspective, that's the hardest thing.

Having Grey with me helps too. The walk to the bus stop is almost pleasant with him strolling right next to me, and I feel pretty calm standing there, maybe because no one else is waiting. A couple of times he starts to speak—I hear the faint click of his mouth opening—but then he stops himself. I would like to say something, put him at ease, but all my attention is focused on waiting for the bus. Whether it's in sight or not shouldn't matter, but somehow I need to concentrate my mind on the horizon, wait for the route display to appear over the hill.

When the bus doors open, we can't decide who should get on first: me because Grey is gentlemanly or Grey because I am scared? Me, in the end, maybe because I am brave. I have the change already counted out, sweaty in my hand, and dump in enough for both of us. This is the first time I've made it this far. I let the accordion doors shut behind me.

The bus is a tight hot box of strangers. There are men with hair on the backs of their necks and tucked-in shirts and women with silver and black nail polish. Any of them, all of them, could turn on me at a moment's notice, digging, smacking, whatever it took to make me fall, vulnerable, available to be carried away. Sweat slicks the underside of my bra, the waistband of my tights. Everything is damp, cold. My wet palm slips out of the rubber loop hanging from the ceiling, but the hand that grips Grey's is tight.

I can't even look at Grey. I wanted him to be proud of me, but now I'm worried that my knees will buckle and I'll collapse onto the gritty bus floor among the spike heels and stroller wheels. He'll have to carry me off, carry me home. And we'd be back where we started from.

When I turn to tell him I need to get off, need to give up for today and maybe try again tomorrow, Grey is making faces at two tiny children sitting behind and slightly above us, up the little flight of stairs. He tips forward on his toes, wiggles his eyebrows, sticks out his tongue. The older girl has cornrows with pink-and-purple bobbles at the ends. She grins and waves both hands at Grey. He glances at me, smiles a more dignified smile, and then goes back to his clowning. The children at the back of the bus don't terrify me the way most other humans do these days. They are something else, alarming and charming, both at once. The little one squirms away from her sister and dances in the aisle, staggers as the bus stops, bangs her head on the pole. Her mother pops up from the seat behind, tugs the little girl back into her wool-coated arms before the child can weep, and in fact she never does. Magic.

As we travel downtown, I try to remember the thing in me that once wanted to be a mother. That sweet ache in the middle of my chest that made me want to hold a baby there. I can't quite feel it over the rough breathing of my fears, but I can imagine. When Daria came by with a frozen poundcake and her little Stevie, I was overwhelmed just watching him wriggle on the floor and squawk at the vase of daffodils on the coffee table. He was so bright and loud, so unstoppable and incomprehensible. "Do you want to hold him?" Daria asked because in my previous life I always wanted to hold him. But we were both different people then, Stevie a cuddly infant and me all excitement and biological-clock ticks. Now Stevie's eighteen months old and able to run from my limp hands and pounding heart, and that seemed about right, honestly. Kids are more perceptive than adults; most people would have run from what I felt at that moment, if they knew. I would have.

Out the front window of the bus, I can see the stone buildings of the university, the tangle of bare wet tree branches over the brick wall at the edge of campus; we're almost at my stop. This used to be the point when I'd put the bookmark in, take out my gloves, make sure I had a clear pathway to the bell pull. But it's too warm for gloves and I'm not reading anything, and the calm routine is gone—I've been staring at the yellow pull-cord, waiting to reach out and grab it since we got on. When I pull it, I'll be getting off the bus alone.

Grey leans toward me, staring too hard, and whispers, "Are you sure? You're shaking. Tomorrow's Saturday—you wouldn't have to wait for me to get home. We could go out first thing."

To walk out into the navy blue evening by myself, vulnerable to anything and anyone, seems the most impossible thing. I shake my head, and a hank of hair falls out of my ponytail and lashes across my face. "We've made it this far. I'll go. It won't kill me."

"Do you want me to get off with you? I can wait at the gates, or somewhere?"

I do want him to do that, but I say no again. He pats my little black purse, where he knows my new cellphone is.

265

"Call me and I'll come pick you up in the car in a millisecond, if you want."

"I'll be all right. I can just get a cab."

Then I hear it— someone has *pinged* for the university stop. It's like we're in a Second World War movie and I'm shipping out. No, it isn't; it's like Grey and me on the bus, and I'm on my way to school and he's going to work or to Evan's house, like we've done a thousand times before. Like the way we used to move through the world, living our lives. Like us.

I lean forward and kiss him on the mouth—our first kiss since I've been back. It was something Dex never tried with me, wasn't his thing. And Donny I kissed so many times, but always on the cheek, the forehead, shoulder, not the lips. In this kiss on the bus, there is no memory except for other kisses with Grey—his chapped winter lips on mine at the movies, running out the door at home, the first time on the steps outside the restaurant where I used to work. This one little act, untainted by memory.

As I move toward the back doors, Grey's hand is resting on my shoulder, not grasping or holding, just touching. We lose the connection when I have to walk round someone's bundle buggy. The bus jerks to a stop and I lock my gaze on Grey as I push out the doors. He looks the way I feel, scared and trembling, like I'm stepping out into the sea and not a curbside slush puddle. The pause where the doors hang open is the worst because I could dart back on if I wanted to. And I do want to, but I remind myself that I am getting off at the university, once one of my favourite places on Earth. That thought takes me through one breath in and one breath out before the doors flap shut.

And then I am standing alone on the edge of main campus. The lawn is stiff and yellow, recovering from winter. Spring is coming. Dex took me right before the spring thaw last year. Today the trees are naked and wet, making a brittle rustle in the wind. Around me, younger people in slouchy wool coats float through the gates in both directions. The day is ending, evening classes beginning. There's no reason to be terrified, except I'm surrounded by all these strangers, all this space, and anything could happen. I feel my boots clinging to the sidewalk; I can't move. People just keep walking past me in the fading light; it's nearly six now and the sun is giving up. A girl with a glittery scarf and a tuque pushed back on her head catches my gaze accidentally as I stand there, staring into space. She just smiles and shrugs.

No one here knows who I am or what happened to me. Or if they know, they either don't notice me or they don't recognize me from the newspapers and posters. The blank, pleasant faces around me are focused on wherever they are going, only seeing some simple outline of me—a student, typical enough, but moving slowly. No one is worried, or menacing, or paying attention at all, and that lets me turn toward the gates and finally walk onto campus.

I want to be the person these people imagine me to be. Normal, friendly, functional. Sometimes I can even convince my mom this is true. She watches me constantly when we sit in the living room, her with *The New Yorker* on the couch, staring over the tops of her pages at me with some novel on the floor. I miss her, even though I see her all the time. I miss the way she used to watch me as if I were a fascinating TV show instead of a terrifying one—we both miss all the things I used to be able to tell her about my life. I would love to tell her things now, but I feel like I'm having to learn our language all over again, figure out how to navigate her gestures and glances, cultivate my own. I think a lot about how I used to climb that tree up to her apartment. I don't remember the handholds anymore, but they weren't that hard to learn the first time. I'll get them back, I think. I'd love to see her face when I slip through her window.

Grey is better at pretending he isn't watching me, but still I can sense it, that concerned and tender glance. And I know he feels what I feel—homesick for the lives we used to have. The kiss was like a flashback to a time when I didn't flinch when he brushed against me, when I could make conversation without having to push myself from sentence to sentence. That kiss was hopeful. It was hope.

Walking through campus is easier than getting on the bus, since it's a place I loved. Love still. I wander through the teenagers with their bulky backpacks, the continuing education students with grey hair and briefcases, jocks throwing footballs, couples holding hands. I stroll past the wishing fountain, the enormous Engineering building with its slit windows and tiny doors. I wanted to come here today for the same reason I always wanted to be on campus—it makes me feel like I'm on my way. Even if I wasn't all that smart yet, I was getting smarter, learning things, meeting people. I read, and listened, and wrote, and talked to people. I had hoped Donny would come here, someday. I really thought I would meet him for coffee on campus and we'd talk about what we were reading while eating giant stale muffins. I can picture his long skinny body loping over the lawns, ignoring the pathways, rushing to class or basketball practice, grinning at everyone.

I step carefully over a slick of dead leaves in a puddle and gaze up at the library—the sunset is bright behind the building, bright enough that the windows are just glossy shadows. In an hour, everyone inside will be clearly visible as they pass in front of the windows. Professor Altaris told my class that Julianna Ohlin went to this school, took English classes, same as us. At the time I didn't understand why he was so excited about it, but now it does seem amazing to me that she could have sat in the library at one of those big wooden tables with sixteen chairs, and read some of the same books I did, *The Stone Angel*, or something by Hemingway, or P.K. Page, with her feet propped on her backpack under the table. Maybe this is where she started writing poetry. How does anyone start? How do you build something more than reality if reality is all you have?

I keep walking, toward the Humanities building. Professor Altaris's office is on the third floor. It's probably too late in the day for him to be there, but it's good to have a destination, even if I just walk up the stairs and then back down. Altaris is on my mind because I've been thinking so much about Julianna. I think he thought a lot about her too; the way he taught her poetry made it seem like he did, like he was just giving us a few little notes from a giant book on her that he kept in his head. Now that I'm reading her poems again, though, I wish he'd talked more about them specifically, about individual lines and what they mean, and how they seem to mean different things depending on where you pause, where you breathe. The versions I told to Donny in the basement felt right, even though I got so much wrong. When I read the real poems, they still sound like what I whispered to Donny. The heart of them is still the same.

What makes a poem what it is? And how much can it change before it becomes something else, someone else's? That's what I'd like to know. I wonder what Julianna would think of my versions of her poems, the ones I scribble out in the back of my journal when I can't think of anything else to write. I wonder if she would recognize them.

Sometimes I wish that I didn't know she was dead, or at least not how she died. It's hard not to think about it whenever I read her work. One moment of violence is not what matters about her, yet it is the shadow that's cast back over the poems. She couldn't know how she would die, but certain lines feel ominous to me, like signs. Sometimes I look back on that last day at the restaurant—a dropped knife, the sunset seemed so early—and wonder if I should have known what would happen. That's crazy, but once you've been through the worst things, it colours every memory.

Is the person I was before dead? Or will the worst things that happened to me eventually get diluted by the rest of my life, become just a part of the story that I've always been writing? That is what Grey, my mom, everyone is waiting to find out. Even me.

I am so tired of interior monologue. I wish Grey were here so I could tell him what I'm thinking. I'll tell him when I get home, even if I'm tired. I will.

I want to just go back to being the person I was before, but you can't stop being the person you've become. You just have to keep going forward. Which is why, though my stomach wobbles at the thought of the poorly lit, echoing hallways, I find myself going up the stairs in front of the Humanities building.

At the top of the steps, I turn and look back. It's nearly full dark now but the bright windows of the library stay where they've always been, and behind the light, I can see all the books I haven't yet read.

I'm gathering myself to open the heavy wooden door when a group of laughing and yelling students pours out and around me. A boy in a leather jacket hangs back to hold the door for me, so I have to go in. His hands are thick and I don't look him in the eye. In my head, Donny whispers, *Just go ahead, you can handle this*. Donny is still taking care of me, or at least I like to feel he is. Inside, dull yellow lights seem to not quite fully illuminate the stone hallways. People feel closer indoors, and it's more terrifying to see the men walking toward me, bros in their hoodies and warmups, hipsters with skinny jeans and scarves. But they don't see me, not really. A female body, maybe the soft blue coat that Grey bought me, at most. Maybe I won't really see them either, someday. For now, the details press in on me.

Winter term is ending, a year after I failed Professor Altaris's class because I was locked in a basement on the east edge of town. I will only last a few more minutes in this building. My heart is pounding and I'm sweating beneath my coat. But I think I'll be ready to be a student again by the fall. There's a lot to do between now and then—so many journal entries, therapist visits, dinners. I will call Kyla back at last, and we'll talk about Donny. I will tell her whatever she wants to know, if I can. I'll tell her the stories he told me about her, the things he remembered most and best—the flashcards she made to help him with organic chem, them riding doubles on his bike, the way they sang little melodies to each other when there wasn't anything to say. And then I'll ask her where she's going to school in the fall. Donny said she's smart. Maybe I'll see her here someday, walking down these same stone halls. Maybe if we can work through the weight of all that history, we could even become friends.

Upstairs is quieter, and even darker. I can see Professor Altaris's door is ajar, light spreading yellow into the dim corridor. I stand beside the doorway to see if he has a student with him, and find myself admiring all his shelves and stacks of books. So much to read. He is alone and reading a book flat on his desk.

I had thought my shadow in the doorway would make him notice me but it doesn't. "Hello, um, Professor Altaris." He looks up immediately, startled the way he always seemed startled, even when he was lecturing. "I'm Catherine Reindeer. I was in your Canadian Poetry class last year."

"Yes, I remember you," he says hurriedly, starting to stand up and move toward me. I'm not ready to talk to anyone at close range, so I wave for him to sit back down and he does. "I remember you." And he clearly does know me, who I was then and everything that's happened since. His eyes are wide behind his narrow glasses. I've seen this look before, from people so certain I was dead that my living self is hard to process, even if they're glad to see me. You can be happy and still be afraid of ghosts. There's a long pause. He could easily mention the news reports, all the horrifying things this whole town has probably imagined happening to me. Instead he says, "You were a good student."

"I know." I think for a second and realize I do know it. "I'm planning on coming back to school in the fall. I've missed it."

He grins. "That's wonderful. There are some great new classes next—"

I step forward and shake my head, and he understands, falls silent. It was too hard to get here not to talk about what I want to talk about. "There were some poems I read in your class that I've been thinking about. I have some ideas about what they mean that I wanted to talk over with you. I have a lot of ideas."

Acknowledgements

I am sincerely grateful to the Canada Council for the Arts, the Ontario Arts Council Writers' Works in Progress program, and the Toronto Council for the Arts for their financial support during the writing of *So Much Love*.

Early readers helped the work immeasurably. They are Carolyn Black, Kerry Clare, Brahm Nathans, Nadia Pestrak, Ben Rosenblum, Mark Sampson, Elizabeth Ross, and S. Kennedy Sobol. Prior versions of the book were supported and encouraged by my teachers and colleagues at McGill, Concordia, George Brown College, and the University of Toronto. I appreciate all the support I received on this very long road.

Various research elements were aided by Aaron Scott MacRae, Mike Butler, and Jaime Murdoch and her family. Miranda Hill's suggestion helped greatly with the chapter "Long Live Home." In very different ways, this book was supported by the Toronto Women's Writing Salon and the Nelson gang, particularly Lunch Club and Jane High. Many thanks to you all!

Several chapters were published previously, in much different form: "Marriage" (*The New Quarterly*), "The House That Modern Art Built" (*PRISM international*), and "At the End of Breath" (*Ars Medica*). I am grateful to those editors for helping me strengthen these pieces. I also must thank the editors of *The Rusty Toque* and *Little Fiction* for working with me on and publishing other chapters from this narrative that were not included in the final novel.

Thanks are due to my wonderful agent, Samantha Haywood, for her forthright critiques and warmhearted support of this difficult book.

So Much Love would be an extremely different and poorer book without the deft and untiring editing of Anita Chong, who shouldered the burden along with me for more than two years. Working with her was a relief, a joy, and an education.

I am indescribably lucky in my family, and wish to thank Barbara, Gerald, and Ben Rosenblum for their support of this book, during all the fits and starts and failures and successes.

I owe so much to my husband, Mark Sampson, for his love, his insightful reading (and rereading) of my drafts, his own inspiring work ethic, and his incredible patience with this protracted effort.

And finally, though this book and all its characters are a work of fiction not based on any real persons or events, of course I read a great deal by and about victims of various forms of violence, in particular kidnapping victims like Catherine. Though much of the media coverage of that type of crime is sensational and disturbing, the actual voices, when I could find them, were incredibly, shockingly quiet, still, and true. Their words stay with me, and I am thankful for them.

—ᴍ—

The lines from *Hamlet* that Donny recites on pages 78 and 79 are from Act 3, Scene 2, lines 334 to 338, from page 1716 of *The Norton Shakespeare* (W. W. Norton and Company, 1997).

The text on Archie's tag described on page 102 is from the poem "The Largest Life" by Archibald Lampman, which can be found in *The Poems of Archibald Lampman* (ed. Duncan Campbell Scott). (General Books, 2009)

The translation of Leo Tolstoy's *The Death of Ivan Ilych* that Kyla refers to in "Youth Must Have Its Day" is an amalgam of those by Richard Pevear and Larissa Volokhonsky (Vintage Books, 2012) and by Louise and Aylmer Maude.

A NOTE ABOUT THE TYPE

The body of *So Much Love* has been set in Perpetua, a typeface designed by the English artist Eric Gill, and cut by the Monotype Corporation between 1928 and 1930. Perpetua (together with its italic partner Felicity) constitutes a contemporary face of original design, without historical antecedents. The shapes of the roman characters are derived from the techniques of stonecutting. Originally intended as a book face, Perpetua is unique amongst its peers in that its larger display characters retain the elegance and form so characteristic of its book sizes.